FEAR NO TRUTH

A FAITH MCCLELLAN NOVEL

LYNDEE WALKER

First edition 2018.

Severn River Publishing
www.SevernRiverBooks.com

ISBN: 978-1-64875-463-0 (Paperback)

ALSO BY LYNDEE WALKER

The Faith McClellan Series

Fear No Truth

Leave No Stone

No Sin Unpunished

Nowhere to Hide

No Love Lost

Tell No Lies

The Nichelle Clarke Series

Front Page Fatality

Buried Leads

Small Town Spin

Devil in the Deadline

Cover Shot

Lethal Lifestyles

Deadly Politics

Hidden Victims

To find out more about LynDee Walker and her books, visit

severnriverbooks.com/authors/lyndee-walker

For Lynnda, who taught me to stand up for what's right and drag dark truths into the light wherever I found them. A great teacher's impact stretches far beyond the classroom door.

The man who fears no truth has nothing to fear from lies.
—Thomas Jefferson

PROLOGUE

He'd never seen a bona fide angel before.

Funny, just when he'd decided the angels had forsaken him, that he would stumble across a living, breathing one in the craziest time and place: along the top of Mansfield Dam smack in the middle of the inky-black hours lesser mortals slept through.

Destiny. Sent there, led there, just for him.

Nobody ever came out here this time of night but him and the katydids. Even the coyotes didn't venture so close to the edge of the tree line. Night after night sitting in his spot, headlights off and engine long cold, and she was the first soul to cross his path.

A reward.

A test.

A deliverance?

No way to tell which, but bushels of time to figure it out.

God knew he wasn't going anywhere. He couldn't look away.

Her skin glowed silver in the perfect shaft of moonlight, her long, shimmering hair the color of heaven.

She paced a short section of the roadside, between a bag she'd dropped near the north end of the dam wall and the first floodgate. Up the hill on tiptoe, arms out like she was walking a balance beam, down in a cold sprint, her shape a luminescent blur against the darkness. He caught every breath, every blink, waiting for her to fly away.

So beautiful. So graceful. The stars dotting the purple-black Hill Country sky had diddly-squat on her. Nothing had ever caught his attention so completely.

The tingle started in his core, spreading slowly to his fingers, his toes, the ends of his perfectly gelled hair.

No.

Just breathe. Calm. Slow.

The tingling receded to his knees and elbows. The monster slumbered on, the angel safe.

Her legs pumped as she ran, her arms rising as she turned to survey the dark expanse of the lake below. Christ, she was immaculate.

Had she been sent to save him? The perfect offering. The monster couldn't possibly want anything more. Was her skin as soft as the wings she had to be hiding under those gauzy layers of blouse? As sweet as vanilla ice cream?

How strong was she?

She was fast.

Maybe faster than him, even.

The tingle flared into a slow burn as his breath quickened.

What if it wasn't so easy this time?

What if the angel didn't just stare in wide-eyed terror when the monster brushed two fingers over her face and whispered what was coming?

Would the angel fight?

Dear God. His blood rushed, roaring in his ears.

Could she win?

His hand slid between the front seat and the console, fingers finding the cool hilt of his favorite hunting blade.

She knelt on the edge of forever.

Perfect.

Waiting.

He slouched into his seat. His hand closed around the knife, eyes locked on her lithe form.

The monster shifted, resettling.
He could wait, too.

1

"You must miss me something fierce, New Girl." Archie Baxter's long, sun-leathered face spread into a grin when I stopped in front of his battered metal desk. "Weren't you just here? I guess I'm too damned nice for my own good these days. Going to ruin my reputation."

"Only if I tell people. Which would be difficult since nobody talks to me but you." I flashed a smile as I dropped a thick blue folder on top of the thinner open one in front of him. "Tox and DNA on the DuGray murder."

He snatched the file up and flipped it open, scanning the reports. "Nothing? They got nothing conclusive, even under her nails? And they took six weeks to let me know?" He leaned back in his black mesh chair, lacing his fingers behind his head. "I swear, sometimes the lab nerds hate me."

"In fairness to the lab nerds, her remains were half-cremated when those hikers found them." I swiped a peppermint out of the star-shaped crystal dish next to his phone. "The report does show accelerant in the tissue and on her clothing."

"Whoop de shit. I knew someone set her on fire when I saw the park ranger's report two months ago. Damned jurisdictional red tape and under-funded labs. It's been almost a year since this girl disappeared, and we still have nothing." Archie sat up straight, shaking his head. "What the hell am I supposed to tell her parents? 'We appreciate you sending your child and her tuition money to our fair city. Sorry we can't tell you why she never made it home'?"

"That is a pretty shitty thing to live with." I closed my eyes when Archie sighed at the melancholy floating under the words.

"Damn. Faith—"

I cut him off with a raised palm before he could get another syllable out. I couldn't take one more well-intentioned "At Least We Know She's at Peace" speech on the twenty-fourth of April. What the hell did that even mean, anyway?

"Disregard." I fixed a smile in place, the peppermint's cellophane crinkling under my fingers as I untwisted the ends. "It's just another Tuesday, and I'm determined to make it a good one. So, you've got another dead end on Miss DuGray. Which trail are you following next?" Living vicariously through Archie's workload was the best thing about this job so far. Which was way more depressing than I would ever admit.

Archie raised two fingers to his temple. "Whichever one looks like it'll keep Skye from having me crucified on live TV? She's up to five interviews with the parents, and it's spreading. The paper gave it a full page in Metro last Sunday. Even called an FBI expert to offer long-distance critique of my investigation."

"And whose fault is that?" My nose wrinkled almost reflexively. Skye Morrow. The one good thing about not living in Austin anymore was not having to see that woman's smirking face every time I turned on the TV. Texas's "most award-winning" investigative reporter had never given a single damn about the people trapped inside the nightmares she took home trophies for exploiting. Skye was all about the ratings. "I told you calling her was a bad idea. Did selling your soul even get you one solid lead?"

Archie snorted. "Five hatchet jobs in the press, four raving nutcases, three bullshit sightings, two false confessions, and a partridge in a pear tree."

"Christmas was months ago, Arch."

"How come birds only get to be in lyrical trees at Christmas?"

I popped the peppermint into my mouth and touched my index finger to the end of my nose. "You always have the best questions." My words came out slurred around the candy. Pushing it into my cheek, I tried to smile. "Guess that's why they give you the fun stuff."

His eyes softened. "You'll get there, McClellan."

"Some days, I think I was there. Why'd I need this again?" I flopped into the gray polyester-upholstered chair next to his desk, my scratchy, super-starched indigo jeans practically cracking at the knees when I crossed my legs.

"This place is a meritocracy, Faith. Give it time."

"This place is a good old boys' club, Arch. Emphasis on the *boys*."

He tipped his head side to side. "Then prove them wrong."

"Working on it. You said three people called in sightings of the DuGray girl?" Broadcasting calls for information tends to bring out the crazies, but reports of sightings generally produce the best leads. "From where? And how do you know they were bullshit?"

"I pulled surveillance video from all three places: a tattoo parlor, a coffeehouse, and a lingerie shop. Stared at it until my eyes were about ready to bleed. She wasn't in a single frame."

I tapped my index finger on the edge of the desk. Huh. One of those, I might buy, but three? "You checked the traffic cams for her car?"

"Her car didn't move for nine days surrounding her disappearance. Her father took it home a week after she was last seen."

"Cause of death?"

"A brain bleed." Archie sat back, nodding, when my eyes popped wide. "I know. But Jim Prescott did the postmortem, and he's about the best there is. He couldn't say conclusively if it was from a blow or a stroke. The burns were too extensive to be sure."

I shook my head. "Someone hit her. They must've. How in the hell does a nineteen-year-old girl have a stroke?"

Archie threw up his hands. "That is number thirty-seven on a long list of bizarre questions around this case. I have turned every rock from here to Oklahoma. Jessa was happy. Bright. Good student. Quiet. Nobody noticed anything off, but I didn't find many people who noticed her much at all. It seems she had a hard time making friends here."

I sucked on the peppermint-flavored inside of my jaw. A quiet girl with few friends. Trouble fitting in. "A boy? Is that what's under your magic rock?" That's what Archie called the one he didn't see until it seemed like it had been the obvious choice the whole time.

"Damned if I can tell you. The search stretched on for weeks—droves of volunteers, dogs, air support. Candlelight prayer vigils. Her family buried an empty box on live TV, a hundred mourners at the service for every friend Jessa had on that campus. And three months later, there she is—what's left of her—in a place we checked during the initial search. Where was she for all that time? How did she get to the cave? Why did she get to the cave?" He shook his head. "I'm trying to dig a diamond out of a pile of horse shit here, kiddo. Story of my life."

I plucked a pen from his desk, rolled it between my fingers. I knew the feeling. "She wasn't dating anyone? Or recently not dating anyone?"

"Not that I've been able to find. But I started this one in a hole. Hell, nobody even really looked for her until three days after she was last seen."

Damn. The first twenty-four hours of a murder investigation are the most crucial. Fresh memories mean hot leads.

"Too bad the legislature never seems to have the cash for that early-warning network. If her roommate had known to call sooner, and we had an alert system for victims over eighteen, we might've found her. Or found who did this to her, at any rate." Archie flipped the folder open again and turned a few pages before he spun it around and slid it toward me. "See? They couldn't even get a short range on time of death."

"That's difficult when the remains are so damaged." The words sounded far away as my brain switched gears from police work to politics. He was right—the Amber Alert had saved countless children in two decades of operation, but anyone of legal age still wasn't considered missing until forty-eight hours after their disappearance. We needed the reporting network. Jessa's case highlighted why in bright-pink neon—especially with the right person to argue for it, and arguing is in my blood. Who did I know with a seat on the Homeland Security and Public Safety Committee? Maybe a little lobbying would help pass these damned mindless workdays.

"I see wheels turning in there." Archie waved a hand in front of my eyes. "What're you thinking?"

"That I'm so desperate for something besides not-so-glorified secretarial nonsense I might try my hand at lobbying?"

He shook his head. "Politics is like a roach motel—folks go in, but they don't come out. Not the same, anyway."

I snorted. "True story."

"I'm beginning to think I could use your psychobabble crap on this one. Want to help me out?" The creases at the corners of his eyes had deepened with time, but the smile was the same one that came with surprise lollipops and bubble gum when I was a kid. I let the dig at my master's in criminal psychology slide. Archie was proud of me—maybe the only person alive who'd ever been truly proud of me—and I knew it down to my bones.

"Can I do that without causing you trouble?"

"Somehow, I'm sure. Let me think on it."

I stood, grabbing another peppermint. "Think fast. I'm going to lose my touch before too long."

Archie tapped a pen on the desk blotter. "Hang in there, kiddo."

"My arms are getting awfully tired, Arch." Stashing a third peppermint in my pocket, I saluted as he wished me a safe drive.

Weaving through the gray maze of desks on my way out of headquarters, I tried to ignore the noise. In every direction, people bustled, phones bleated, brains stormed. Red and black ink transformed the ordinary whiteboards lining every wall into timelines and evidence trails that mocked me every step of the way to the doors. I was here, but I wasn't. I'd made it, but I was still an outsider.

Meritocracy, my ass. How the hell was I supposed to "prove myself" playing courier for the lieutenant? I shoved the door a little too hard but managed to catch the edge before it slammed into the brown brick of the outside wall.

Coffee. The long, monotone drive back to Waco would be shorter and less hypnotizing with a little more caffeine on board. And in Austin, decent coffee is never more than a few minutes away.

I grabbed a newspaper from the rack outside the Starbucks up the street and flipped to the Metro section as I walked in. A property tax hike, the latest miracle cure for homosexuality, and day 167 of the drought, one away from the record. Not a single column inch on Jessa DuGray. Archie was in luck, at least for today.

A half sip into my Pike Place—no cream, two sugars—a scanner alert bleated from my back pocket. Setting the paper on the counter, I pulled my phone out and swiped a thumb across the little red box in the center of the screen.

Unresponsive female. Mansfield Dam Road, just up from the park.

Twelve years in police work, ten of them in homicide, meant the words missing from the screen told me more than the ones screaming from it in all caps. No ambulance requested. So, more "dead" than "unresponsive." And that address sat behind a posh marina on the shores of Lake Travis.

Drowning? I drummed two fingers against my cup. Nah. Who was swimming out there in April? What water the lake had left after six months without rain had to be sixty-five degrees tops.

I read the message again.

Not a single detail offered.

Scanner reports aren't renowned for their prose, but age ranges, race, and circumstances aren't uncommon. Busy dispatcher? I touched the button to see all incidents. Five calls in two hours. So no. Which left two options: new personnel, or a more interesting than average corpse.

"Prove them wrong." Archie wasn't known for bad advice.

I sipped my coffee. The corner chair looked comfy. I could settle into it. Read about the new legislative session. Maybe contemplate making a few calls about that suspicious disappearance alert network.

My eyes went back to the phone screen, my feet moving almost involuntarily away from the inviting leather chair.

I paused, shaking my head. Not my town anymore. Not my job anymore. Could very well land me an ass chewing as a bonus.

All valid points. None as important as a dead woman at Lake Travis on April twenty-fourth. Not that the date meant one damned thing to anybody but me.

Chance, coincidence, plain old lousy luck—that had to be all there was to it.

But today, that was enough. I stuffed the phone back into my pocket, my black boots echoing off the tile, coffee sloshing, as I half ran for the door.

Sliding behind the wheel of my pickup, I flipped the visor down against the spring sunshine and swerved into traffic, earning four middle fingers amid a slew of honked horns and squealing brakes. I waved and pointed the truck toward the lake, my attention already fifteen miles down the road. The scene would be a jurisdictional battle to rival the Alamo—I could name four different departments that would claim rights to the investigation, especially if it could bring good press.

After slamming my brakes when the light at the 2222 intersection flipped yellow to red in a split second, I pulled the phone back out and touched the screen. A good subordinate would call her lieutenant before she moved another inch.

Let them do their jobs, McClellan, I could practically hear his gravelly growl. *They'll ask for our help if they want it.*

But even if they asked, what were the chances anyone would put "New Girl" on anything important? Downright laughable, that's what. I was on my fifth overnight to deliver paperwork to headquarters in as many weeks, for Chrissake.

The shore was probably already crawling with cops and coroners—most of them lacking my uncanny eye for detail and scary-specific memory.

I could help. Razzing aside, I wasn't new—I was a hell of an investigator who'd saved 119 families from the bitter, gnawing hell of not knowing what had happened to someone they loved.

I checked the light, my fingers drifting to the silver star pinned over my heart. My lone goal since I was fourteen years old. Some days it was still hard to believe, even etched in metal: the Texas Rangers.

I had worked damned hard for that badge, and stood proud as one of fewer than twenty women to ever wear it. My chin jutted out, my jaw setting as I stared at the red light. Lake Travis was well within my sector. Technically, all 270,000 or so square miles of the Lone Star State were in my jurisdiction.

Lieutenant Boone didn't strike me as a technical sort of man, but would his irritation simply land me a yellow reprimand slip, or were a million burpees and a whole 'nother year of shit detail closer to his idea of punishment? I didn't know him well enough yet to venture a guess.

Worth risking?

Deep breath.

Green light.

I dropped the phone into the cup holder and laid on the gas, speeding past the luxury-car gallery clogging the city-bound lanes.

Forgiveness was indeed harder to come by, but infinitely easier to ask for. If anybody drawing breath ever knew that, I did.

2

The dead girl's face was flat-out perfection.

Ignoring the burgundy-black blood seeping into the debris-littered, boot-sucking lake bottom revealed by the drought, I studied the rest of her: arms folded across her ribs, clothing neatly arranged, legs slightly cock-eyed, glittery peep-toe heels stretched toward the retreating water.

Blue light skated across a three-hundred-foot wall of concrete behind me, the flashers atop two marked Travis County Sheriff's Office cruisers slingshotting color through the chilly gray shade lining the midmorning waterfront.

"How did you get here?" I murmured, eyes locked on her unnaturally pale face. My habit of talking to dead folks had earned me plenty of funny looks and whispers, but I'd swear on a stack of Bibles it was the reason I'd never missed a collar. I never forgot that the case numbers we assigned victims didn't replace their humanity—someone's child, someone's husband, someone's sister. Caring who they had been, what had stolen their lives, pushed me to keep digging when others wanted to give up. I tiptoed closer, scanning the ground for anything I might disturb before each half step.

"We swept around her first." My favorite coroner's voice came from behind my right shoulder, tipping my lips up into a smile as I turned.

"Good to see you, Jim."

"Back at you." He patted my shoulder. "That star suits you, McClellan. I knew you wouldn't stay with the troopers long when you left the SO. I bet the Rangers are thrilled to have you."

My eyes rolled up so far, I caught a glimpse of my hairline. "So thrilled they've got me fetching coffee and guarding folders," I muttered, letting my boots settle into the mud as I gestured to the lithe body sprawled across it. "How long has she been here?"

My eyes trailed the nearly waist-length blood-tinged blonde hair, my heart rate kicking up too many notches for Archie's peppermints to calm. I dug in my pocket and came up with a crumpled pack of Marlboros.

"Hasn't anyone told you those things will kill you?" Jim shook his head, stringy hair blowing straight up off his comb-over as he turned to look up the face of the dam. "Less than eight hours. Almost no scavenger activity, minimal rigor."

I plopped the smoke onto my lower lip and patted my pockets in search of a lighter. Which I didn't have because that straggly pack was supposed to be there to remind me of why I didn't need them.

Jim pulled a Zippo from his jacket and handed it over without a word. I inhaled, handed it back. Held my breath for a ten count and let my eyes fall shut.

Blonde. Beautiful. Laid bloody at the edge of the water.

Like Charity.

So much for quitting this week. But there was always next week.

"Somebody's going to miss her," I said through a stream of smoke, my nerves jangling a tad less as my eyes roamed the rest of the scene. An espresso-colored Louis Vuitton tote rested at the foot of the dam, a half dozen brightly wrapped packages peeking out the top.

"Where'd that come from?" I jerked my chin toward the bag.

"Uniform found it up at the top of the dam about an hour ago. Brought it down to check for prints."

"Hers?"

"Can't say for sure yet. But probably."

I nodded, turning back to the young woman: toned limbs, eyes the color of a latte. Probably warm when there was life behind them. Now they just stared at nothing.

One last drag and I pinched the butt out and tucked it into my pocket before asking Jim for gloves. Pulling them on, I knelt next to the girl. The answer to everything always lies with the victim. Whatever happened here —murder, suicide, accident—this young woman held the key.

Finding it was the tricky part.

Using two fingers, I closed the girl's eyes, my own moving down a long torso to longer legs. Week-old scabs decorated both knees, but there was no visible blood anywhere except under her head. No bruising on her throat or arms.

Faint pink-red splatters on her gauzy cream blouse caught my eye—not blood, or at least probably not fresh blood, but worth having the lab check the fabric. Sitting back, I ran a gloved finger along a ragged spot: her blouse was ripped, a long strip gone from one of the sheer layers.

Before I could get my mouth open to ask Jim if they'd found the missing scrap, the sun peeked from behind a cloud, angled rays glinting off something in the sand. Something nearly under the dead girl.

I reached for it, my fingers closing around cold metal.

It stuck. Like she didn't want to give it up. Which was stupid—I'd devoted my life to death and disaster and truth, and this beautiful young woman didn't want anything. Not anymore.

Tugging a little harder, I rocked back on my ass in the sand when the metal thing popped free.

It glittered against the blue-gray glove in the shadow-filtered sunshine. A locket. With a broken chain, though whether it was that way before I pulled on it was impossible to guess.

I pressed the clasp hidden in the outside edge, the weight in my palm and a practiced eye telling me this wasn't a cheap piece of jewelry.

Yep—her eyes were warm. They stared from a bitty heart-shaped photo, her laugh lighting a face even prettier than her long, shiny curls. A boy stood behind her, both arms folded around her shoulders, his smile as easy as hers. I glanced back at the girl on the sand. The boy in the photo had to be a foot taller, and she wasn't short.

Raising the locket, I poked my nose a fraction of an inch from their teeny little faces, trying for a better look at his minuscule features.

Oh, sweet Jesus.

I knew that boy.

And the whole goddamn city knew his father.

This wasn't just going to be a jurisdictional nightmare—the clock was already ticking on a full-blown media circus.

Scrambling to my feet, I started for the forensics truck parked near the boathouse like I still wore deputy gray. Halfway there, I spun back to the girl, my gloved fingers tightening around the smooth, cool gold.

As soon as Captain Jameson saw that picture, this girl would be all over the news. Prints would come before five, sure, but maybe my ridiculously cluttered memory could spare this family finding out their princess was dead via the TV. Given any shot at scoring a few political points, Jameson wouldn't even try to find her parents before he leapt in front of the nearest camera.

Except I didn't have to let him. Because I didn't answer to him anymore.

Squeezing the locket tighter, I pulled my glove off around it and slid the little makeshift baggie into my pocket. It wasn't compromised. It'd be a cinch to slip it into evidence later.

Sprinting to my truck, I waved a *See you later* to Jim. He was too busy photographing the contents of the designer tote bag to notice. Probably just as well, with the stolen evidence burning a hole in my Levi's.

I ran every red light between the lake and the South Congress DoubleTree, and whispered a prayer as I loped up three flights of stairs two at a time: *Please let me get to them first.* I'd never make this right, but I could soften the blow.

I flipped my laptop open and clicked to the university's homepage.

Fingers steady, I shook the locket from the glove onto a plastic bag I'd swiped from the ice bucket. It landed facedown, revealing one last secret: *TA* etched into the back.

I dug a pair of rubber-ended tweezers and a magnifying glass from my overnight bag and picked the locket open with the tweezers.

Google.

News.

Sports.

Images.

Yep: Darren Richardson, the most decorated men's basketball coach in NCAA history, accepting a lifetime achievement award in a banquet hall filled with stars, politicians, and professional athletes. And the kid from the locket—Nicholas Richardson, recently crowned state 5A wrestling champ—smiling as he lifted his dad's trophy high.

A four-second search produced the name of Nicholas's school. Of course. Marshall High, educating the next generation of Westlake Hills's country club set since 1896. Charity and I would've gone there, if private school hadn't been deemed superior for "security" (read: image) reasons.

Student directory.

A.

There she was.

My breath stopped. Tenley Andre. Track phenom. List of activities longer than her gorgeous golden hair.

Damn, damn, damn.

Talk about clickbait. A beautiful, accomplished dead girl with ties to a prominent family would get Skye Morrow hotter than George Clooney headlining the next *Magic Mike* movie.

I folded the plastic around the locket and tucked the bundle into a small drawer in the desk, one eye on the clock. Forty-one minutes until the noon newscasts. Marshall High was twenty-five minutes away in normal traffic. Fifteen with the siren.

I slapped the computer shut and ran for the door.

3

It took the vice principal four rounds with a secretary to get Tenley's mother on the phone. I stood at the woman's elbow, shaking my head at the tension in her voice.

"The last thing we need is for her to cause an accident trying to get here. Lighter," I whispered in her free ear. She nodded.

"Don't speed. Just come straight in when you get here," she said. Still tight, but better. She crumpled into her worn leather office chair as she replaced the receiver, turning wide eyes on me. "You're sure it was Tenley?"

I nodded. Like I'd be there asking them to call her mother if I wasn't.

She folded her arms across her desk blotter and dropped her forehead to rest on them, deep breaths moving her suit-jacket-padded shoulders in a slow, steady in-and-out rhythm.

I paced the short stretch of worn carpet to the side of her desk, one eye staying on her tiny frame in case she started to hyperventilate or needed to vomit. I nudged the trash bin closer to her chair with my boot on the next pass—people often get sick after hearing tragic news, and I was wearing the only clean pair of jeans I'd brought.

"What are we going to do with this?" The words were directed at the desk, muffled by her arms. Before I could formulate an answer, she sat up. "Things like this don't happen here at Marshall. Tenley Andre can't possibly be dead—she's president of the senior class, an accomplished athlete, the reigning queen of an impressive group of students. What will people say? How will this make us look?"

I blinked, sucking my cheeks in to keep my mouth shut and continuing back over my last run of steps. No two people take this sort of news the same way, but I'd only ever seen one other human treat death like a PR problem. If I didn't know my mother wouldn't be caught dead in a Donna Karan knockoff, I'd swear she was the one speaking.

The doorknob rattled before the *I'm so sorry this young woman's death is inconvenient for you, Mrs. Bauer,* snuck between my lips, and I turned, leaning one hip on the edge of the desk.

A tall, elegant woman with Tenley's spun-gold hair, hers swept back into a perfect chignon, stepped into the room. Her smile faltered when her eyes landed on me.

"Mrs. Andre?" I glanced between the newcomer and the vice principal. Got a nod from both. "Come on in. I'm Faith McClellan, Texas Rangers."

"Call me Erica. Nice to meet you, Officer. Hello, Sarah." Her voice trembled as she put a hand out for the vice principal to shake.

The older woman took it. Tried to smile. Didn't quite pull it off.

Erica's pale, dewy skin flushed yellowish green.

I waved one hand at a chair, putting the other out to help her if she needed and wishing I hadn't kicked the trash bin toward Vice Principal Image Is Everything.

Tenley's mother ignored the offer of help, holding herself steel-beam rigid as she stood next to the chair.

"Thank you for coming down, ma'am." I let my arms drop to my sides, keeping my posture easy and open. "I have a few questions for you, if you don't mind." Leading with bad news often makes it difficult to collect crucial details, and unraveling Tenley's death would require examining every little thing, no matter how inconsequential it seemed out of context.

She nodded, making a jerky move for the chair. Her face kept the sallow green hue but was otherwise unreadable. Did she know something already? I made a mental note to check police reports for a call.

"When was the last time you saw your daughter?" I asked as the back of Erica's linen skirt hit the black plastic seat.

"This—" Erica stopped before she got the "morning" out.

I raised an eyebrow when her eyes went to the matte beige wall behind Sarah Bauer, her hands twisting in her lap.

"I guess I didn't see her this morning," she whispered. "I heard her in her bathroom right around sunrise, but I shut my alarm off and caught an extra twenty minutes. She was gone when I got up."

I drummed my fingers on my thigh as Erica recounted that, her words directed at the flat-gray industrial carpet, strands of burnished gold falling around her heart-shaped face.

She paused, her gaze drifting to the vice principal. Not that I needed to worry about her letting anything slip—Sarah Bauer's blank mask had been hardened by years of disciplining wayward teenagers, and she was more concerned with discerning a way to preserve her school's sunshine-and-state-champion reputation than she was with Tenley, anyway. She met Erica Andre's pleading eyes for a half second before she dropped hers to her hands.

Tick. Tick. Tick. The second hand on the wall clock was louder than a hundred church bells in the tiny, silent room.

"So yesterday, then?" I prodded gently.

Erica nodded. "I cooked her breakfast, fueled her up for her meet." Her words came quicker as her eyes darted from the clock, to the wilted school official, to me, and around again. "She took first in everything. She always does. 'Nobody catches Tenley Andre' is practically their team slogan, right, Sarah?"

Sarah Bauer nodded, not raising her gaze.

Erica's flicked to the flat-white door. "Where is my daughter?" It came out clipped, but steady. Controlled.

A strangled half sob escaped Sarah.

Erica's shoulders heaved, and I dived for the trash bin, whipping it across the room and landing it at Erica's feet.

She locked her jaw, her nostrils flaring as she pulled in a slow, deep breath.

Swallowing hard, she tilted her face up to look me dead in the eye. "Please. Has there been an accident?"

My lips tilting down automatically into a sort of pitiful upside-down smile that rookie deputy Faith had once practiced in the mirror for hours, I knelt next to the trash bin in front of her, puke zone be damned.

"I'm afraid I have some bad news, ma'am." I pulled my breath in for a five count. A well-executed pause lets folks steel themselves for having their world turned on its head.

Erica's hands set to trembling, her lips rolling between her flawlessly whitened teeth. She shook her head—slowly at first, then fast enough to dislodge her perfect updo. Hairpins flew.

Her eyes tried to widen, her hands going to her throat as she fought for air, and I laid a reassuring touch on her knee.

Every time I sat on this side of a tragedy, this part put me right back in my father's office, bare feet cold under my rose nightgown, his monotone words stripping my world away one layer at a time. The air flat vanished from the room. I knew exactly why Erica Andre couldn't breathe.

I reached for her hand and squeezed, and the pressure let her pull oxygen back into her chest.

"Tenley has died, Mrs. Andre." Best to be blunt here, rip that Band-Aid right off. It's everyone's least favorite part of this job—except me. Because it's not about me and my comfort level, it's about how I can help this person who's drowning under waves of fresh grief. "A jogger found her at the foot of the Mansfield Dam this morning. I'm so sorry for your loss."

I kept my grip on her hands, her fingers going cold under mine, wishing I could read something—anything—through the emotionless mask that betrayed her Botox devotion. Her eyes fixed on a bitty silver nailhead in the school office wall and stayed there, filling so slowly I watched the tears well, and my heart suddenly felt too big for my chest.

"How?" Erica whispered.

I swallowed hard, shaking my head. There was no room for tears here—not from me. Not once in more than a hundred cases had I broken that rule. I always talked to the families. I was damned good at it. And yet here I was trying to cough an answer around a softball that had found its way into my throat. Maybe it was the date—this random Tuesday in late April would now be the same fault line for her it was for me. A break in her timeline, a shift to a new, dimmer reality she'd never wanted to imagine.

I moved onto my knees, raising my head to catch her gaze. "I don't know. But I will find out. You have my word." I was a peon with no clout, a boss who barely trusted me to get his coffee order right, and no jurisdiction here, but I meant every syllable. I could figure out how to deliver on it later.

"Thank you." Her fingers closed tight around mine as the first tear escaped her lashes—and three sharp raps rattled the door.

4

I jerked Sarah Bauer's office door inward with a stern *Not now* ready on my lips. The words died when Graham Hardin's mouth dropped open and hung there like he'd forgotten how to close it.

Scuttling through the door, I pulled it shut before he could get a look behind me, keeping my voice low and hoping he'd follow suit. "Hey, Graham."

"Faith?" It came out an octave too high and at least twice too loud when he figured out how to make his jaw work. The gray-green eyes that so perfectly matched his Travis County Sheriff's Office uniform shot from my face to the name on the door to my badge a half dozen times in as many seconds.

I didn't even need my six-plus years as his partner to see his temper spiking with each pass. His pinched lips and drawn brow screamed "not amused" to the three secretaries and four teachers clustered around the desk outside Mrs. Bauer's door. I grabbed his sleeve, hauled him into the copy room next to the principal's office, and shut the door. No lock to be found. I leaned against it just in case anyone was brave enough to try following.

"Before you—" I began.

"Just what in the blue hell are—" he angry-whispered.

We both stopped, eyes narrowing.

"Ladies first," Graham bit out.

I wanted to tell him where he could shove the patronizing bullshit, but perhaps this wasn't the time. Hauling in a deep breath, I tried for a smile. Not at all sure I pulled it off, I plunged ahead anyway. "I'm just trying to help, Graham."

"With what? We don't need the Rangers to tell us a girl jumped off the dam, Faith. We might not be elite"—he squiggled his long fingers in the air on the last word, throwing in a derisive tone and an eye roll in case I missed the sarcasm—"but we can still manage a simple suicide case."

Not that I needed the scorn to know he was pissed at me. His total radio silence for the two years since I'd left the sheriff's office was a pretty solid clue. I got it, but I didn't deserve it. And I didn't have time for it. Not today.

I checked my watch. "Got it all figured out in two hours, huh? That's convenient. The captain looks good for the cameras, and folks don't get nervous about going to the lake right before the busy summer season."

"That theory might fly further if there was any lake left for people to go to. The back of her head is bashed in. Evidence indicates she was at the top of the dam carrying a very expensive bag that wasn't stolen. Now she's at the bottom. But we appreciate your loyalty." He didn't bother to whisper that time.

I pulled in a deep breath. *Recenter.* Time was, I'd have been plenty pissed at the Rangers stepping on my case, too. "This isn't about loyalty, it's about a young woman who's on her way to the morgue when she shouldn't be, and a family that will never be the same. I'm not trying to steal your glory, Graham. I couldn't give a shit if anyone with an audience ever knows I put a toe in this. I just want to get these people an answer. Same as always."

"We have an answer. She jumped."

"What if she didn't?"

"What if potbellied pigs fly out of Skye Morrow's ass on live TV at ten o'clock?" His eyes flashed, the words razor-sharp.

"It would probably raise her ratings and make her day." I folded my arms across my chest. "This girl had college plans, Graham. Big ones.

Signing day is next week. Nothing matches the suicide profile, at least not yet. Why would she want to die?"

"Same reason the other two kids did last year. Damn cell phones let bullies at them around the clock. Depressed teenagers can't see past the end of next week. They think it's never going to get better."

"Bullies? You saw her, right?"

"Come on, Faith. You went to high school. Jealous teenage girls are meaner than hungry rattlers."

I shook my head. It didn't feel right. "She was a high-profile VIP around here. Even if the parents wouldn't notice something off, the school staff would've. Or her friends. I can't just take the easy answer as the right one. We owe her more than that."

Graham's turn for the deep breath. "You can't make every dead girl a personal crusade."

Says who? I wanted to snap, but I squished the words under my tongue before they could annoy him any more. I didn't care what Graham thought about me. I cared about Tenley. But Graham could shut me out of the case with a quick phone call if I didn't play this just right. Not that I wanted him to know that.

"You know I'm a good cop. And that girl's mother is on the other side of this wall"—I laid a hand on the cool beige plaster to my left—"trying like hell to hold what's left of her shit together long enough to get out of this building. I just wrecked that woman's whole life with a forty-five-second conversation, Graham. I cannot leave her without an answer. Without the right answer."

"I guess you might know a thing or two about that." His voice lost its edge.

"I wish I didn't." I blinked hard. Damned if I'd have him think I was resorting to tears to get my way.

He met my eyes, his softening. "Me too. I mean that."

"I know you do. And I know you know I cannot walk away until I've done right by these people. While you try to prove she jumped, whoever killed her could vanish. Leads cool quickly." Just ask Archie. "We don't have time to prove there's a killer to look for before we start looking."

"We?" Graham raised one eyebrow, his low tone dangerous. "Are the Rangers taking over this case?"

Oops. Back it up a bit.

I shook my head. "Of course not." I smiled. "But I'm not buried at the moment." To say the least. "I'd like to help."

He tapped two fingers on his lips, telling me he was thinking. "You do have that creepy memory thing," he said finally.

Score. "It comes in handy occasionally. Like, say, for identifying victims."

"Aha." He shoved his hands into his pockets, rocking up on the balls of his feet so he towered over me. I stood up straighter. "I wondered," he continued. "We don't even have the print run back. How'd you find her mother?"

I tucked a wayward strand of hair behind my left ear. Taking that locket wasn't terribly legal. But Graham knew I thought rules were stupid when they got in the way of justice, and I was stepping on his case—well, someone's case. The sheriff's office holds jurisdiction over every waterway in the county, but Tenley wasn't in the water because of the drought. Not that the captain would let a technicality stop him once he knew who she was.

"I asked the principal to call her?" I let my voice tick up at the end like he should've known that.

"But where'd you get an ID? I'm waiting on prints. We didn't find a wallet."

My eyebrows pinched together. "If you don't have her name, why are you here?"

"We found a bag full of gifts at the scene. Two of them addressed to students here and one to the track coach. Looking to see if they can shed some light on anything." He crooked his index finger. "How about you go ahead and flip that switch for me?"

"I found a locket."

Graham stuck his hand out.

"I didn't bring it with me. It's at the hotel."

"What did it tell you?"

"Tenley Andre. Senior track phenom. Class president. Girl with no visible reason to leap off the dam. What was in the packages?"

Graham rolled his eyes. "We can't open them until the lab screens them for prints and fluids." He'd grown up enough to leave off the "duh, McClellan" at least.

"Thought you said she jumped?" I softened the jibe with a smile.

"You're not the only one who likes to check all the boxes." The corners of his lips tipped up. "But two and two is usually four."

"Until it's six." Or 230. "Didn't you look at her? How could she have jumped and landed so straight? It looked like she lay down, not like she fell. Remember that jumper we had at Pennybacker Bridge? Her hips were twisted around like she needed an exorcist."

Graham offered a slow nod. "That is weird. Not impossible, but weird."

"Worth having its own box to check. Especially when you have a ready volunteer helper."

He scuffed the toe of his boot on the worn green linoleum, tracing the edge of one whole square before he spoke. "The most pigheaded volunteer who ever raised a hand."

I grinned. "Think of me as your new assistant. Pinkie swear."

His big laugh filled the tiny room. "The day you willingly sign on as anyone's assistant anything, I'll turn in my shield."

Never mind that that was pretty much exactly what my so-called dream job had turned me into. I stretched my face into the smile that used to be reserved for my mother's cocktail parties. Back when I'd still been invited.

"I hear you're the new apple of the brass's collective eye, future commander Hardin." I raised one hand when his cocoa cheeks went peachy pink as he shook his head. "Look around you, Graham. Do twelve seconds of research on Tenley Andre and her friends. This could be big. The kind of big that makes careers. I'm offering you every bit of credit if I'm right and none of the hassle if I'm not."

He folded thick arms across his broad chest. "You're taking care of the family?"

And there was my way in. Graham hated that part more than anyone else did—he tried to look tough, but a soft heart lurked under all the muscles and bravado. Both were reasons we'd always made a good team. "Got it covered. See? I'm helping already."

His eyes crinkled at the corners when he grinned, butterflies flapping in my middle at the flash of bright-white teeth against his dark skin. My hand went to my stomach, my eyebrows puckering. I'd seen Graham smile too many times to count, with nary a noticeable twinge. Then again, last time I saw Graham, he was my partner. Noticing my partner's smile in a butterflies-inducing sort of way was the short road to getting myself fired. Maybe him, too.

"I'll let you do your thing, then," he said. "All I needed to walk out of here with was an ID. Get me contact information for the parents when you're done here, and if you can't manage to fly under Jameson's radar, I didn't see you today."

I shook his hand and promised to call him later, then watched him all the way out of the building before I turned back to the office door.

With more time, I could get Graham on board—provided I was right.

My gut was good, sure. Even so, the best instincts can be jammed by lesser interference: the day, the lake, the pretty teenage girl. Bad memories never stay buried forever, no matter how deep you dig or how far you run.

But chasing a ghost beats the hell out of missing a murderer.

5

Tenley Andre was more phenomenon than actual person—at least to the crowd of school officials in the little beige office, which included the principal and the track coach by the time I'd finished arguing with Graham.

Hushed conversations about spin control and counselors practically overlooked and definitely dehumanized the superstar Marshall High had just lost. And with her mother still sitting in the big middle of it—nice, folks.

"I just got a call from the athletic department at Stanford yesterday." Jake Simpson shook his head, one hand running through his thick chestnut hair. "They want to finalize the formal signing for her scholarship. What the hell do I tell them?"

Simpson oozed smarmy self-importance, from his "Four-Time State Champions" hat to his designer sneakers. So far, his talking wasn't making me like him any more.

"Nothing." My reply had a tinge too much edge.

He blinked. "I'm sorry?"

"You'll tell them nothing. Don't call them back yet."

"But I—"

I raised one palm, leaning in and lowering my voice. "Priorities, Coach. I shouldn't need to point out that this woman just lost her child—never mind that no one has had a chance to speak to Tenley's father. I won't have this all over the TV before he knows about it. Which means what you've learned in this room today stays in this room until further notice."

He shrugged. "Whatever you say, ma'am." My bullshit detector flipped right on over to truckload of steaming manure.

"Thank you so much." I smiled. "I'd hate for you to spend the end of your season tied up in court because you interfered with an open police investigation."

Well, I wouldn't hate it, but it wouldn't happen, either—without an injunction, I couldn't keep him from running straight down the hill to channel two and jumping on the air with a photo of Tenley.

I'd bet he didn't know that.

His blue eyes widened as he nodded. "Of course not."

Looked like I'd won that hand.

Turning my best no-nonsense glare on the rest of the room, I repeated the request for confidentiality. "I understand y'all want to help your students through this," I said before the school administrators could speak. "But I need you to keep it quiet as long as you can. If anyone asks, you don't know where she is."

Principal Shannon nodded. "Of course, Officer."

Tenley's mother raised her head from the principal's shoulder when he spoke. "I have to go home." Her voice faded. "Please."

The track coach started to reach for her, stopped midstep, and shoved his hands into his pockets, his shoelaces fascinating all of a sudden. Huh. I watched for three more ticks. He didn't move again, so I stepped to Erica's side and laid a hand on her shoulder.

"I'll be happy to take you. Is there someone I can call to come sit with you while you wait for your husband to get home?"

Simpson looked toward Erica. "Is Brent flying this week?"

She nodded, her eyes staying on the carpet.

"Her husband is a pilot," the principal told me. "Continental."

"We'll find him," I said, sneaking a last glance back at the coach, who was looking everywhere except at Erica Andre.

The principal stood and helped Erica to her feet, and I offered her an arm. She hesitated, only taking it when her knees began to shake. Pulling in a slow breath, she stared down at her strappy pink sandals. "I need to go home," she repeated.

My chest tightened around my heart as I contemplated the difference between the pitiful woman hanging on my arm and the one who'd arrived an hour ago, the picture of West Austin privilege from her every-strand-in-order hair to her cost-more-than-a-month-of-groceries shoes.

The Botox left her brows unable to move enough to reveal actual emotion, but her puffy, crimson-rimmed eyes and blotchy skin told the story well enough.

I nodded to the school officials huddled around the desk. The vice principal brushed fresh tears from her cheeks, her boss blinking hard as they looked over assembly schedules.

Coach Simpson leaned on the edge of the desk on two hands, his lips stretched into a tight line, eyes hard as blue granite.

"Thank you for your time and your help," I said, handing the principal a card I'd fished from my back pocket and taking one from the little silver stand on the corner of Sarah's desk. "I'll be in touch."

I patted Erica's hand, took a half step toward the door. "You ready?"

Erica didn't move. "Does it matter?"

I put a hand on the knob. "You just tell me when, ma'am."

"Wait." Erica's voice trembled, her fingers going to her hair. She pulled the last three pins and dropped them to the carpet, running her hand through the length and hiding her swollen face behind a curtain of shining bronze.

I could've heard a gnat sneeze as we left the building, but Erica kept her head down and I helped hold her up until we reached my truck. I secured Erica's seat belt before I climbed in and started the engine, then idled to the parking lot exit and pulled my phone from my pocket to look up the Andres' address.

GPS set, I turned left out of the parking lot. Erica's head lolled across the back of the seat, looser than a rag doll's, her glassy eyes staring at nothing.

I focused on the road, ticking back through people and conversations and letting the silence stretch. There were no words that would make this woman okay today. Or tomorrow, or next year.

Getting her an answer was the only thing that might help, however little. So that's what I would do. I stopped at the corner of Redbud and Forest View, started to reach for the radio, changed my mind.

"She was early." The words rasped out on a whisper, pulling my eyes from the road to my passenger. Fresh tears spilled down Erica's cheeks. "Always early, and so strong. I felt her move for the first time when I was just thirteen weeks pregnant. By sixteen weeks, Brent could feel her kick. The doctor said it was impossible, until she landed a swift one to his arm while he measured my belly."

I nodded, the kind of awkward half smile that comes with not knowing if or how to reply uncomfortable on my lips. The Benz behind me beeped, and I was so glad to have something that needed my attention I almost waved a thank-you. Turning left on Westlake, I let Erica's words build a picture of the young woman behind Tenley's beautiful face.

"She was born in late August, due October first. They took her to the NICU and put her in an incubator, told us the first week would be crucial to how well she'd fare, and the degree of mental retardation she'd suffer from lack of oxygen during the delivery." Erica snorted. "She was in my arms less than twelve hours later, breathing fine on her own. She talked at six months. Walked at nine. By ten, she was running, and she never stopped. My miracle. My supernova. Always fastest. Always first. For her whole life."

Her voice dissolved into a harsh sob as we turned onto her street, stately homes set far back in the low Texas trees flashing past the windows. The sadness in the truck was heavy. Permeable.

Familiar.

"Her whole life," Erica repeated. "Her whole life . . . is o—" she didn't get the last part out, turning her face to the window. I knew she didn't see what was on the other side as I turned into the driveway at number 19. We rolled past brick columns, under an arch dripping with blooming wisteria, and around a massive concrete fountain that hadn't been notified of the drought.

I stopped in front of imposing ten-foot oak double doors. "I'm so sorry for your loss, Mrs. Andre. Are you sure you don't want me to call anyone? Family? A neighbor? A friend?"

Erica stayed still, eyes on the house, questions falling around her unnoticed.

I let the pause stretch a day's ride into awkward territory before I cut the engine and hopped out of the truck. I rounded the front bumper and pulled her door open. I started to speak. Thought better of it. Offered a hand.

Erica's thin shoulders shuddered. Her mouth opened for a scream, no sound escaping.

I rested pale fingers on her spray-tanned golden-brown arm, nearly landing on my ass when she plunged headlong for the polished-stone drive. Thanks to somewhere around a million hours of suspension core training, I managed to keep us both upright as Erica crushed my shoulders in a desperate, sob-riddled embrace.

A stranger's face buried in my neck, my thoughts whirled with a thousand things I needed to do before I slept and ten thousand questions clamoring to be asked first, the steely resolve I'd missed for months settling heavy in my chest. No matter what Graham or the lieutenant had to say, I was in this. I belonged here.

I would find this woman an answer or die trying.

But right then, I patted Erica Andre's back and let her cry.

6

She couldn't go in the house.

She had to go in the house.

She never wanted to go in the house again.

I remembered that sinking dread like it had been nineteen days and not nineteen years—the knowledge that Charity's absence would sting warring with a need to be in her spaces, to keep her with me a bit longer. Indecision radiated from Erica Andre's face like a neon billboard as she lifted her head from my shoulder and turned her eyes to the flawless white stucco facade of her home.

I reached for a box of tissues and blotted tears and snot off my neck and collar, watching her for a cue. Her eyes fell shut, and she tensed from hairline to heels. Three deep breaths later, she met my gaze.

"I'm—" She cleared her throat when the word came out on a croak. "I'm sorry."

I pressed the tissue box into her hands. "Don't apologize, ma'am."

Erica mopped at her face. "I don't know how to do this. How am I supposed to feel? How am I supposed to be?"

I leaned back against the truck, my shoulders going up before I got any words out. "However you feel is how you're supposed to feel. However you get through the next days and weeks is the best you can."

Erica laid the tissue box on the seat. "I'm still hoping this is a nightmare and I'm going to wake up any minute and hear T—" She swallowed hard. "Hear my daughter in the bathroom, singing while she puts on her eyeliner. But if I were dreaming this, I couldn't have dreamt a more compassionate person to be here for it. So thank you."

"I'm truly sorry I have to be here, Mrs. Andre."

Erica squared her shoulders, nodding to the front doors. "I have to do this, don't I?" Her voice cracked.

"No."

"I'm sorry?" She blinked, turning her head.

"You don't have to do anything, ma'am. If there's one thing I know that I know, it's that when life throws you something this horrifying, most of the rules you live every day by no longer apply. You don't have to go in there. I am happy to drive you anywhere else you'd like."

Erica tipped her head to one side. Shook it. "I appreciate that," she said. "But if I don't do this now, I may never do it again."

I put out a hand. "Ready when you are."

The lock squealed a protest as Erica turned the key, the alarm yakking and beeping when she opened the door. Her sandals seemed rooted to the marble as she stared at me with wide eyes and barked a short laugh.

"I can't remember the passcode."

The beeping picked up speed.

"Let it go off." I patted her arm. "That, I can handle."

"This is so stupid." The words came through her manicured fingertips, muffled. "Oh-eight-two-nine. It's always been Tenley's birthday. I'm losing my goddamned mind."

I shook my head, crossing to the touch screen near the hallway and poking at it. The house fell quiet after the first peal of the siren.

"Thank you." Another tear escaped Erica's lashes.

"No problem." I wrapped my arms around myself, eyes roaming the immaculate copper and white-marble foyer: smooth eggshell walls rose to a domed two-story ceiling accented with copper-cast molding, and a large leaded-glass window above the heavy front doors tossed a thousand tiny rainbows over the room in the afternoon light. Directly across from the doors, a pair of art niches occupied by cream-and-peach Ming vases flanked the entrance to the family room. A massive claw-footed mahogany table with burnished copper overlay dominated the floor space, a Waterford vase full of spring wildflowers in the center lending the room a pleasant scent. Down a short hall to the right, French doors guarded a library that would do a bookworm Disney princess proud.

My mother would love this room. But the reflexive *Your home is lovely, Mrs. Andre,* that was as much a part of me as my deductive and observational skills didn't make it past my lips. On a normal day, a woman like Erica would be insulted by my lack of comment on such a stunning showplace.

Today was not a normal day. I turned back just in time to see her yank one foot from the Venetian tile and stride toward the archway opposite the front door. I followed, stopping when she pulled up short in the doorway before she broke into a run.

The sharp heels on her sandals left divots in the wide-plank walnut floor as she half flew across the room. She gathered a gray cashmere throw into her arms, burying her face in it and breathing deep, before she sank into the short end of the sprawling chocolate leather sectional.

I took a seat next to her and caught a waft of vanilla and lavender from the blanket. Tenley's perfume, I'd bet.

"Can I bring you anything?" I asked.

Her shoulders hitched, face still hidden by the throw, her words muffled. "Yesterday," she said. "Bring me yesterday so I can lock her in, sit on her, keep her safe here with me."

"I wish I could." I patted her shoulder, letting her sit for another minute before I dropped a question on her. "Mrs. Andre, it's pretty important that I get in touch with your husband."

She raised her face and nodded, looking past my shoulder at a twenty-by-twenty-four canvas hanging over the fireplace. A younger, even thinner Erica and a tall, fit man in a white linen shirt that had to be the husband, laughing in front of a sinking violet-pink sun flanked by low aquamarine waves on a beach.

"Chelsey Davies." Her words dropped heavy. "If you find her, you'll find Brent. I'd say let me call, but I tried him this morning when I saw the news about the storms in Louisiana and Mississippi. Wanted to make sure he was okay. He didn't pick up."

Fantastic. What could I say to that? I studied her face, my heart twisting at the anguish even the Botox couldn't hide.

"When was the last time you saw your husband, Mrs. Andre?"

"Last night. It was late. We had yet another fight. I went for a drive, he went to bed. The house was quiet when I got home."

"Was Tenley home for this fight? Did she know about Miss Davies?"

Erica shook her head. "Tenley adores her dad. Utter mutual admiration society. I wouldn't take that from her. They even have a standing lunch date every week. They've been doing it since she was twelve."

"When?"

"Every—" Erica stopped, her hand moving back to her mouth. "Monday."

Hmmm. I pulled a pad and pen from my hip pocket and scribbled that down. "Is Tenley's car still at school?"

"It's in the garage. But she rides with friends sometimes. I didn't think anything was wrong when I saw it . . ." More tears swallowed the "this morning."

"Mrs. Andre, I know this is difficult, and I appreciate you hanging with me for just a few more questions: Who were Tenley's closest friends? Is there anyone you can think of she might have confided in? Anyone who might know what could have happened this morning?"

Erica shrugged. "Tenley and Nicky Richardson have been practically joined at the hip for almost as long as I can remember, but even he hasn't been around much in a while. They've all been so busy, finishing up school, getting ready to leave home . . . She did say she was going to his house to hang out on Sunday, though. Nicky knew her better than anyone else but me."

That was the boyfriend from the locket photo. Good enough. I nodded and stood. "Thank you, ma'am. This gives me a few places to start. Are you sure I can't get you anything?"

Erica started to shake her head. Paused. "Boo bear," she whispered.

"Stuffed animal?"

Erica nodded. “If you go to the top of the stairs and take a left, in the room at the end of the hall, there will be a pink teddy bear on the bed. If you could get me that, I’d like to have it. I can’t go . . .”

A free pass to poke around Tenley’s room? I was already halfway up the stairs when Erica’s sentence dissolved into another sob.

7

A bedroom fit for a princess, right down to the mahogany canopied bed dripping floaty pink and lavender muslin. Tenley Andre had slept under that canopy. Read on that thick, plush gray velvet window seat. Done her homework at the carefully distressed chic white desk.

My eyes skipped from the wall unit full of trophies to the Stanford pennant that stuck out so much it had surely been a fight to get the mom to agree to hang it.

Tenley had lived in this room.

Could anything here tell me why or how she'd died?

I put a toe onto the pale-gold wood floor, my boot issuing the faintest *click* against the tenpenny nailhead glinting out of the board end.

Crossing to the window, I surveyed the grounds, straining for a glimpse of the street through the trees. All was quiet, but it wouldn't stay that way for long. I was kind of surprised Graham wasn't already there, really. "Probably tied up with the press," I muttered, thankful for any small favor today.

Desk first. The surface was tidy—a stack of bright folders and papers in a dusky purple tray, a pink cup sporting a Taj Mahal silhouette full of pens and highlighters, a fancy graphing calculator, and a sleek silver MacBook.

A toile-covered memo board hung nearby, dotted with ticket stubs, ribbons, and photos of Tenley with her mom, with the track coach, and with the man from the portrait over the fireplace downstairs. I slid my phone from my pocket and snapped a photo of the board. Why no pictures with friends?

I bent to check the drawers: mail in the top one, three large envelopes from Wells Fargo under several smaller ones from Stanford; a stationery box filled the middle drawer; the bottom held tissue paper and rolls of ribbon.

I flipped the laptop open with the nail of my index finger, my silent prayer answered as the screen brightened, a neat row of program shortcuts running across the bottom.

Sometimes it was hard to remember that not everyone guarded information the way I did.

Photos of Tenley and the boyfriend peppered the screen's background. Skiing, boating, dressed up in formal wear, standing on a bluff next to bikes . . . there had to be forty snapshots of them doing everything under the sun, dazzling smiles lighting every single one.

Next up: I needed to find this kid.

I clicked the Safari logo and scanned her favorite sites, then the recently visited. Instagram, school, YouTube . . . and realtor.com?

I opened the history, scrolling faster as the days went back.

Every day for the past several weeks, Tenley had looked at apartments in Palo Alto. She was headed there for school in the fall, the track coach said. Dorms must be passé these days.

YouTube recents had a KT Tape how-to for a sore calf, a cat fails compilation, and a *Futurama* episode.

No "How to jump off a dam." No "Suicide methods of the rich and famous."

Who looks at apartments when they're not planning to be alive for the move?

Social media might know. Tenley was the poster girl for the selfie generation, every moment, every smile, caught on camera and shared with the world. I clicked to her Instagram: 389 notifications. How often did she check it, for crying out loud?

I clicked the little red badge and scrolled through the first hundred—all less than twelve hours old. Back on the main feed, I trailed my fingers over the trackpad and watched images flash by. A party. A big party for a random Monday night. And Tenley was tagged in what? Almost four hundred of these?

Good Lord. Selfie generation, indeed. Slowing my scroll, I looked for Tenley and Nicholas. Found them both, but not in the same frames. Were they fighting? I didn't want to think a girl as smart as Tenley would jump off the dam over a boy, but evidence doesn't always tell the story I want it to.

Damn, what I wouldn't give for time to go through these carefully. I stopped on an image of a group of kids laughing, raising red Solo cups at the camera. Tenley was the only one who didn't have a cup. Or a smile.

I zoomed in, picking apart Tenley's flat, uncomfortable expression. Her eyes weren't on the camera, but cut to her right, glaring at a tall, muscle-bound boy with dark hair. He wasn't Nick Richardson, but he sure appeared to have his hand on her ass, and she sure didn't look happy about it.

I snapped a photo of the screen with my phone and kept scrolling. Wait. There they were, Tenley and Nicholas, her easy smile back in place, his arm slung over her shoulders, cheek resting on her hair, as they overlooked the city from what appeared to be a very large deck. I went back, comparing the time stamps on the photos. The sullen one was posted almost an hour before the more relaxed one. I snapped a shot of it, too, glancing at the others as they blurred by and wishing I had time to review them all.

But I didn't. Did I?

Tapping a finger on one side of my phone, I looked around. There, on the nightstand. I grabbed the iPhone cable and plugged my phone into Tenley's laptop, clicked "No" when it asked if I wanted to sync them, and touched the phone screen to open my password thief. One by one, I navigated to Tenley's social media bookmarks: Instagram, Twitter, Snapchat. One by one, checkmarks flashed on my screen.

It was the first time I'd tried the app, poached off a corner of the dark web I didn't feel all that bad for perusing if the up-to-no-good inventions lurking there could help me unravel a murder. Hopefully this particular cyber criminal was actually worth the fifty bucks he'd charged me.

Unplugging the phone, I tapped a pencil on the desk blotter, imprints on the surface catching my eye. I bent closer, running one finger over an off-color blotch with ragged edges. Another. And another. She'd been writing. And crying.

Who was Tenley Andre when the cameras were off, the winners' circle was dark and silent, and the whole world wasn't watching?

I pulled a notebook from my back pocket, laid a thin sheet over the impression, and ran the side of the pencil back and forth lightly. Learned from Nancy Drew and still useful decades later.

Well, sort of useful—I lifted the paper, but the white lines standing against the gray were so convoluted, I couldn't make out anything.

Like many things had been written over the tearstained blotter.

The letters Graham found with the gifts?

I held the page up to the light. Nothing.

Damn.

I closed the notebook and the laptop, returned the charging cord to the nightstand, and let my eyes roam the room again. Directly across from the desk, in the middle of the built-in bookcase, sat the trophy shelf, a gilt-framed photo front and center: neck heavy with gold medals, Tenley hoisted the state track-and-field trophy high, her grin threatening to split her gorgeous face clean in two.

I crossed to the shelf, shaking my head at two-dimensional Tenley, Graham's suicide theory rattling around my head. "I don't buy it. You weren't sad, you weren't slow, you weren't hiding from the world. What happened, Tenley?"

Wishing I'd thought to bring gloves, I turned for the bed. Made with military precision, the thing didn't look like it had ever so much as been sat on.

I dropped to my knees, sliding the back of one hand under the lace dust ruffle. Cliché, hiding stuff under the bed, but that doesn't stop it from being common.

Laying my head on the thick floral-patterned rug, I clicked the flashlight on my phone.

Tenley Andre was not common. Not even a flipping dust bunny.

The closet?

I stood and moved to the double doors on the opposite wall. Nudged one open with the toe of my boot.

Bathroom.

Resplendent in gold and white, it even sported a chandelier over the huge claw-footed swimming tub, crystals swaying in the current from the air vent overhead. They speckled the marble sink with tiny rainbows, courtesy of the skylights.

Same care and precision as the rest of the house, not so much as Tenley's toothbrush out of place. The closet door lay open on the opposite wall, and I crossed to it, pausing when I heard a rumble that sounded an awful lot like an engine.

Shit. I might not get another chance to look around Tenley's room. But pissing off the wrong people would cost me any ability to help Tenley's family.

Yanking my phone back out of my pocket, I fired off a photo of each wall. Nothing jumped at me from the rows of neatly hung designer apparel organized by season and color, but maybe the photos would pick up a clue that panicked, in-the-moment me didn't see.

I spotted the bear on my way back through the bedroom and snagged it, pulling the door shut behind me with the back of one finger. Better if Erica didn't walk by an ambush eyeful of her daughter's things.

I hurried back to the stairs—just as chimes drifted through the house.

So close.

Turning my back flat against the wall, I watched a tearstained Erica Andre cross the foyer.

The door clicked. Hinges squealed.

Muffled voices. I strained, but couldn't make out what they were saying over the blood rushing in my ears. Dammit.

I put a foot on the top stair. Pulled it up again. Squared my shoulders and stepped away from the wall.

What the hell was I hiding from? I was a goddamned Texas Ranger, with the badge and the slightly bruised ego to prove it.

It's not your case, I could practically hear Lieutenant Boone's voice.

It is if I make it my case. Not that I would dare talk to him like that in real life, but boy it felt good to do it in my head.

Erica walked back into my sight line toting a square end table finished to a high shine with cherry lacquer.

And no cops. Thank God for small favors.

I cleared my throat before I started down the stairs.

Erica looked up, her eyes widening at the bear, table crashing to the marble floor. "You found him."

"He was hiding." I flashed a half smile as I stepped off the bottom riser and handed the toy to Erica.

"Thank you!" Erica hugged the thing to her chest with a force that would put an unfortunate end to any actual critter that size.

"Of course." I bent and reached for the table, moving it to the hallway off the left of the foyer.

"My neighbor refinishes antique pieces for my studio." Erica sniffled.

I nodded absently, my thoughts still on Tenley and the photos chronicling the last few hours of her life. Damn, I hoped that password grabber was the real deal. I pulled my buzzing phone from my pocket, wincing at the channel two news notification.

EXCLUSIVE: Marshall High track star found dead near Lake Travis. News2 *standing by for details. Click to stream live.*

My lips folded between my teeth as my eyes went from the screen, to Erica, to the portrait of Tenley's parents smiling from another lifetime.

Damn Captain Jameson and his monstrous ego.

"I'm afraid I have to go, ma'am. Will you promise to call me if you think of anything that might help me figure out what happened to Tenley?"

Erica's eyes spilled over again as she nodded. I gave her fingers a last squeeze and strode out the door, checking my watch.

The last bell would ring at Marshall in sixteen minutes. A pinch of luck, and I could still get to the boyfriend before the press did.

8

A jackass is still just a jackass, no matter how many diamond bridles you dress it up in. Larry Jameson was preening, posturing proof my granddaddy was right about that.

Stopped at a light halfway to the high school, I banged one palm against the steering wheel, shaking my head at a text message from Graham: *As soon as Jameson gets done with his TV strutting, he's going to tell the family himself. When he finds out they already know . . .*

Shit. Of course the cameras were the captain's first priority when someone had lost a child—but Jameson's particular brand of sadistic narcissism meant he'd find delivering tragic news to the Andres nearly as much fun as talking to the press. While I was too invested in Tenley's story to care about saving my own ass from hot water, I couldn't let Jameson's temper keep me from finding her family an answer.

The light changed. I checked the rearview. Empty. Bending my head, I ignored the light, thumbs flying over the screen. *I haven't talked to her father. He's out of pocket. Pilot for Continental.* The captain was the kind of man who would consider notifying Mr. Andre "informing the family" whether he talked to Tenley's mother or not. Problem solved.

I dropped the phone in the cup holder and hit the gas when the light flashed to yellow.

Bing. *10-4.*

I swallowed a smile I didn't have the time or energy for. Graham was willing to help me nose around in this case. That could mean something interesting. But we could figure out how interesting after we had Tenley Andre's death unraveled.

Blowing right past the secretaries, I barreled into Sarah Bauer's office with two minutes to spare—and found exactly what I was looking for, with an unwelcome bonus: the boy from Tenley's locket, the hair longer and shaggier but the face unmistakable, sprawled across the chair Erica Andre had vacated an hour earlier.

Three heads turned when I opened the door without bothering to knock. In half a tick, I knew three things: Nicholas didn't know yet. Sarah had every intention of telling him. And, with Darren Richardson in the other chair, this was about to get complicated. Hadn't I been clear with the "Please don't talk about this yet"?

"Officer McClellan, I didn't expect to see you again today?" I couldn't tell if the rise in Sarah's tone was more question or guilt—or a little of both. I held the woman's gaze for a ten count before I answered, my voice tight.

"So I see," I said slowly, turning a smile on Nicholas and his father. "Coach Richardson, it's nice to meet you. Faith McClellan, Texas Rangers."

"Come in, Officer." Sarah Bauer's voice was at least an octave too high, and my smile faded when I turned back to nod a curt thank-you.

Damn this woman to the very tip-top ring of hell. Kids are tricky—interviewing anyone under eighteen requires a parent's presence, unless of course it's a casual conversation and not an official questioning. Add even a little bit of money or a hint of celebrity to the room, and tricky becomes downright impossible because the lawyers have to have their hands in every damned thing.

I had walked right into the exact situation I was trying to avoid by hauling ass up there. Not only was Coach Richardson present but he'd have legal counsel at his side in twelve seconds if I so much as thought the word *investigation*.

The kid sat up straight and shook back bronze curls, his smile fading. "Mrs. Bauer?" he asked as his father shot out of his seat with a too-loud, too-fast "The Texas Rangers? Is this a joke? Dammit, boy, is it possible for you to not be an embarrassment for more than five minutes? All I'm asking is a little effort."

Mrs. Bauer's awkward half smile didn't flicker. Neither did Nicholas's stony mask. Darren Richardson's cheeks and forehead, however, went from ruddy to an alarming shade of magenta during his tirade.

Damn. Whether the kid was a troublemaker or not—and by the sympathy pouring from the vice principal's eyes, my money was on not—that was quite a flying leap off the handle.

I shut the door behind me and stepped forward, narrowed eyes on college basketball's best-loved coach.

"Nobody is saying Nicholas has done anything, sir." I gave the words a little volume and a lot of edge, pulling every eye in the room my way. Standing up to my full nearly six-foot height, I met Richardson's scowl with one of my own. "While I believe I know why Mrs. Bauer asked Nicholas in here, as you just heard her say, she was not expecting me."

"Fine." Richardson sank back into the chair, his color fading to near normal. "What, then?"

Mrs. Bauer opened her mouth, snapped it shut, and closed her eyes.

I reminded myself that she'd found Tenley's mother for me and held my tongue.

I crossed to Nick and knelt in front of him the same way I'd knelt in front of Erica. "Nicholas—" I began.

"It's Nicky," he interrupted quietly, guarded green eyes fixed on a spot above my left ear.

"Only because you want to aggravate me any way you can," his father muttered.

Hot damn. Yes, let's.

"Nicky." I cloaked the word in chirpy brightness. "When was the last time you saw Tenley Andre?"

"Why?" Pretty sure that was a chorus of Richardson voices, but I stayed focused on Nick.

"Can you tell me first?"

"Last night. This morning, I guess, technically. It was after midnight when I took her home."

The party. I was itching to ask, but I needed to let him tell his story.

"Home from where?" I kept my eyes on Nick and my tone light, well aware that his father would holler for an attorney at the first breath of interrogation. Not to protect the kid, of course, but to protect his image. That's a much more urgent concern for a narcissist of Coach Richardson's caliber, and I've known my narcissists inside out and sideways since long before I graduated the academy.

"We were at a party. Somebody's parents were out of town. Everyone ended up there. Same story, different day."

"You don't know whose house it was?"

Nick shook his head, his eyes finally meeting mine. "I think the kid was like a sophomore or something. Why are you asking? Is Tenley okay?" His eyes went wide, his nostrils flaring, breath speeding.

Never gets one teeny heart tear easier.

I sucked in a long breath and reached for his hand before I shook my head. "I'm afraid not. She was found dead near Lake Travis early this morning."

Mrs. Bauer sighed. Coach Richardson's breath hissed in through his teeth.

I only saw Nick, whose whole face had gone slack and unfocused, a single tear disappearing into the four-day scruff lining his jaw.

"No." He shook his head. "No way. We were going to Stanford together, me and T. Getting out of all the bullshit here."

The room was cemetery silent for a full second before it exploded.

"Like hell you are!" Richardson jumped back to his feet, a big vein popping out of his temple to highlight the magenta flooding his face this time. "I gave Mo Owens my word. Your ass will be right here come September. You want to stick with your faggoty sport, fine, but you're not going anywhere."

Dad of the year right there. Flinching at the hateful words and tone, I watched Nicky's eyelids drift down before I stood slowly and spun to face the coach. "Sit. Down. And shut. Up."

"Excuse me?" he roared, his cheeks going from magenta to plum.

I took a step forward and lowered my voice. "Your timing might be great on a basketball court, but it's shit in the real world. I just told this boy his girlfriend is dead. Can't your diatribe about college choices wait?"

Richardson's face stretched into a grin, a single boom of laughter sliding through his bonded teeth. "His girlfriend?" He shook his head. "Some Texas Ranger you are. If you can prove this kid of mine isn't a fucking fairy, I'll let him go to college anywhere he damn well pleases. Owens will live."

Wait. What?

I turned back to Nicky, who made no move to acknowledge that his father had spoken, his head still shaking slowly back and forth. "She was the only person who ever loved me just for me. Jesus, Tenner, what did you do?"

I pressed a clenched fist into the side of my thigh to keep from slamming it into the top of Mrs. Bauer's desk. First order of business: Did Tenley kill herself? While my gut said that was the easy solution to what was becoming a more convoluted equation by the minute, Nicky's accusatory words were enough to give me pause.

Ignoring the blustering asshat to my left for the moment, I knelt in front of Nicky again. "Can you tell me what makes you think she did anything?"

"Do we need a lawyer for this?" That came from the coach, low and threatening.

Dammit. I swiveled a withering look at Richardson, not bothering to stand. "I guess that's dependent on whether or not anyone here has done anything you think might require legal advice. At the moment, the Travis County sheriff is pursuing a suicide investigation in this case." Every word true.

Richardson moved to the wall and leaned against it, cocking one leg up to flatten his shiny brown wing tip against the beige paint. "I see."

When he stayed quiet, I turned back to Nicky.

"Can you help me understand this? Because from where I sit, it makes very little sense."

He shrugged his broad shoulders, his eyes still distant. "I've been so wrapped up in my own bullshit I didn't try hard enough to find out what was bothering her." He slumped forward and buried his face in his big hands, fingers digging into his scalp. "God, what if I could've stopped it?"

I left him to his grief for a moment, turning back to Sarah Bauer. "Had you seen any evidence that Tenley was unhappy?" I asked, trying to keep the irritation I still felt with the woman out of my voice.

Sarah's carefully shellacked, teased brunette hairdo didn't budge as she shook her head hard. "Tenley was a model student athlete. Our track season isn't even over, but we've already qualified for the state meet on points, most of them from her blowing every other kid in the district straight off the track." She punched a few keys on her computer and tapped a finger on the space bar as she waited for something to load, then shook her head again. "Near-perfect grades. She's solidly in our top five seniors, battling for the salutatorian's seat at graduation. No discipline issues."

"Visits with the counselor?" I asked.

"I can't see that here," Mrs. Bauer said. "And unfortunately, Tenley's counselor is on personal leave for her daughter's wedding in Jamaica this week."

Of course she was. My eyes went back to Nicky, who was still hiding his face. I laid a hand on his shoulder. "I'm so sorry for your loss."

He looked up at me. "She told me she loved me about a hundred times last night. I loved her so much. How did this happen?"

"We don't have all the facts yet." The kid didn't need the gory details.

"You said she was at the lake?" Nicky's brow furrowed. "Why else would she go alone?"

I tipped my head to one side, itching for a pen and paper but choosing to push my freakish total recall ability because I didn't want to spook Coach Richardson. Why didn't he have somewhere more important to be?

"I saw lots of photos of you guys on her laptop," I said. "The lake was special to her?"

"We ski off the coach's boat every week in the summer. But the best memories I have of Tenner and the lake will always be of sitting up on the dam talking all night."

The dam. I couldn't ask, though. Better to let him fill the silence.

"She loved it there. Said it felt like she was on top of the world, but the world felt big. Big enough that she couldn't break it. We'd sit up there, right off the edge of the old closed road, and just spill our guts until the sun came up." He let the sentence trail, his attention going to his long fingers, playing with a fat platinum class ring.

When he'd been silent for a full minute, I cleared my throat. "Have you been there recently?" Like maybe this morning?

Nicky shook his head. "I haven't seen much of Tenley since . . . well, most of this year, really." His eyes flicked toward his father. "I've been busy. I was actually glad to rescue her from Davenport last night. At least I got to talk to her for a while."

Rescue? I felt my brow furrow. The kid from the Instagram photo, maybe?

But what of the rest of that? From what I'd seen and heard so far, Nicky was the most important person in Tenley's world. So why had they lost touch for one of the biggest years of their young lives? Two and two here was anything but four.

"Why hadn't you seen her? Did you two have a fight?"

Nicky shook his head. "We never fought. Not since we were kids."

Richardson snorted. "Easy to avoid fighting with a girl you're not screwing."

And here I'd almost forgotten he was there. Probably what made him pipe up in in the first place. I closed my eyes and locked my jaw for a five count so I wouldn't tell him which orifice he could shove his useless bullshit into.

Ignore him. That was certainly the thing that got under my father's skin best.

I stayed on Nick. "Can you tell me what happened?"

He scrubbed both hands over his face, hooking a thumb toward the coach so subtly I wasn't sure it was on purpose until he met my eyes with widened ones and a barely whispered "I can't."

He could. But wouldn't with his dad there. *Ten-four, kid.*

I turned a pleading glance on Mrs. Bauer. *Get him out of here,* I mouthed.

Sarah Bauer offered a small nod, clearing her throat. "Coach? Principal Shannon was just telling me the other day we should discuss adding you to our hall of fame, even though you didn't attend Marshall, because of your extraordinary accomplishments and devotion to the school. I wonder if you'd have a minute to talk with him about that, as long as you're in the building?"

Richardson's mouth curled up on one side. "About time you people recognized greatness when you see it. Especially after everything I've done for this place. Is he in his office?"

I swallowed a laugh. Sarah Bauer might be good at dealing with wayward teenagers, but her smoke-screen skills needed some work. Even Richardson had to know he was being played—he was just too damned self-centered to pass up the ego-stroking.

Mrs. Bauer rose, patting my shoulder on her way around the desk. "Right in here, sir." I could hear the tension in the older woman's voice on that last word. God bless her. Every ounce of irritation in me followed the two of them smack out the door.

I took the other chair and turned to Nicky. "Better?" The word floated in empathy, bringing his eyebrows up as he sat back to look at me.

"Spoken like a woman who understands."

"My dad is . . . well." A harsh laugh escaped my throat. "My dad is Chuck McClellan."

It had to roll around for a minute for a kid Nicky's age, but his eyes popped wide when he got it. "Governor Chuck McClellan?"

"Former governor."

"Didn't your sister—" Nicky cut the question off halfway out of his mouth, shaking his head. "Sorry. I'm sorry."

"No worries." I patted the back of his hand. "I'm not here to talk about my dysfunctional family. Just wanted you to know I get it. I really, really get it. What was going on with Tenley? I want to help, but you have to tell me the truth. Even if it's ugly. Drugs don't fit because she wouldn't have been able to keep up with school and sports."

He shook his head, hard. "Tenner would never. She didn't even drink. Her mom taught her better. She didn't do chemical enhancement." He sighed. "Didn't. Past tense. What the fuck?" His head fell back and he sniffled, his right foot knocking his backpack over as he raised it to cross over his left knee. His phone, an Altoids tin, and a fancy-looking pen tumbled under his chair. He didn't move to pick them up.

I pulled out a notebook and a regular ballpoint. "So she wasn't drinking at the party, either?"

"I just saw her. We talked. She was fine, chattering about a test today and being young and rich and free." His head sank to his knees, the next words muffled, aimed at the floor. "She was warm and soft and she smelled so damned good. God, I can't . . ." He sat up, fingers sliding into his thick curls, his face sinking hollow with pain. "I can't get my head around this. I loved her so much. I wanted . . . I tried to love her the way she deserved. Do you think she knew that?"

No idea, but he didn't need honesty right then. "Of course she did." I chased the platitude with a soft smile before I turned back to business. "She didn't mention anything lately about being sad, or seem anxious?" My words came faster, eyes darting between Nicky, the door, and the clock. The press conference had to be going strong. Hell, Jameson could show up here with cameras any minute. Richardson I wasn't worried about anymore. He could probably give my father a run for his money in the let's-talk-about-me department. "No new people in her life?"

"She had a guy."

Bingo. "Who?"

"She wouldn't tell me." Nicky pursed his lips, the sour look twisting his gorgeous features. "It hurt, too. Tenley and I told each other everything. By the time I got my head out of my ass and quit pouting long enough to realize if she wouldn't tell me, there had to be a reason, she was different. Distant. Like she'd figured out she didn't need me as much as I needed her. I've spent my whole life being afraid she'd see that someday. Then last night I saw a scuffle on the deck and walked out to find her getting pawed by Davenport." His face scrunched up, disgust coating the other boy's name.

"Is that the secret boyfriend?" I jotted the name down.

Nicky shook his head. "No reason to hide that. The guy is a douche, but he's a rich, popular douche. Quarterback. Lives across the street from her. I'm sure she just caught a ride to the party with him."

"Why didn't she drive herself? Especially if she didn't drink?"

His fingers drummed against his knee. "She didn't like to drive at night. Not since her accident at the end of sophomore year."

"Accident?" I hadn't had time to run records on anyone.

"She was driving her dad's truck, singing with the radio. She missed a stop sign. Caught the driver's front corner of a Camry."

Jesus. I held my breath until he spoke again. "The woman driving it was paralyzed from the waist down. T's been to visit her every week since."

"What is this woman's name?" I asked, the plastic of the pen biting into my fingers from my grip.

"Stella Connolly. She lives in Tarrytown. Runs a gymnastics school. Nice enough lady."

I made notes, raising serious eyes to Nicky. "Truth: Do you believe in your heart that Tenley could have killed herself? Was her behavior lately really that odd?"

"No?" He slumped back into the chair, tapping fingers moving to his rock-solid thigh. "I don't know. I mean, if she didn't, then what? Who would want to hurt Tenley? Everybody loved her."

I stood as the door opened to reveal a petite woman with a blonde bob and a purple pantsuit. "People who are well loved are often the most afraid of secrets getting out." I handed Nicky a card. "Call me if you need anything, or remember anything—no matter how small you think it is. My cell is on the back."

He nodded, not looking at me, his fingers still keeping a frenetic beat against his leg.

I turned to the doorway. "Can I help you?"

The woman's mouth popped into an O, her eyes darting from my badge to the back of Nicky's head on a loop.

She blinked and coughed out a laugh that sounded forced. "I was looking for Mrs. Bauer."

"She's not here." I kept a smile locked in place, shoving my hands in my pockets so I wouldn't gesture to the nearly empty room.

"Of course. I'll just come back later." The woman backpedaled until she nearly fell when her heel caught a plastic power cord cover running across the floor. She gasped, then spun and strode away.

Nicky didn't move, didn't seem to even notice anyone had come or gone. I studied him from the side, noting the drying track where the tear had rolled down his chiseled-from-perfection face. His fingers moved to a beat only he could hear, one Nike-outfitted heel picking up a bounce.

I turned for the door without another word. I liked the kid. Any idiot could see he loved Tenley Andre. And his single tear and fidgety manner could very well be as emotional as he was capable of getting, given his douchebag dad—everyone grieves in their own way.

My gut said Nicky knew more than he was saying, which didn't surprise me given his dad's temper tantrum. I didn't have time for secrets, though, and now I had another question for my list: Was Nicky protecting Tenley's memory, or someone else's reputation?

9

A stocky man outfitted in khaki from hat to hiking boots studied half of a pair of Japanese false cypresses flanking the foot of the Davenport family's wide polished-stone drive, snipping new shoots with the pointy tip of his shears like he was trimming a bonsai.

"Pardon me," I said, stopping to his right with a smile. "Can you tell me if Zayne is home?" The kid's name was easy to find, thanks to the unofficial-religion status high school football enjoys in Texas.

The man didn't look up from his work, the dark eyes peering from under his broad-brimmed safari hat fixed on the branches. *"No hablo inglés,"* he said, so careful and quiet I couldn't tell if he was talking to me or the plant.

"No hay problema." I switched to Spanish and repeated my question. Practically raised by nannies in central Texas, Charity and I spoke Spanish before we spoke English. We spent elementary school forever in trouble with the grammar teachers for switching nouns and verbs in our writing.

The shears paused, his eyes sliding to me. Stopping on the badge.

"Lo siento. No se." I'm sorry. I don't know.

I scanned the yard. Grass freshly cut. Piles of bitty clippings around the foot of the hedge. He'd been out here all day. So either Zayne had been home a while, or the gardener wasn't getting between the kid and the cops.

Probably the latter, but there were easier ways to my goal than trying to coax him into the middle of this mess.

"Gracias." I waved to him and strode up the drive, a massive house hiding behind lush trees and hedges that seemed immune to the city's drought-emergency water restrictions.

Chimes rang Beethoven on the other side of the ten-foot embossed cherry double doors. I turned away from the camera in the right corner of the porch, keeping my badge out of sight.

Almost a full minute passed before I heard footsteps. They paused behind the door, then a lock clicked free and the left side cracked open.

"Can I help you?" The petite woman's green eyes were almost as big as her blonde hair, her linen shorts and silk top straight off a Dallas runway.

"Good afternoon, ma'am. I'm looking for Zayne Davenport." The cocktail-party smile stretched my face too wide.

The green eyes narrowed to a quarter of their width, locking on my badge. "I'm Zayne's mother, Bethany. Why don't you tell me what you want with my son, Officer . . . ?"

"McClellan." I nodded when the green eyes widened again as the name hovered in the air. When Bethany opened the door a little wider and leaned on the edge of it, I gestured to the house across the street, catching a glimpse of the gardener out of the corner of my eye when I turned. He'd moved on to trimming the azaleas in the bed off the porch. I wrinkled my nose at a waft of sharp chemical, refocusing on Zayne's mother. "I'm afraid one of Zayne's friends has passed away, ma'am. Tenley Andre?"

One polish-free hand flew to Bethany's throat. "No!" She leaned forward, her voice dropping to just above a whisper. "Another accident? I always wondered if she wasn't drinking the first time, you know. Her mother and all."

One raised eyebrow was the only reaction I gave her words, but I didn't miss the bit about Erica. Worth checking out. "No automobiles were involved. Is Zayne here?" I peeked into the cavernous house over her shoulder. Miles of polished wood, a museum's worth of antiques, and a set of top-dollar golf clubs—but no teenage quarterback.

Bethany stepped onto the porch, pulling the door shut behind her and keeping one hand on the knob. “He’s not, I’m sorry. But he was home all night last night.”

I kept my face neutral, studying hers. Liars always have a tell. It’s reading it that’s tricky sometimes. The Richardson kid was easy: When he told the truth, he looked me in the face. When he lied, he averted his eyes and fidgeted. The bigger the lie, the more he wiggled. Like he’d walked straight out of a psych textbook.

I knew Bethany was lying now because Nicky was looking dead in my eyes when he told the story about finding Tenley with Zayne at the party the night before.

“You didn’t see him leave the house?” I asked.

“If I had, I wouldn’t have said he was home all night,” Bethany snapped. Her nostrils flared.

There. That was it.

“And he didn’t say anything about Tenley?”

Bethany shook her head, the nostrils going out again.

Better than a polygraph.

“What about this morning? Do you know what time Zayne left for school?”

Bethany settled one shoulder against the door. “Usually around six. They make them go so early.”

I pulled a card from my back pocket, the chemical singeing my nose hairs again. “I understand Zayne is a popular kid. If he hears anything, could you ask him to call me?”

Bethany took one corner of the card with two fingers, her nostrils going wide as she flashed a Splenda-coated smile and said, “Of course, Officer.”

She disappeared inside before I could get the “Thank you” past my lips, heels receding across the marble behind the door. Probably headed for the phone to call her husband. Google said Quentin Davenport was a partner at the biggest law firm in central Texas. Which meant if I wanted a shot at talking to Zayne, I needed to find him right quick.

Where do teenagers with too much money and no responsibilities hang out? The mall?

Probably not anymore. Not that I could find one kid in the Galleria anyway.

I jogged down the steps, taking a zigzagging path back to the street and scanning the polished stones for anything that resembled blood.

The gardener caught up to me as I crossed to the truck.

"Señora?" he said in a harsh whisper. "*Lo siento* . . . I just . . . Señorita Tenley? She's really . . ." His dark eyes filled as I nodded. So he did speak English. Not that I could fault him for the lie.

"You knew her?" I asked.

"She would run here along the street in the mornings. Always stopped to say hello to me on her way home. Ask about my babies. My little girl, she's a runner, too." His chest puffed up with pride as he pressed his fist to his lips, his Adam's apple bobbing with a hard swallow. "What happened?"

"I'm not sure yet. I was hoping talking to Zayne could help me figure it out."

The gardener bit his lip. Looked over his shoulder. "He had on his gym clothes when he left."

Hot damn.

"Do you know where he works out?"

He shook his head, shuffling his feet. "*Lo siento.*"

"No apologies. That's very helpful." I pulled out another card and pressed it into his hand. "I'm Faith. If you see or remember anything, will you please call me?"

His brow furrowed. "The police around here, they don't like us much." His tone was cautious, his dark eyes hooded as he looked up at me. He wouldn't give me his name, and I knew better than to scare him by pressing. Hell, I couldn't even say he had no reason to be afraid—not all cops are assholes, but we have our share just like any other group.

I smiled, laying a hand on his arm. "I like you just fine, and I appreciate you coming to talk to me." I took the card back and jotted my cell number on the blank side. "All I care about right now is getting Tenley's family an answer. That's my cell number. You use it anytime."

He nodded. "*Gracias.*"

I watched as he turned back toward the Davenports' drive. So Tenley Andre was the kind of girl who stopped to speak to people most of her peers didn't even see. Gardeners and maids were as much a part of the landscape in this part of town as the expensive bush this guy was babying with teeny snips of his shears. Tenley was the kind of girl who cared about their feelings and families. The kind of girl Charity and I would've liked.

I climbed in the truck, putting the window down as I started the engine. Across the way, the gardener's head and shoulders slumped, his ribs expanding slowly as one hand went to his face. Letting my foot off the gas, I stopped the truck behind him for one last question. "Sir? Would you leave your daughter alone with Zayne?"

The broad shoulders stiffened, his head beginning to shake as he turned. "*Dios mío*, no. I replanted the bed in the backyard last month and found pieces of . . ." He paused, glancing over his shoulder again. "Pieces of several animals. Buried all through there. The high pH in the soil is what killed her roses."

"What kind of animals?"

He grimaced. "They'd all been cut up. Skinned. At least one was a cat."

Jesus.

I swallowed hard and nodded. "Thank you."

"*Adiós*, señora. *Con cuidado.*" *Be careful.* He turned back to the bush. I grabbed my phone and searched for nearby gyms.

West Hills Country Club, just up the road. Golf clubs in the Davenports' foyer.

My foot dropped hard on the gas pedal, all the things I loved most about my job thrumming through every nerve ending: the witness who's invisible to everyone around them, the rush of a quick rapport, the way a case can go from the-North-Pole-in-January cold to El-Paso-in-August hot in one chance conversation. For the first time in months, I had an honest-to-God potential suspect in Zayne Davenport.

10

Makeup lost its mystique long about fifth grade, thanks to the upper-crust pageant circuit that required my ten-year-old wannabe-tomboy body to sit still in a salon chair for hours on end. A little tinted moisturizer and some eyeliner and I was good to go these days, but that didn't stop my face from coming in handy occasionally. Like when I flashed my brightest the-judges-are-watching smile at the mountain range of muscle behind the club's front desk and asked if the Davenport kid was on the premises.

"In the weight room, ma'am." Biceps grinned. And flexed. "I can show you back if you'd like."

I waved one arm. "After you."

A pounding drumbeat rattled the mirrors lining the gray-and-black room, the tops of the walls proclaiming *your gain, their pain* in two-foot-tall all-capital letters.

Biceps turned a knob on the sound system and the music stopped, the pack of teenage boys draped over various machines turning with a collective groan. "What gives, G?" The tallest one, with perfectly coiffed black hair nearly hiding a Band-Aid over his temple, ducked out of a shoulder press. I recognized the smirk from the Instagram photos Tenley looked so miserable in. Jackpot.

"Zayne, this lady wants to speak with you," Biceps said.

He turned, his mother's green eyes staring from perfectly symmetrical sockets. They raked me from head to toe, moving slower on the return trip. A grin spread across his face. "And just what can I do for you?" He licked his lips.

Dream on, kid. I ignored the innuendo he layered clumsily into the words, turning to Biceps. "Is there a place we could speak privately?"

"The trainer's office is empty." He pointed to the back corner of the studio, and I glanced at Zayne.

"Nice big desk in there, Z," one of the other boys called, inciting a couple of whoops and a cackle. I kept my head high and walked on. Didn't even kick anyone as I passed them.

Standing to the side, I let Zayne enter the room first and pulled the door shut behind us. He rested against the corner of the desk, puffing his shoulders out until it was impossible for me to move without touching him. The "office" was a converted closet jammed with two file cabinets, a tiny desk, and two chairs. I kept my back against the door and one hand on the knob.

"What's up, Officer?" he asked.

"Where were you last night, Zayne?" I kept my tone conversational.

His eyes flicked to the desk. Then the floor. "Home."

"You sure? Because I have witnesses who say otherwise."

He glanced up. "I was home," he said.

"You weren't at a party up the hill with Tenley Andre?"

He didn't answer. I let the silence stretch.

"Don't I get a lawyer or something? On TV, you get a lawyer if the cops accuse you of doing something bad," he said.

"Who's accusing you of anything?"

"My dad is a lawyer. He says you never talk to cops without your attorney."

I pulled in a slow breath. Counted to ten. Blew it out. "You're entitled to an attorney, though you don't need one if you haven't done anything wrong."

Zayne scuffed his foot on the carpet. "I saw it. On the news this afternoon. I know what you think, but it wasn't me. Tenley was frigid. Like kissing my grandmother. People thought she was so hot, but she was messed up. Too hung up on her little flaming friend, Richardson, if you ask me." He looked up. "She left with him, you know."

I nodded, keeping my face blank. "Messed up how?"

Zayne spread his arms. "Are you looking at me? I asked her out nine times in the past ten weeks. She blew me off every time, and then suddenly yesterday she texts me and asks me to take her to the party. Then the whole way there she was emailing that lady she almost killed. She said three words to me in the car. Wouldn't put her phone down."

"That make you mad? I mean, you must not get turned down too often." Not counting the girls with at least half a brain, that is.

He pinched his lips together. "She was fine when she left with Richardson. Hand to God. You want to hook me to a machine?"

Not yet. I shook my head, eyes scanning Zayne for a giveaway I couldn't find. If he was lying, he was good—but that could be genetic, with dad being a hotshot lawyer.

"You see her after that?" I asked.

He rolled his eyes, letting his head fall back. Didn't reply.

"Zayne?"

He kept his face tilted toward the ceiling. "I want to talk to my dad. Can I go now?"

"Of course you can." I pushed the door open and stepped backward. "Your mom has my card, if you decide you want to talk."

He was already to the lobby door. He flung it open hard enough to shatter that end of the mirror wall on his way out. I watched him go, the other boys murmuring as their eyes skipped between me and the broken glass littering the black rubber flooring.

No alibi and a temper. Plus the dead animals in the flower bed. Promising. But a kid with an A-list lawyer for a father was an awfully big fish. I needed better bait.

Thanking Biceps on my way out of the club, I watched Zayne leave a quarter inch of his red Camaro's fat Michelins on the parking lot's asphalt. I reached for my notebook and scribbled down his plate number.

The kid was shaken.

The mom was lying.

Which meant the lawyer dad would be pissed.

I needed something more solid before I went in for round two with Zayne, but the interview was helpful in more ways than one. Climbing into my truck, I tapped Stella Connolly's name into the search bar in my phone. Tenley emailing this woman hours before her death made her worth a visit.

Google said I'd find Stella at Lone Star Gymnastic Studio. I hadn't been in a gym since before Charity died.

"Suck it up," I scolded my reflection in the rearview. "Tenley Andre doesn't have time for your baggage today."

11

"What?" I asked the empty truck, stopping in a parking lot on Exposition and pulling my phone from the cup holder when it rang for the fifth time in five blocks.

Three calls from the lieutenant. Three-minute pause. Two back-to-back from Archie.

Fantastic.

My finger hovered over his number, but before I could touch the screen, the thing set to buzzing again, a Rangers shield flashing up behind his name.

I hit the green circle and raised the phone to my ear, cutting the truck's engine.

"Hey, Arch." I tried to keep my tone light. Breezy. Nothing to see here.

I suck at lying. Archie has said for years I ought to practice if I want to be a truly great cop, but I've always figured an affinity for the truth can't be much of a handicap in law enforcement.

Times like this, I wish I'd listened.

"Oh, good. You're not dead. Boone says you were supposed to drop off papers and go back to Waco. Thirty-five is moving like the damn autobahn, so you're not sitting in traffic. What gives?"

I bit my lip. I trusted Archie more than any other soul walking this planet. He wasn't yelling. He didn't even really sound mad. That was his Faith voice. The one that said I was driving him nuts but he was worried.

My eyes landing on the Starbucks sign overhead, I sucked in a deep breath. "Can I buy you a cup of coffee?"

"Why do I have a feeling I'm going to want something with more of a kick than a latte?"

I snorted. "You and me both. But I'll settle for some tea. Starbucks on Exposition across from Casis Elementary. Just come."

He paused so long I might've thought he'd hung up, save for the background noise. Sighed. "On my way."

The call cut off. I crossed my fingers and hoped I was doing the right thing.

Before I got the door open, a music-box-variety tinkling started to my right.

Was that . . . the *Peter Pan* song? "The dreams that you wish will come true," I sang under my breath, diving for the passenger floorboard. Where the hell was it coming from?

My fingertips brushed butter-soft leather, found a grip on a thin, cold piece of metal.

I hauled a Prada bag across the muddy floorboard of my truck and sat up just as the tinkling stopped.

Erica Andre left her purse.

Once upon a rookie time, fresh-faced TCSO deputy Faith would've called Archie to postpone and driven right back out to the hills to return it without another glance, because due process said she couldn't look in it without Mrs. Andre's permission. Today? I knew due process didn't always land the bad guy where he belonged, and what nobody else knew couldn't hurt my case in court.

The bag's interior was no different than the Andre house: "A place for everything and everything in its place" was surely coined by one of this woman's ancestors. Nestled in a little pocket in one side of the silk, I found Erica's iPhone.

With a tissue from the box still resting in the passenger seat, I worked it free. Touched the home button and held my breath.

Missed call and two texts from someone named Melissa.

Can you pick up the Stickley table from Beth . . . was all I could see.

Not helpful.

But.

I bit my lip and stared at the screen. In twenty-first-century America, nothing is a more powerful reflection of a person than their iPhone.

"Three tries," I muttered.

It was right there.

Six little magic buttons away.

But which six?

I tapped my index finger on the side of the OtterBox encasing the phone.

This woman loved her kid with a fire that made my heart ache. So most obvious first.

"T-E-N-L-E-Y." I touched the numbers that would correspond with Tenley's name on a telephone dial.

Incorrect passcode attempt flashed at the top of the screen.

Shit.

Enter code or touch ID replaced it.

Wait.

The alarm code. It was the girl's birthday. August twenty-ninth. But this needed six numbers, not four. Eighteen back.

I tapped it in.

Incorrect passcode attempt. This iPhone will be locked after 2 more.

Damn. I clicked the power button. One shot left meant I needed to think. I could try again later.

A tap next to my ear sent Erica's pocketbook flying into the passenger seat, the phone landing next to it. I turned to find Archie smiling from the other side of the window.

I shoved Erica's things into the glove box and grabbed my own phone before I kicked the door open and hugged him. "Thanks for coming." My voice thickened and he didn't miss it, patting my back.

"You're scaring me today, kiddo." He pulled back and lowered his sunglasses to the end of his nose, studying my face. "What's going on with you?"

I squeezed his hand. "Coffee first."

"Will it come with a shot of answers?"

I smiled and turned for the door, waving for him to follow.

The shop was empty save for three shirt-and-tie businessmen with headphones in and laptops open, and the two college kids working behind the counter. We got drinks and settled into the leather club chairs in the back corner.

"I can't believe Boone even missed me." I shook my head. "Maybe they're out of toner for the copier or something."

Archie sipped his coffee. "I'm sorry they're giving you shit, Faith, but it's not like you didn't know it was coming. Boone thinks you slid in on your last name."

I rolled my eyes. "Because a woman couldn't possibly be as good a cop as he is." That came out a little too sharp.

"Preaching to the choir." Archie raised both hands in mock surrender. "I like to think I had a hand in training you."

I smiled. "You call letting me tag after you all those years training?"

He chuckled. "It flew both ways. You learned a few things from me, and you girls made being on your dad's detail bearable. Fun, even. I'll never understand how your folks ended up with kids like you."

A tear escaped before I could stop it. "I miss her, Arch."

"I know, kid. Is that what this is all about? You going AWOL today because it's today? I get that. And I can keep Boone off of you. I'll tell him the captain sent you on an errand. They hate each other. He won't dare call to verify."

"Did you see a call this morning? Out at Travis?"

Archie's eyes fell shut as he set his cup down. "I was too buried to pay it any mind. But you weren't." His big hand closed around mine. "What happened?"

I sniffled, shaking my head. "Pretty blonde teenage girl, smart, superstar athlete. Dead for no reason I can see."

His breath hissed in and his fingers tightened around mine. "I'm so sorry, honey."

"I have this feeling that it happened for a reason. I can't shake it. I'm here. I saw it right when it came in. I have not another damned thing going on right now, work-wise. They're basically paying me a field salary to be a courier. I've made some headway already, even. I'm supposed to work this case, Archie."

"She was at the lake? What does the SO have to say about that?"

"Graham thinks she jumped."

"I remember a time when you thought Graham Hardin was smarter than Sherlock Holmes." Archie's bushy gray brows went up. "Do you really think he's wrong?"

"My gut says something is off." I wasn't proud of the defiant edge in the words. I was just tired of everyone looking at me like I needed to be handled.

Archie's eyes shone with sympathy. "You can't catch a monster that's not there, honey."

"I'm looking for the monster nobody wants to see. Charity's is somewhere, isn't he?" I wanted to stuff the words back into my throat as soon as they hit the air.

Archie sat back in his chair, and I shut my eyes. "Dammit. I'm sorry, Arch."

"There's not a single day that's passed in the last nineteen years that I haven't wished I could do a hundred things about that case different. That I haven't felt every dagger you could throw. I couldn't have loved Charity more if she was my blood daughter, Faith. You know that."

I nodded.

"Your father . . ." Archie started the sentence and then let it fade when I put my hand over his.

"Believe me when I say I know."

We retreated into our lattes and our thoughts. I couldn't cry for my sister. Not now. But beating myself up for snapping at Archie was perfectly acceptable. It had damn near ended him when Charity's killer was never caught. He'd fought his way back through injury and alcoholism, been publicly booted from the governor's honored detail when I knew he'd bailed in private because my father kneecapped his investigation at every turn, terrified that any conviction without a capital rider would hurt him politically as the governor who'd executed more inmates than any other in Texas history.

This man sitting across from me was the closest thing I had to real family. I knew he wished he were in a position to get me off the shit detail I'd been assigned to after I'd all but forced my boot in the Rangers' door.

"I didn't mean any disrespect." I squeezed his hand.

He returned the pressure. "I know, honey. I don't suppose I have to ask if you went out to the scene this morning?" His blue eyes sparkled when I batted my lashes and smiled sweetly.

"Who, me?"

"You did." He rested his elbows on his knees, steepling his fingers under his chin. "So why do you think there's a monster here to chase? What did you see?"

I shook my head. "I'm not even sure I can explain it . . . Something isn't right here, Arch. Suicide is too easy. This girl had everything in the world. Why would she jump?"

"Boy trouble. Pressure she couldn't handle. Knocked up. Bullying." He ticked points off on his fingers, and I sighed. Did I have to fight the whole damned world on this?

"I don't think so. I've already found too many other things that are off. Like, the kid who was pawing her at a party last night is clearly dealing with some anger issues, and doesn't seem the type that gets told no often."

"Sometimes coincidence is just that in a city as big as this one." He leaned back in his chair.

"But sometimes it's not." I set my cup on the table.

"True. Figuring that out is the tricky part."

"Especially when it's not your case?"

Archie laughed. "You haven't backed down from a challenge yet. Can I help?"

"Graham is covering for me at the SO, but I need the lieutenant off my back—and I really need for him to not know what I'm up to."

"Tell him you need some leave."

"After three months?" My eyebrow cocked upward. "Yeah. That'll go over well."

"He might bitch, but given the absolute bullshit he's been assigning you, he won't do it too loudly, or he might bring trouble on himself, and he knows it. Everyone starts with a week. You got plans for it?"

I smiled, pulling out my phone and opening a text to my boss. "I do now. What would I do without you?"

He reached for his cup. "I like problems that solve themselves. Makes me feel smart."

"You're the smartest guy I know," I said. "I assume that's why they keep you up to your eyeballs in impossible investigations."

Archie snorted. "Joys of budget cuts. God forbid a company move to Texas and actually have to pay any damned taxes."

"Seems about as likely as Boone giving me an actual case to work," I agreed.

"I wasn't kidding when I said I could use a fresh set of eyes on Jessa DuGray," he said. "I've been through everything we have a hundred times, I scoured the labs you brought me this morning, and I still have exactly jack shit. My gut says I'm missing something. You feel like working two cases on your un-vacation?"

"I'd take actual police work over any beach you can name right now. I guess you know you've chosen the right career when you miss it this much after a few weeks." I drained my chamomile chai and stood. "I love you. You do know that, right?"

Archie nodded, slower to rise on his bad knee, and ruffled my hair like he used to when I was a bored tween following my parents from stuffy event to stuffy event, scolded every time my smile was less than camera-ready.

"I love you too, kid. Come by the office tonight and we'll see if you can find our magic rock. And be careful nosing around this dead girl. If your monster is there and managed to make Graham Hardin think she was a suicide, that means this particular beast is smarter than average."

"Noted." I gestured for him to go to the door ahead of me. "I'll see you at six thirty? I can bring Chinese."

"You know I'm not turning down a good egg roll."

"I'm on it." I stepped through the door he held open, my throat tightening again, making me turn back. "Arch—"

He let the door fall shut behind him and nodded. "I know, honey."

Of course he did. But that didn't mean I didn't need to tell him anyway.

Not that I had been able to find the right words a single damned time in going on twenty years.

"Thank you," I whispered, blinking.

"Watch yourself."

I strode back to my truck and slid behind the wheel with Archie's warning looping through my thoughts on repeat. *Smarter than average.*

Nothing about Tenley Andre's life—or death—was average.

I clicked my Maps app and pulled up the location of the gymnastics school again.

Superstar kid from privileged background hurts middle-class small-business owner in accident and volunteers time to help said accident victim? Really?

There was more to this story than the sum of the surface events. There had to be.

I started the truck just as my phone binged a text arrival.

Boone: *I'll see you Monday, then.*

Looked like Archie was right. As usual.

Now—was I right this time, too?

Did something about Tenley Andre's life cause her death?

Five days to find an answer.

12

Thwack. Pause. *Thwack.* Pause. *Thwack.*

I stepped through the door at Lone Star Gymnastic Studio to the long-familiar sound of a bars routine in progress, pulling in a lungful of sticky air laced with a somehow inoffensive fusion of rubber, chalk, and feet, a tsunami of memories rattling my resolve.

Breathe. Smile. Charity loved few things more than being the girl who could fly. Gymnastics held happy memories, if I could choose to see them that way.

A muffled *thud* and a hasty "I thought you had another layout?" drew my eyes to the floor, where a little blonde pixie limped out from under the bars.

"Dammit, Lena, 'spot her' means *don't* let her break her leg!" A booming shout echoed off the metal warehouse walls as another girl jumped to grab the low bar. "Gretchen, are you all right?"

I leaned on the granite countertop of the tall reception desk, watching tiny girls in shiny leotards defy gravity twelve different ways.

A petite woman with a neat brunette bob shouted corrections and praise from a sporty fuchsia wheelchair at the edge of the mats lining the balance beam. I crossed the space and touched her shoulder.

"Stella Connolly?" I flashed my ID before I tucked it back in my hip pocket.

Stella nodded, her brow furrowing. "Is something the matter?"

"I'd like to ask you a couple of questions about Tenley Andre if you have minute." I kept my face neutral, my words and tone walking a line between businesslike and friendly. Every bit as tricky as the uneven bars the tiny blonde had crashed from moments before.

Forgetting to breathe, I stared at Stella and waited for my score.

The other woman's face smoothed and she shook her head. "This was all taken care of more than a year ago. I'm good with the settlement. I don't want Tenley to be in trouble."

I nodded, because while curiosity about the car crash burned, I needed Stella to think I was an insider. "I'm not here about the accident." I looked around. "Is there someplace more private we can talk?"

Stella pointed to a door behind the counter. "My office is right through there." She turned and told a teenage gymnast to watch the little ones before she waved for me to follow her. "Is everything okay, Officer?"

I stayed quiet until the office door was shut tight. "When was the last time you saw Tenley?" I pulled out my notebook and pen.

"Yesterday."

"Was she upset about anything?"

"On the contrary, she seemed more sunny and—I don't know how to say this . . . in the moment?—than I've ever seen her. She was happy. You could feel it just being in the room with her. Why? What's the matter?"

"I'm afraid she passed away early this morning." I watched her reaction, unblinking.

Stella's eyes popped wide, her mouth opening in a neat little O.

She shook her head. "I'm sorry, what? No! How?"

"That's part of what I'm trying to find out, ma'am. You said Tenley was happy when you saw her yesterday?"

"She was. She brought my dry-cleaning in with her yesterday afternoon and hung it there." She waved a hand to the back of the office door, where a plastic bag from Jack Brown's still swayed slightly under the air vent. "She kissed me on the cheek and asked how my weekend was, and then she went in to help the girls."

"Which girls?"

"Tenley tutored five of the girls on my elite team. One hour every Monday afternoon on math, one on English."

"And none of the girls noticed anything out of the ordinary?"

"Not that any of them mentioned to me."

"Would you mind if I asked them?"

"I won't. They will." She smiled when my brows shot up. "That's why Tenley was so good for this place. I used to do it all myself—figured I could get some use out of my teaching degree—but they resented being pulled away from practice, and it started to hurt my coaching relationship with them. These girls are so damned focused it's disturbing. So much pressure. Push, practice, compete, win. Repeat. Tenley got it. She was one of them."

"It certainly seems she was a talented young woman."

"She was all about her grades, too, though, which I can't get my highly competitive girls to give two figs for. I was hoping she'd be a good example for them."

"The only thing I excelled at in high school was annoying my mother."

Stella laughed. "Girls like mine—like Tenley—are a special breed. They don't crack easily under pressure, and they drive themselves harder than any coach or teacher would ever think about driving them. They're their own worst enemies in so many ways. Nobody is harder on herself, win or lose, than an elite athlete. But that generally comes from a desire to please. They want to hear the applause, feel the hugs, see the pride on everyone's faces."

I kept my face blank, nodding. She could've been talking about Charity.

"Lord, if there's anything Tenley wouldn't do for a kind word from her mama, I'm sure I couldn't name it." Stella shook her head. "Thicker than mud, the two of them. Tenley cares more what her mother thinks and worries more about her mother than any ten kids do. Or should."

"Worries about her mother?" The same mother I'd met earlier? In the two minutes I'd had with Erica Andre before I'd shattered her world, I could tell the woman was practically a force of nature.

Stella tapped a finger on the wheel of her chair. "I get the feeling her mama isn't happy."

Mrs. Andre did seem convinced that Mr. Andre had a girlfriend. "Did Tenley confide in you about other things?" I asked.

Stella held one hand up and twisted her wrist side to side. "I wouldn't go so far as to say she confided in me. I hear a lot, though. People tend to forget I'm in the room." She flashed a smile. "It's the chair. Handy for eavesdropping. Tenley's been glued to her phone lately."

"Talking to anyone in particular?"

Stella pinched her lips between her teeth and shook her head. "Just that she talked a lot about wanting someone to be happy."

"No indication who or what she might have felt this person was unhappy with?"

"Complaining wasn't in her. Rainbows and unicorns, at least as far as she wanted most people to know." Stella's lips stretched into a line, her eyes going soft and unfocused. "I wanted so badly to hate her. She was the last thing I saw before I passed out and the first when I came to that night. I thought for a minute I was dead and she was an angel. The doctor came in and said she'd insisted on sitting with me. All night. Like I was supposed to thank her or something. Then he asked her to excuse us, so he could tell me I'd never walk again. From out in the hallway she started bawling and telling me how sorry she was, how she'd make it up to me, anything I wanted. I told her to get the hell out and leave me alone."

Stay quiet. Let her talk.

"She wouldn't budge. I screamed until the doctor rang security. Called Tenley everything but a white girl. She just stood there, tears running like a faucet, nodding her head and repeating, 'I know. I'm so sorry.' By the time the cop got up there, I told him to leave her alone."

"Why?"

Stella hauled in a deep breath, a short cough issuing back. "All I saw when I first set eyes on Tenley was a spoiled brat who didn't want to get in trouble. But watching her just stand there and take the vile things I said to her . . . I've worked with teenage girls for nearly thirty years. And I never set eyes on a kid so broken as she was. Not before, not since. That little girl needed a friend way worse than I needed a whipping post."

Wait. What?

Popular. Confident. Strong. Beautiful. That's what all the other adults in Tenley's life had to say about her.

And Stella saw "broken"? How?

"I'm not sure I follow." I stretched the words. "Tenley was popular and bright. She was gorgeous. You said 'rainbows and unicorns' five seconds ago. How can that kid and this kid you're describing be the same kid?"

Stella rolled the chair back and forth in tiny increments. "For these girls, knowing they're good at a sport works for the sport. But when things shake them, it almost seems like they feel it deeper than regular people, and Tenley was in a bad place when I met her. It got better. Then worse again last fall, and then a bit better, and yesterday she was as happy as I've ever seen her. Real happy. Genuine joy." The last word faded into a sob, her fist going to her mouth. She looked up, her eyelids batting back tears. "And now she's gone? How?"

"I wish I knew." I shoved my notebook back in my pocket, staring at the team photo gallery on the wall. In all but the last two, Stella stood next to the girls.

Tenley had come here to do penance. The kind of girl who talked to the neighbor's gardener wouldn't have burdened Stella with her problems.

But, kindred spirits and all . . . what about someone else here?

"Which of the girls was she closest to?" I asked.

"Lena. She's more competitive and focused than anyone else. Like takes to like, my grandmama always said."

"Is she here today?"

"I think she's here more than I am." Stella gestured for me to step aside and rolled her chair out the door and toward the mats. "Lena!"

A petite, muscle-bound brunette with a short ponytail and huge eyes over her high cheekbones practically floated in our direction. "Yes, ma'am?" Her voice was so squeaky sweet I blinked.

"Sweetie, this is Officer McClellan with the Texas Rangers." Stella reached up and grasped Lena's dangling hand. "Come into the office and let's talk."

Lena's wide eyes got even wider. She jerked her hand away. "No! I tried to talk her out of it, I swear. I didn't do anything." She leapt past me and snatched a bag off the floor, her bare feet pounding a path to the door.

"Nobody is saying—" I called to Lena's back as she shoved the door open and disappeared. I turned to Stella. "Well then."

Stella's mouth hung open. "What in the name of heaven?"

"Sometimes flashing a badge gives you information you didn't know you were looking for. I don't suppose you'd save me the trouble of tracking down her address?"

"Happy to. As long as you tell her to get her ass back here when you're done with her. We have a tournament coming up." Stella rolled the chair back to the desk, shaking her head. "She's such a quiet, focused girl. I don't know how she could have time to get into trouble."

I didn't answer that. Seemed several teenagers had more ways into trouble than I would've thought possible just yesterday.

She found the file in the computer on the desk and copied the address and phone numbers onto a turquoise Post-it. I tucked it into my pocket with a thank-you and a promise to pass along the message about coming back to practice.

As I shook Stella's hand, I met steely, determined eyes and a stronger grip than most men had. Stepping back into the sunshine, I wasn't sure what to make of her. I still felt sorry for her, of course, but the granite stare and viselike grip stayed with me. Was Stella really as forgiving as she wanted people to think?

I punched Lena's address into my GPS. Four blocks. Flipping the visor down did nothing for the low-hanging western sun, sending my hand digging in the console for my sunglasses as I glanced at the clock. Just enough time to maybe get one answer today before I needed to grab food and go see if I could help with Archie's murdered coed. Police work provides little rest for the weary.

God, I had missed it.

13

Twenty minutes and a half dozen futile jabs at the doorbell later, I left Lena's house with no answers and a rumbling stomach.

A quick pit stop at Wu Chow, and I found Archie in the conference room at headquarters standing over a tabletop completely obscured by folders and photos, his left foot tapping like it always did when he was trying to figure something out.

"Dinner delivery," I said, setting the bag on a chair. "Orange chicken and beef lo mein. And extra spring rolls. I didn't know what you'd like, so I brought options."

He nodded, still focused on the table. "I'm missing something, Faith."

"Stop staring and tell me what you know." I stepped to the edge of the table, swallowing hard at the photos even all these years into police work.

"I told you about all I know already." He ran a hand through his thick silver hair. "It's like digging in bone-fucking-dry sand. They didn't even find what was left of her until six months after she disappeared, and the park rangers aren't exactly crime-scene experts. I've been praying every day that the labs would turn up a lead, but we hit another wall there. I can't let myself believe a person who could do something like this is just going to get away with it. There has to be something I'm not seeing."

I sipped my soda, nodding. There always was. I believed that with every fiber of my being, and had the perfect record to prove it.

Which was the only reason I was there—Archie loved me, sure. He also worked alone. Had since forever. But he was on the verge of giving up, and he knew I wouldn't let him.

"Walk me through it from day one," I said.

He pointed to the left end of the table, where the thinnest folder lay. "Missing person's report called into the university PD by her roommate on July twenty-seventh. Jessa went to meet friends for pizza and a study session the evening of the twenty-sixth. She didn't go home, which was unusual, but not alarming." He sipped his Dr Pepper. "When the roommate didn't see or hear from her all of the following day, she started to worry, though. She called and texted, but didn't get an answer. So at six forty-seven, she called the campus police."

I picked up the folder. It contained three sheets of blue paper: one dispatch report of the first call, one officer's incident report from an interview with the roommate on July twenty-eighth, and one disposition form showing they'd referred the case to Austin PD when Jessa's parents came looking for her on the thirtieth.

"Four days. It took four days for anyone to do much of anything." I shook my head as I murmured. "Cutting-edge technology at our actual fingertips, and nobody moved on this until the trail was practically frozen."

"College kid, summertime . . . nobody took it too seriously."

That was usually the first mistake in cases like this one. People don't tend to want to think the worst until the worst has happened to them. They let precious time tick by, squandering the minutes and hours when a trail is blistering hot on poor assumptions and positive thoughts. By the time anyone really started looking for Jessa DuGray, she could've been in a hundred different kinds of trouble in a thousand places nobody would ever find her.

Dammit.

Psychology would have to ride shotgun to superstition, then. I could study every detail in every folder here, and I could build a pretty good profile of Jessa's killer, but we'd need some luck, too—and that was harder to come by.

Running a finger over the gold charm bracelet that had been my sister's most prized possession, I wished for a little divine intervention. I put the file back on the table and gestured to the food containers. "Chicken or beef?"

"I feel like I'm back on your father's detail." Archie chuckled. "How many hotel ballroom dinners did we eat?"

"Too many."

He nodded. "Beef."

I passed him the container and opened the spring rolls and a bowl of sesame noodles for myself, handing him the plastic fork before I tore open a set of paper-wrapped chopsticks.

"How'd it go this afternoon?" he asked. "You get anything new on your dead girl?"

"Nothing that's going to change anyone's mind about the whole suicide thing."

"But you still don't buy it?"

"Everything around this feels weird to me, Arch. I went out there, and Graham is right: She was near the base of the dam. Damage to the back of her skull consistent with a fall from that high. But I can't let it go." I dropped a tangle of noodles into my mouth.

"Where's her car? The SO impound?"

My hand froze, a spring roll halfway to my lips. "No."

Archie furrowed his brow.

The roll fell back into the container, followed closely by the chopsticks. "Her car is at home in her garage. Her mom said she thought someone picked her up this morning, but she couldn't say who."

"Did she go up there on foot?"

I shook my head. "Not likely. It's, like, fifteen miles from her house, and she's a runner, but she wasn't dressed for a workout in those party heels."

Party.

"Shit." I put the container down and jumped to my feet, striding to the far end of the table. Moving works like a bright light for my brain, sharpening connections and making answers clearer.

"What now?" Archie asked.

"I missed a ton of intersections here. The car was at home, and she wasn't dressed for school in that teeny-weeny skirt. Her friend said they went to a party last night."

"So she didn't make it home?"

I bit my lip. "He said he took her home."

"Anybody who can vouch for that?"

I spun on my heel and paced the length of the room again. Erica Andre said she hadn't heard her daughter come in. But she also said she'd heard Tenley in the bathroom before daylight, and the husband was still out of pocket. "I haven't had a chance to talk to her father. He might know." I turned again, still walking. "I don't like the boy who took her to the party, but he's not the same one who took her home."

"Oh? The one who took her can't be happy about that."

"You can definitely say that again. And then a few more times after that. He played it off, though. Captain Her Loss, quarterback of the football team. But I rattled him. Trouble is, mom is swearing he was home all night and dad is a partner at Carrey and Minor."

Archie winced. "That sounds less fun than chasing a rattler through a cactus field."

"I know."

"My quarter's worth of free advice? Keep him on your list and keep digging," Archie said. "If you get anything else that pulls him in, it's worth going after, even with a hotshot lawyer in the mix."

"I got his plate number. I'll see if that turns anything up." I gestured to the folders. "I didn't come here to talk about Tenley, though."

I plucked a tangle of noodles from the carton and bit into it, barely noticing the tang as I chewed, my eyes on the photo of Jessa clipped to the front of the APD jacket. I reached for it, memorizing every contour of a pretty, earnest face that didn't need much makeup.

"How did you end up at the caverns?" I asked, my gaze locked on Jessa's wide blue eyes.

"I'm guessing not for a study date. Beyond that, your guess is as good as mine." Archie slammed his carton onto the table, sloshing sauce over one edge.

I watched the brown droplet slide toward the shiny tabletop. "Did they get anything useful from her phone? Texts about plans, social media posts?"

He flipped open a thicker file folder, already shaking his head. "Nobody ever found her cell phone."

Damn. Strike one. I chewed a bite of spring roll.

"APD ran a standard missing person's." He fanned a stack of papers and photos across the table between us. "Her debit card was swiped at a gas station on Sixth not long after she left the dorm, and then at a pizza place in Tarrytown an hour later. ATM camera across the street from the pizza joint puts her entering a bar next door just before eleven."

"When did she leave?" I tapped one finger on the table, pushing my food away.

"That's the first place it gets sticky." Archie sighed. "She didn't, that we can see."

Um. "What? Is there a back door?"

"There is, but there's no camera back there. Add to that, there was a storm after midnight that night—the last storm we saw, if I'm not mistaken. A transformer two blocks over took a lightning bolt, and the power surge fried the circuit the ATM camera was on. So there's no footage from 12:38 until noon the next day."

Double damn. I shot to my feet and paced the length of the floor. "Witnesses?"

"Bartender pointed us to a handful of regulars. The place has a mostly older crowd, not really a typical hangout for kids that age. One woman remembered seeing her, but didn't notice when she left or with who."

I folded my hands behind my back, fingers wrapping the bracelet again. So far, its mojo wasn't helping tonight.

"Who'd she go in with?" I stopped, picking up a series of four grainy stills that showed Jessa, dressed in a short dark skirt and a floaty transparent top, approaching and entering the bar.

"It's hard to tell if she was actually with anyone," Archie said as I flipped from the first image to the second. He was right. Between the crowded sidewalk and the southern propensity of any given person to open the door for another, the photos couldn't tell us who was in a group and who was a polite stranger.

I shook my head, dropping them back to the table. "This really is kind of impossible. So far."

Archie shoveled another forkful of beef into his mouth and nodded, chewing. "And yet we can't say that," he said around the food.

"Sure we can. We just can't believe it." The words hung in the air around us, seeping into the wood-paneled walls, the weight of what I didn't add out loud pressing in, heavy and constricting, as I surveyed the table. It was all there, every variable in a long, complicated equation that only had one right answer. Photos. Hours of detective legwork and interviews. And the whole thing stopped right here. Archie's desk was the last exit on the cold-case expressway. Jessa would end up in victim purgatory if we didn't manage to dig out what everyone else had missed. I hadn't ever met this young woman's parents, but I would pour everything I had into saving them from getting that phone call. The Rangers run Texas's cold-case unit, but with nine investigators and about three thousand cases, successes are few and country miles between.

I shut my eyes. Focused on my breath. In for a five count, out for seven. The answer is always somewhere. I'd spent more than half my life believing that with the fire of ten thousand suns. It got me through the rougher days.

Thirty feet or so below my boots, a file cabinet held the known facts of what happened to my big sister. And someday, I'd be down there leading a team that would finally put an end to my wondering. My fears. My nightmares.

Someday.

But today, Jessa needed my help. And so did Tenley. Clapping my hands together, I resumed pacing. "Fast-forward to the hikers."

Archie grabbed a third folder, the fattest on the table. "February twenty-fourth, 9:48 a.m., Parks and Wildlife responds to a call from two hikers, both male, who spotted, quote, 'what looked like somebody's head' near the mouth of Whirlpool Cave. Hiked back out to the road to get a phone signal and called 911."

I knew most of the rest of the story already—everyone did. Jessa's remains had been burned; her dental records needed to identify her. Archie went on TV asking the public for help. Her folks put up fifty grand for any information that led to the arrest of her killer. Crazies came out from under their rocks and clamored for attention or money or both.

The investigation went nowhere.

Which brought everything back to this room. A last shot at justice for this pretty coed.

"I'm tired of young women disappearing and nobody ever having to answer for it." Archie blew out a long breath, reaching for the middle folder, holding the snapshot of Jessa in both hands. "I've been in this game a long damned time, kiddo. We fail these women. Maybe not us personally, but our system. Every single day."

Truth. And I knew that look.

Archie wouldn't rest until every last *i* was dotted, the case locked down tighter than Luke Bryan's jeans. So neither would I. Jessa deserved no less than every last drop of what I would give Charity, when I got the chance.

Texas didn't have enough hidey-holes to keep whoever had done this safe.

"We got this, Arch." I laid a hand on his arm before I turned to the whiteboard on the long wall behind me, picked up a dry-erase marker, and scribbled two bullet points:

• *Location*

• *Labs*

"What else was in the lab report?" I tapped the cap end of the marker against my thigh. "Did they get a type for the accelerant?"

Archie nodded, fiddling with his fork. "Kerosene, with traces of paint thinner."

Paint thinner? I added another bullet point to my list.

"Who uses paint thinner to set a fire?" I wobbled the marker between my index and middle fingers, pacing again.

"A painter? Handyman?" Archie's eyes followed me for two lengths of the room before they went back to his fork. "Construction worker? They use it to clean equipment."

"Why the mixture, though? Kerosene would do the job." I spun and started back for the far end of the room. Paused. "Where did the samples you sent them come from?"

He picked up the fat folder again. "Back lower right of her skull, left middle and right index fingernails, front and back of right and left arms and thighs, genital area, left cheek."

"Did they all test positive for paint thinner?"

Archie sat up straighter in the chair, his left hand snagging the blue folder I'd dropped off that morning. He flipped pages. Paused. "Boone is a fucking idiot, wasting your brain on running errands," he said as he looked up with a grin. "Only the samples that came from her back had the paint thinner."

"So it wasn't dumped on her . . ." I raised the marker and turned back to the board.

"She'd lain on something that had been treated with it," Archie finished.

I stepped back and surveyed my list.

• *Location*

• *Labs*

• *Paint thinner on surface*

"No viable DNA from the genital samples?" I asked.

"Jim managed to get an inside swab, but CODIS didn't have a match."

Never one single goddamn easy answer.

I resumed my seat and fished a few lukewarm noodles from the paper carton, swallowing them before I pulled the photos from the remains recovery out and spread them across the table. Every possible angle of the cave's exterior in more than a hundred shots. My eyes went first to the ground around Jessa's body, green grass sticking up every which way, speckled with early crocus buds. "The area isn't disturbed."

Archie dropped his fork into his empty food carton with a sigh. "Because she was dumped there."

"That place isn't that secluded."

"Right. So where was she from July to February? And why did someone want her found?"

"No. Earthly. Idea." Every bit of the lift from figuring out the paint thinner vanished, and I stabbed a chunk of tofu with one chopstick. "Somebody was careful."

"Somebody is smart," Archie said, standing to throw away his carton and leaning over the photos on the table.

I went back to the earlier folders, studying the stills from the ATM camera again.

When I flipped to the third one, I caught a sharp breath.

Archie turned as I coughed up the bite I'd half inhaled, raising his eyebrows when I brandished the photo as I wiped at my watering eyes.

"I know this guy," I sputtered, plopping the photo on the table and pointing to a man coming from the right, entering the bar behind Jessa. "I met him this afternoon."

Archie's eyes popped wide. "You're kidding."

I shook my head, my fingers going to the charm bracelet, a silent thank-you floating through my head. "He's the girls' track coach at Marshall High School. Tenley Andre's coach."

"No shit?" Archie's face spread into a grin. "You have gone from pestering me for gum to being damned handy to have around."

I smiled. "I could still use the gum. I haven't had a smoke break since before noon."

Archie flipped open his laptop and pulled a pack of Doublemint from his shirt pocket. "Good girl. Chew on this and let's see what we can dig up on your girl's coach."

Holy shit. Was it possible Jessa DuGray and Tenley Andre had more in common than neighboring ZIP codes and much-too-short lives?

14

She stayed on the edge of the dam, perfect ass nearly brushing her stiletto heels, long arms hugging her knees tight, completely unaware that she wasn't alone, until she demolished him.

Darkness seeped in from every side, blood rushing to his core, zipper straining to contain his want as he memorized every last flawless inch of her.

Underneath his soul, in the darkest place, the monster stirred. Yawned. Focused on the angel.

Oh.

Oh my.

God, yes. What the hell are you waiting for, you coward?

The monster willed his hands to the door handle. Wanted his long legs to close the space between them and the angel. Wanted to twist a hand into her impossibly moonlight-colored hair. Trail the two honored fingers over her satiny cheek. Whisper to her. Rip the gauzy blouse and find her wings.

The monster wanted inside this angel.

It craved her cries, wanted to feel her fight fade, taste her tears.

That would send this ugliest part of him that couldn't really be part of him at all back to sleep. Maybe even satisfy it. Banish it entirely. Surely, the monster would give up on him eventually. Everyone always did.

But there had to be another way.

He was so hard it hurt. The monster roared.

Get up, you whiny little bitch! *The words were so clear, so loud, inside his head. He heard them all over again. Like they were playing on the stereo. Which of course was impossible. He was alone here, the peace of this place special. Calming.*

What's the matter? She doesn't do it for you?

He flinched, electricity racing through his core. Shook his head. The darkness spread until he couldn't see the angel anymore. A girl lay spread before him on a scarred, messy table, her skirt ripped. Her hands tied. Her pleading eyes streaming tears.

Please no. Please help me. *Her mouth made the motions but he couldn't hear her voice over the others.*

You want that? Take it. *Her skin was so soft. So smooth.*

The monster was born in that moment. Willed to life as the cries fell around him. He pushed, pushed, pushed until the unthinkable was done and the monster was gone.

He told himself he loathed the monster. But somewhere deeper and darker than most people dare to go inside themselves, he also knew he'd come to need it.

Because of moments like these. The monster might be howling, clawing—but he wanted her, too. And hating the monster was so much easier than hating himself.

The girl vanished, fading back into memory. His vision cleared. Still there—his very own celestial wonder, serene as a monument on top of the dam.

So damned easy.

Just creep across the road and touch her . . .

Silence the monster. Silence them all.

Right now.

The knife practically jumped from its hiding spot, his palm slick with sweat around the hilt.

Later.

Now.

Wait.

For what?

He knew there was something. Staring at her perfection with the monster growling in his thoughts made it impossible to remember.

Couldn't be very important, then.
He gripped his forehead in one hand.
"Shut up!" The words slid through clenched teeth.
The monster growled. Showed fangs.
He raised the blade and made his call.

15

Two close-to-dead laptop batteries later, Archie and I had almost enough for a warrant. But not quite.

Turned out, Jake Simpson's all-American apple pie image wrapped a long string of past indiscretions in sugary stars and stripes.

"Ten years ago, he was fired from Dakota High School in Ardmore, Oklahoma for sleeping with a student," Archie read aloud from a police report. "Went by Bob Jacobs back then—his legal name is Robert Jacob Simpson, according to vital records."

"Then how in the hell did he get hired at a school like Marshall?" I asked. "To hear my mother tell it, blue blood and an Ivy League degree are required to take phone messages there."

I touched a few keys on my laptop, navigating to the school database. Simpson's personnel file had to be a work of top-tier fiction, and I wanted a look. I tried the obvious passwords, starting with the mascot and working my way to *password*. No luck.

"Their security is better than average." I sat back in my chair, stretching my arms over my head.

Archie stuck his fingers in his ears. "La-la-la-la, spare me your amateur hacking adventures," he said.

"I resent the 'amateur' part of that statement." I poked my tongue out at him. "I still have a forensics certification, even if I'm not currently using it." Officially, anyway. "Without seeing the employment records, I'm going to guess he got a fake ID. It's not like they're hard to come by—I can find you two dozen kids on Craigslist right now who could make one that would fool us all day long."

"How would he explain not having a social?"

"He made one up? I mean, if statutory rape doesn't bother him, why would violating the tax code be an issue?"

Archie nodded, drumming his thick fingers on the table. "And you spoke with this guy?"

"Briefly." I picked up a pen, rapid-fire clicking the button on one end. "I didn't like him. Couldn't put my finger on why at the time. He has a sort of smarmy-behind-the-handsome, car salesman-y vibe. Makes you wonder what he wants out of it when he speaks to you."

"Charming. How did he react to the news about the girl?"

I paused the clicking. "Oddly." I stretched the word. "I mean, it didn't jump out at me, because he was kind of a douche. But he seemed more concerned about what he was going to tell Stanford than the fact that she was dead. And there was something weird between him and the mom. I thought they were sleeping together, maybe . . ." I let the words trail off, my thumb picking up the rhythm with the pen button again as the room around me blurred out of focus, everything in me zeroed in on the theory taking shape in my head.

Archie stayed quiet.

"What if Tenley was sleeping with the coach?" I asked finally.

"Where'd we jump on this train, again?"

Hours ago, it seemed, but I didn't know where it was headed at the time.

"Her friend said she was seeing someone but she wouldn't tell him who." The room snapped back into sharp focus as I shot to my feet. "And the lady at the gymnastics school said she was all the time whispering into her phone. Why would she be so guarded about a normal relationship? There had to be something she didn't want anyone to find out. Something that could've cost her boyfriend his job?"

Archie's brows drew down and joined as one, his head bobbing faster and faster. "He's got a history of it."

"And maybe the weirdness with the mom was that she knew? Or suspected?"

"So he took the girl to the dam and killed her? What for?"

I spun slowly on one heel, reaching for the photo of Simpson following Jessa DuGray into the bar. "Because of this. Suppose Simpson did know Jessa and didn't want people to know that after she went missing, because of his past. Or he maybe actually was involved in Jessa's death. What if Tenley found out he was connected with Jessa somehow?"

Archie slid one hand down his face, his words muffled by his fingers. "And he thought she was going to turn him in."

"It would explain the detailed effort at making it look like she jumped —whether he meant to kill Tenley or not, even. If they were up at the dam, and she confronted him about Jessa and they argued . . ."

Archie's head bobbed. "It's not the craziest theory I've heard. What'd this guy say about Tenley today? Anything that would push the suicide story?"

I flipped back through my notes. "Just that he thought she was 'handling the pressure' better."

He banged one palm onto the arm of his chair. "I'll be damned. I like this train. Can we ride it all the way to the courthouse?"

"Not on a photo and a hunch." I leaned on the edge of the table. First rule of an investigation: don't get ahead of the story. My gut was useful, but we needed to focus on facts. A theory is just that until the facts are there to support it—and this one wouldn't hold weight with a judge yet. No matter how much I'd love to take off, siren screaming, to slap handcuffs on Coach Smarmy, there was a smart way to handle this, and that wasn't it.

Simpson's whole being, from his look, to his focus, to his middle-age preoccupation with beautiful young women, howled, "Look at me."

And a decent narcissist will hang himself if you just give him enough rope. "We could pick him up for questioning," I said. "Tell him we want to get more information about Tenley and let him sweat a while."

"If this guy knew Jessa DuGray, he's been smart enough to keep that to himself for months, even with half the city talking about her disappearance and death," Archie said. "It'd be hard to crack him without tipping our hand. Let's dig a little more, see if we can come up with something we can show a judge. The fake ID, a diary, something proving he was involved with Jessa—or with Tenley outside his position as her coach. We should tread lightly." Archie closed the computer. "And we should tread tomorrow. It's past this old man's bedtime, kid."

I flashed a smile. "I could do with a little sleep myself." I started sliding photos and papers back into the corresponding case folders.

Archie gathered them and laid them back in a white file box. Neither of us spoke until he settled the lid in place. "You hold up okay today?" he asked softly.

I swallowed hard and nodded. "Mostly. It's been years. I keep thinking it'll get easier, you know? But sooner or later it always catches up to me." I squeezed my eyes shut tight. No tears.

"Me too. I should've been there—"

I shook my head hard. "This was not your fault, Arch. I miss her every day. But I don't blame you. They took her from her bed in the dead of night, and she was almost nineteen years old. How the hell were you supposed to stop that?"

"My superpowers." A smile ghosted across his face so fast I might've imagined it.

"Well, if you want to bring that into it . . ." I turned and hugged him. He stiffened momentarily at the unexpected gesture. I don't do hugs. Or much of any kind of touchy-feely nonsense, for that matter. It used to bug Archie when I shrank away from him, but he'd long since resigned himself to it. I loved him even more for his efforts to remedy my parents' mistakes, but he just didn't have enough time to make much headway.

He wrapped one thick arm around my waist and squeezed back. "Thank you for your help tonight. Maybe we can save the next one."

"Let's do that." I pulled away, looking up at him. "You don't think I'm trying too hard to see something that's not there with Tenley Andre?"

"I think you grew up to be the kind of cop I'm proud to call my colleague. Photo puts your girl's coach near Jessa the night she disappeared. Witnesses say Tenley was hiding a romance. That's worth following. And if it's not him, we'll move on to the next thing until we find the truth—in both cases. Promise."

Well, hell. I blinked against the unwelcome pricking in the backs of my eyes. Archie didn't throw attagirls around like peppermints—they had to be earned. Warmth bloomed in the center of my chest, rippling outward. "Thanks, Arch," I half whispered around the lump in my throat.

He hefted the box and nodded a *Ladies first* toward the door. I flipped off the light on my way out. "I appreciate your help, Ranger McClellan," he said.

"I can safely say the pleasure has been all mine." I smiled. "I feel like a cop for the first time in months."

"That is a crime in and of itself." He put the box on his desk and smiled when I popped one peppermint into my mouth and pocketed three more. "I'll keep you in mints forever if you'll give up the Marlboros."

"One vice. I eat clean, I run five days a week."

"And you have the lungs of a grandmother at thirty-six."

There was that one unfortunate side effect.

"Yeah, yeah. I'm working on it." I rolled my eyes. "You know I'm happy to help you with any case, anytime. If you ever wanted a partner again, say . . ."

He shook his head, starting for the door. "I'm too old to go changing my routine now. But I'm glad you're sticking around this week. One night and we've got a solid suspect. Nice work if I do say so myself."

I unlocked my truck, waved good night, and slid behind the wheel.

Was Jake Simpson responsible for one or both of these dead girls? Maybe. We needed more for me to trust our theory.

Solve the equation before anyone else gets hurt—that was the never-ending goal of this world we moved in, the variables always shifting for the next sicko in line.

This particular sicko thought he was smart.

So the trick was to make him do something dumb.

16

"'Lo?" the sleepy slur to Jim's single-syllable greeting after four rings made me swear under my breath.

"I'm so sorry to wake you, Jim." It was just past ten, but I feared morning would be too late. Jim liked to get an early jump on available autopsy rooms. "It's Faith McClellan."

"S'okay." A thump in my ear told me he'd dropped his phone. A couple of distant sailor-worthy mutterings later, he was back. "What can I do for you?"

"The young woman from out at Travis this morning—have you started her postmortem?"

"Waiting for an update from the SO to make sure the family doesn't have concerns."

I smiled. Jim didn't need the Andres' permission for an autopsy, but he was a dad, and a hell of a decent guy. Nice of him to hold off for word from them.

"Her mother was in rough shape this afternoon, but she wants to know what happened to her," I said. "Doesn't seem to me like you'll get pushback."

Jim sighed. "I don't want to imagine. I saw Jameson plastered the girl's picture all over the TV. God forbid that jackass miss a shot at a few minutes in front of the cameras." Disdain practically dripped from the receiver. "Why're you asking?"

"I'd like to observe, if it's okay."

"Oh yeah?" Now he was good and awake. "The Rangers taking this over?"

"Not officially, no," I said quickly. "It's been a weird day, and I'm kind of attached, is all. Wondering if you'll do me a solid here."

"I'm always happy to have company. Assuming I don't have to explain why it's necessary to her parents, I'll be on it first thing tomorrow morning. But I got the impression everyone was leaning toward jump. You have other ideas?"

"None I can prove. Something feels wrong, though."

"Is that so? I learned a long time ago that your gut is more reliable than any indictment in this town. I'll call you when I get in tomorrow. Leave your phone on, it could be early."

"Your turn to wake me up?" I laughed.

"Something like that. At least you were warned."

"Thanks, Jim. Sweet dreams."

I touched the "End" button as I turned into the parking lot at the DoubleTree. And stopped short when I walked through the sliding doors to find Graham chatting up the pretty brunette desk clerk.

What did he want this time of night? I fidgeted, wondering if I should scoot into the elevator before he saw me, just in case he was here to tell me to butt out of Jameson's big case. Hiding hasn't been my thing in a lot of years, though. Not having Graham on my side would suck, but it wouldn't make my mission impossible.

Smoothing my hair back as much as I could, I strode across the lobby and tapped him on the shoulder.

He winked at the clerk, turning to me with a smile. "Beginning to think you weren't ever coming back, McClellan."

"It's been a long day," I said, waving him toward the elevators. "I'm kind of afraid to ask what brings you by here."

He didn't answer until the elevator doors closed. "Guess who's lead on the Andre thing?" He grinned.

I caught a breath and held it, sending a silent thank-you to God and my sister and anyone else who might've tossed this break my way.

"I thought you said she jumped?" I didn't bother to try keeping the smile off my face as I cut my eyes to him.

"The official position is that she did unless we find solid evidence to the contrary. But you say she didn't, and you're a good cop." The doors opened, and he followed me to my room, picking up again when the door was shut behind him. Funny how some things, like not talking where other people might overhear, just become second nature after a while.

"I figure I'd be a fool not to ask what you've got, and I generally consider myself pretty smart. So—how long are you in town, and what've you got?" He pulled the wheeled chair away from the desk and turned it to sit, resting his hands on his knees and fixing me with a half smile that made it hard to focus on words. I tried to swallow, my mouth suddenly drier than the drought-starved lake bottom where I'd gotten myself sucked into this case.

I grabbed two bottles of water from the fridge, tossing him one before I opened mine and took a long swig. Graham and I had a long history. I couldn't remember it ever including the interior of a hotel room, though. That had to be it—weird to have him sitting four feet from where I'd slept last night. He looked at me like a kid sister. Partner. Friend. So I should return the favor. I twisted the cap back onto the bottle and nodded.

"I put in for vacation this afternoon, so I'm here all week, and I've got a whole lot of gut feeling something isn't right, but not enough to say how or why. Yet, anyway." I leaned one hip on the edge of the dresser, drumming my fingers on the surface. "The track coach is squicky." I paused. Should I mention Jessa?

Nah. Adding a complication from a high-profile murder might make him reconsider, and I didn't know anything for sure, anyway. It'd keep.

"Care to tell me what makes you think so?"

"He was fired from a district in Oklahoma ten years ago for sleeping with a student. He's working at Marshall under an assumed name. Tenley's friend said she was seeing someone she wouldn't talk to anybody about." I ticked the points off on my fingers.

"Damn. I'd say that warrants a visit." Graham's eyebrows waggled, a grin lighting his whole face. "So I take it your vacation isn't going to be of the lounge-by-the-pool variety?"

I snorted, standing when my elbow bumped the flat-screen and it rocked. "Have you met me? Besides, I've practically been on vacation for three months. It'd be nice to have a purpose again."

"That bad?"

"I'm the low person on the totem pole, and I lack the outdoor plumbing the lieutenant prefers in his officers." For want of another reasonable place to sit, I perched on the foot of the bed. "So I basically spent the last twelve years busting my ass to be a glorified messenger-slash-secretary."

Graham winced. "That blows."

"You have no idea."

"Welcome back, partner." He put out a hand and I shook it, a tingle shooting clear to my elbow when his fingers closed around mine. I thought his eyes widened the barest bit, but I stopped myself short of wondering if he felt it, too. Partner. Friend. Dead teenage girl who needed our help.

Pulling away, I fidgeted with the paper Ozarka label on my water bottle.

Graham folded his thick arms across his chest. "I might've led Jameson to believe both parents were out of town."

Nice. Jameson vastly preferred face-to-face conversations; we used to joke that his demonic powers didn't allow him to feed off people's sorrow via fiber optics.

"Did you find her dad?" I asked.

"I did. Dad flew back from Charlotte this evening." He leaned forward, resting his elbows on his knees. "That's part of why I came by, actually. He . . . uh . . . he wants to see her."

I caught a sharp breath. "Lord, what for?"

"Closure? I drew the short straw on escorting him—supposed to meet him at the morgue first thing in the morning. You want to come with me?"

I nodded. "I asked Jim if I could sit in on the postmortem, anyway. And he did say he'd like to talk to her folks. I don't suppose you want to hang out with us after dad leaves?" A teasing smile tugged at the corners of my lips as I watched his face flush a putrid greenish brown.

He cleared his throat. "I think I'd rather stay with dad." For Graham, that was saying something.

"Wuss." I smiled.

"Freak." He landed a light fist on my knee, and all the awkwardness melted right out of the room. That was more like it. Me and Graham, teasing each other and laughing, as easy and comfortable as breathing.

I laughed. "You know you love that I handle all the pieces you don't care for. Did y'all ever get around to opening those packages recovered at the scene?"

"They turned out to be interesting—we got a clean print off one package that didn't match Tenley."

"Two and two isn't so much four after all, huh? Did you get a hit in criminal records?"

"No. Nothing in DPS, either."

Of course not. Annoying, but not altogether surprising. The Texas Department of Public Safety is one of a handful in the country that collects and catalogs all ten fingerprints, but the practice is still relatively new, so the database is incomplete.

"So someone who hasn't gotten their license renewed in the past three years," he continued.

"Or maybe doesn't have one at all. Not exactly a narrow field." I plucked at a loose thread on the duvet. At least we'd have the print Graham lifted for comparison when we made an arrest. "What was in the gifts?"

Graham pulled out a notebook. "Evidence catalog has one Stanford sweatshirt for the coach, a locket and a scarf for mom, bookends for dad, spiffy sneakers for her teammate, and a photo in a silver frame for Nicholas Richardson—do you know she was friends with Darren Richardson's son?"

I nodded. How was it possible that I didn't know that just twenty-four hours ago? It seemed like a week since I'd spotted Nicky Richardson in Tenley's locket and started down this rabbit hole. But I was too far gone to turn back now, and so glad Graham wanted my help I could almost cry.

"You ever met the coach?" I asked.

Graham shook his head. "But given the tone that's usually reserved for your folks, I'm going to guess he doesn't make a great personal impression?"

I rolled my eyes as I drained the water bottle, then filled him in on my encounter with Nicky and his father.

He let out a low whistle when I got to the part about the kid's sexuality. "Damn. Right in front of you and the school people, too? You know that means the poor kid catches ten times that at home."

Boy, did I know.

I nodded. "After what I saw, I'd buy suicide if we'd found him at the bottom of the dam. I'm not sure I've ever wanted so badly to sucker punch someone I'm not blood related to."

"Your dad isn't that bad." Graham put one hand on my arm when my lips rolled between my teeth. "Faith. Is he?"

"No comment." I ignored the burning in the back of my throat, throwing him a quick smile and a subject change. "You said there were notes with the packages, too?"

Graham nodded. "Evidence has them all bagged and cataloged if we want to look at them tomorrow. Between that stray print and these notes, I almost think you might be onto something. All the letters are about secrets."

My lips popped into a neat little O. "What sorts of secrets?"

"Apparently, the dad is cheating on the mom."

"Oh, that. The mom knows."

"The girl tells them to explore why. A lot of rambling about suffocating and lying to themselves. And something about the mother not falling back into old habits because she'd already ruined enough lives?"

My hairline met my eyebrows. "To hear the people I've talked to so far tell it, Tenley and her mom were tight. Like, almost abnormally so."

"That's there, too. She practically wrote a sonnet on how much she loved her mom, and said twice that she was proud to be her daughter. The whole thing is weird—they read like rambling word vomit in places."

Another miscalculation. "Tenley was a straight-A student." I shook my head. "Nothing here adds up if you look even a little beneath the surface."

"I mean, we can submit the handwriting for analysis, but if Tenley didn't write these, whoever did sure knew a lot about her family and friends."

I nodded. "Let's see what else we have first. What did the others say?"

"That your gut is right about the track coach. Dude is indeed squicky, and does have a girlfriend in the Marshall student body, but our vic didn't say who if she knew. I didn't get the impression it was her, but I might be reading wrong. The other girl on the track team is knocked up, apparently, and hasn't told the baby's father."

"What if one of those has to do with the other?" I asked. "A popular teacher with a cushy job in a wealthy district gets a student pregnant . . . Could be the sort of secret somebody might kill for."

Graham nodded. "It seems the people in this girl's life were hiding a lot of things some folks might kill to keep quiet. Depending on the person. I'm not saying you're right. But maybe two and two is something entirely different this time."

I twisted the lid off and on my water bottle. "What about Nicky? Did he have a secret, too?"

"Dunno. There wasn't a letter with his gift."

My bottle cap fell to the carpet, my stomach following close behind. "Why would she write everyone else and not her closest friend?"

"Either his secret is already out . . . ," Graham said.

"Or his note left the scene with whoever killed Tenley," I finished on a sigh. Shit. I liked that kid. "But the print you got wasn't his, or it would've hit in the DPS database. He's a teenager."

"Correct. I checked that by hand when his note was missing." Graham raised one index finger. "All of this is predicated on a big if: if anyone killed her."

"Oh, come on, Graham." I rolled my eyes. "What else can you possibly need?"

"I need to know you're not bent on making this something it's not because of Charity." Graham's voice softened. "I know this is a hard day for you. And the similarities are weird. You've even got me wondering. But we have no evidence that anyone had anything against the family, or that the girl was out there under any coercion. Presents and rambling notes for her people could very well be parting gifts and advice from a girl planning to jump. I need you to find your objectivity."

I flopped backward, my eyes roving the ceiling. "You might be right. But I just don't see it: Only child, by all accounts lavished with love, brilliant student, star athlete. She was looking for an apartment in California. The new boyfriend is the only thing that sticks out as a red flag for me, and even then, why would a girl as beautiful as Tenley Andre swan dive off Mansfield Dam over any guy? There are a million more where he came from."

"I don't see the motive, either. Just telling you where the evidence is stacking up."

"But why is it stacking up so damned easily?"

Graham tipped his head to one side and waved a *Come out with it.*

"If I were going to murder a bright young woman from a wealthy family, it wouldn't be the dumbest thing in the world to make it look like a suicide." I let my words hang as Graham's head started bobbing.

"Maybe. Minimal cops, no fuss, no worries about getting caught. But why would someone want her dead? Motive is more important to a murder case than a suicide."

"Right now, my money is on a secret. Maybe Tenley's, maybe someone else's. All the trails are still fresh. Something might jump at Jim in the morning." I didn't want to mention Stella Connolly until I knew a little more.

"Let's wait for the postmortem and go from there," Graham said. "I'll pull the photos from the scene in the morning, too—if she didn't jump, somebody either pushed her or planted her there."

"Thank you, Graham." Without really thinking about it, I reached for his hand, his big baseball player fist swallowing my icy fingers in warmth.

"Don't thank me yet. I'm not convinced—I'm saying we'll see. Pick you up in the morning on my way to the ME's office?"

"I'll bring the coffee."

Shutting the door behind him, I felt lighter than I had in months.

A little more proof before morning, and I'd pull him right off the fence and squarely into my camp.

I reached for my laptop, plugged my phone in, and opened my browser. Tenley's Instagram password loaded with nary a glitch—seemed that swiper app was worth the fifty bucks. I opened her recently tagged photos, inching them down the screen as I scanned for any teensy detail that might give me a clue which goose to chase.

Tenley dancing, eyes closed and head thrown back, arms in the air. I zoomed in on her face. Her lashes spilled down her cheeks nearly halfway to the tip of her nose, a small smile playing around her lips. Brows relaxed. Forehead smooth. She was in the moment.

Happy. Like Stella said.

Next.

Twenty shots later, I spotted the Davenport kid. Tenley was talking to a girl whose bright-purple hair matched her bright-purple crop top. Zayne stood behind Tenley, hands jammed into his pockets, muscles coiled. She didn't see him, but he saw her. And if those daggers he was staring were real, she'd have been shredded like last month's bank statement before she made it to the bottom of the dam. Ten more shots down was the image I'd seen earlier, his hand behind her and her angry sideways glare fixed on him.

Five more, someone had tagged Tenley in one corner of a video shot of a bunch of kids drinking straight out of a keg with a funnel. I zoomed again. She looked frightened, running for a set of French doors on the back wall of the large room packed with teenagers.

Next shot. Tenley and Nicky Richardson in profile, standing on a wide stone balcony. Tenley's easy smile was back, her hand on Nicky's shoulder.

So whatever she was scared of, it was in the middle of the beer-chugging jocks and Nicky's appearance at her side. He said he'd "rescued her" from Davenport.

Good enough for now.

I clicked to the department's log-in page, entered my DPS password, and punched Zayne Davenport's plate number into the traffic-cam search. Last twenty-four hours. City and surrounding areas. "Go." The dam was so far from any camera station, it'd take days to search every way to that road for cars belonging to people Tenley might've known, but an affidavit from Nicky about what he saw at the party would get us a warrant to pick Captain Football up if he'd so much as breathed in the vicinity of the lake Tuesday morning.

A little colored wheel spun on the screen as the data loaded. I tapped one finger on the edge of the keyboard and stared at the page like I could will the information to show up faster. There. I scrolled all the way back to the wee hours.

Nothing after he turned right on Rosebud, four blocks from his house, at 1:38.

Damn. What if Zayne was telling the truth? There are a lot of assholes in the world who aren't murderers.

Next up, Simpson. I pulled the plates for the late-model Ram pickup registered to him and ran another search. It seemed like it took twice as long for the data to load that time, my fingers tapping faster until I had to get out of the chair and pace some more.

I leaned over the desk when the fields started to populate, waiting for the early-morning hits.

He passed through a tollbooth on Highway 45 at 1:12. Turned onto University Club Drive at 1:24. And then nothing until he ran a red light on FM 620 at 5:18.

I double-checked his home address. Pulled up a map and dropped pins, first at the dam, then at each traffic cam and Simpson's home.

He lived between the city and the dam. The tollway could take him home, but University Club was past his house.

I went back to the images, checking his trunk against the rising sun in the third one. He was heading away from the school—and away from the dam, in a roundabout fashion—in a big hurry, right around sunrise.

I made a note on my map pin, my eyes jumping between the marked places. It didn't look great for him, but it still wasn't hard evidence. Dammit, why couldn't there be a traffic cam right near the fucking dam? Watch the feed, get the answer, pick up the bad guy, and save or salvage what was left of the week.

It couldn't ever be easy.

I shoved the computer away. Not exactly the ending note I'd choose for my first day on a real case in months, but the truth lurked somewhere, waiting for us to uncover it.

And Tenley needed me to keep digging.

* * *

Face scrubbed and lights out, I turned the covers back as my phone bleated a text alert.

Archie: *Turn on your TV.*

Shit.

Without having to ask, I clicked the set on and punched the buttons for channel two.

Sure enough, Skye Morrow's faux-serious face filled half the screen, quickly replaced by a series of stills of what appeared to be naked women with strategic blurring as Skye's voice droned in the background. "The internet pornography industry has a disturbing underbelly that's closer to home than you'd imagine. Tonight, an exclusive *News2* investigation leads to the man who puts these unsettling images into thousands of homes via the dark web. A warning to parents: this report is intended for mature audiences."

I sat on the crisp sheets, my eyes glued to the screen. The images were fuzzy, but the women in them had one thing in common: wide-eyed terror.

"Hundreds of videos, all apparently depicting violent sexual assault." Skye's words dropped slowly as more strategically grayed-out images flashed by.

"More troubling still? This site, where some of these videos get hundreds of thousands of views every day, originates from a server right here in Austin." Skye's tone was low and ominous. "More on what we found there right after this."

I grabbed my phone and dialed Archie. "Holy shit," I said when he picked up.

"We have three guys who've been tracking this operation for five months, trying to prove any of this is real and not staged," Archie said. "Does she even goddamn care that she's going to up their web traffic and ad revenue with this?"

"No. She cares about keeping her job. I've never seen so many filler injections in one face. And when you think about the people my mother surrounds herself with, that's pretty serious."

"I hate the press sometimes," he grumbled.

"I hate Skye Morrow all the time," I said. "But you know . . . she's not wrong about this, Archie. Just in my time in uniform there's been an uptick in the number of SAs that get reported, and we all know how many more go unreported. The more people there are who watch this bullshit, the more act it out. The link is there."

"I know. I hate walking this damned tightrope between freedom and public safety." He sighed.

"True story."

The commercial faded to black and Skye was back, pacing in front of a giant channel two logo. "*News2*'s cyber investigations team tracked down the website's owner. Ray Wooley operates the site these images came from through a server in this southeast Austin office building." A ramshackle converted warehouse took over the screen. "We caught up with Mr. Wooley yesterday afternoon, but as you might have guessed, he wasn't too happy to see us."

Footage rolled. Skye: "Ray Wooley? Do you own the computer server upstairs that runs a pornography site specializing in videos of assault and torture?"

A middle-aged, middle-height, middle-sized man with an overgrown hipster beard and black plastic-framed glasses looked dead into the camera and told Skye something the station wouldn't air, then turned away and pulled up his hood as he jogged down the street. Skye gave admirable chase in her four-inch heels, shouting more questions, but he slid into a dark late-model sedan and sped off.

Back in the studio, Skye told her audience to stay with *News2* for more on this exclusive investigation. She vanished, replaced by a red-faced man in a Stetson brandishing an AR-15 in his left hand and pounding a podium with his right as he screamed Second Amendment talking points into a crowd of about thirty rifle-toting, camouflage-clad fans. "Authorities were on guard in Hyde Park near the UT campus today as student anti-gun protestors faced off with Senator Bobby Wayne Otis and members of his Guardians of the Second group. Otis has become the staunchest gun-rights activist in the Capitol in the past two sessions—"

I clicked the set off.

"Jesus," I said to no one in particular. And about both reports.

"On the bright side, if anyone comes forward with an affidavit about one of those assaults being the real deal, the cyber guys get their warrant,"

Archie said. "On the darker side, she just told every wannabe sicko in town where to get ideas over their broadband. Like we don't have enough to do."

"Good thing we're smarter than your average sicko."

"Jessa DuGray notwithstanding."

"We're smarter than that one, too. Haven't you heard that the Rangers always get their man?"

"I wish I felt as sure as you sound."

"I am sure," I said, "because I have to be."

17

I was already awake when Jim rang my phone at just past the ass crack of dawn Wednesday. "Morning, sunshine," I said, putting it to my ear.

"I believe that's the first time anyone has ever called me that."

"What a travesty."

"I have an email that says your victim's father is due at the morgue in about an hour."

"So I heard. I'm riding in with Graham."

"Getting the whole band back together here, are we?"

"Going to be a heck of a reunion tour if I'm anywhere close on what happened to this girl."

"Don't tell me. Can't have my conclusions compromised by knowing what you want to hear."

"Check. See you in a bit."

"Yep. I'll leave your names at the desk, just come on back."

"Captain Queasy is taking dad out while I come in with you," I said.

"Oh good. I like Hardin, but mopping up after him twice was enough."

I laughed around the goodbye and put the phone on the night table. Running one hand through my hair, I sat up and surveyed the knotted mess of blankets on the floor next to the bed.

Jake Simpson. The track coach had scared up fitful dreams all night. I didn't like him. Hadn't from the minute I set eyes on him, and not just because of his too-white teeth and too-perfect hair.

I swung my legs over the side of the bed, the hotel-grade carpet rough on my feet as I padded to the bathroom and turned on the shower, replaying every word the guy had uttered as the hot water pounded my shoulders and back.

The thing that kept coming to mind was that he didn't really seem sad. Charity's gymnastics coaches had about lost their minds when she died. And this guy, who saw Tenley every day and had her to thank for his Coach of the Year award, didn't shed a single tear. That should've registered with me immediately, but now that it had, it wouldn't let go.

Tenley knew his secret. That had to be it. But because she was involved with him, or because she knew someone who was?

By the time I shut off the water and turbaned my hair up in a towel, I wasn't closer to an answer.

I leaned toward the mirror, flicking a mascara wand over my long lashes. Not because Graham would be there; because my mother had a lot of things wrong, but she was right about appearances. Pretty gets more attention, opens more doors.

I nodded at my reflection. "Go with the gut, but know it's not foolproof," I said. God knew I'd heard Archie say that enough in my lifetime. When you got right down to it, it was good advice for more than just police work.

My gut leaned Simpson. Maybe it was him.

And maybe it was a coincidence. They were rare, in my experience, but they happened. My gut was rock solid on Tenley, though—the more we dug up, the deeper I dug in against the suicide theory.

Graham knocked on the door just as I pulled my second boot on. I swung it open and smiled when I saw the Starbucks cups cradled in his big left hand.

"Pike Place, no milk, two sugars." He held one cup out.

"I thought coffee was my department." I took it and pulled the little green stick out of the top, then closed my lips over the lid and took a sip.

Graham's eyes stayed on my mouth until he averted them to the wall behind me, rocking up on the balls of his feet and clearing his throat. "I couldn't sleep this morning. Or most of last night. Thinking about what you said. About someone trying to make us think she jumped."

I swallowed the coffee, stepping into the hallway and turning for the elevators. "And?"

"If—I'm saying *if*—that's what we're seeing here, someone went to a lot of damned trouble."

I sighed, opening my mouth before he put one hand up.

"I'm still here, aren't I? But I pulled photos and reports up when I got home last night and . . . if somebody killed this girl, it was really well planned. The gifts. The notes. Someone went pretty far to make it look like she did herself in. Someone who had to know her pretty well, understand the relationships she had with everyone who mattered in her life. Someone she trusted with secrets. Why would someone who loved her want her dead?"

I punched the button for the elevator and took another sip of my coffee so I wouldn't have to answer that. Because beyond what I'd already told him about Simpson, I didn't have the first fucking clue.

The doors whispered open and I stepped into the little box, feeling Graham's stare on my jawline before I slid my eyes to him. "What if the presents weren't what we're seeing them as?" I mused. "What if she was just feeling generous, and we're reading too much into it?"

"You think the fact that she had a bag full of well-thought-out gifts for everyone who was important to her isn't an apology for offing herself? Remind me to talk to you about this bridge I'm trying to sell later."

The doors opened to the lobby and we walked outside in silence. "You want to take my truck?" I pulled the keys from my pocket.

"Still can't stand even letting someone else drive, huh? Gotta have control." Graham smiled and stopped by my maroon F-150. "That's okay. I'm man enough to ride shotgun."

I steered through familiar streets, hitting the gas on the I-35 onramp. "If she was going to jump, why take presents out there with her?" I asked, turning to look at him.

"Good question. Maybe she wanted to make sure they were found?"

"But why not just leave them on her bed or something? Taking them to the dam if she knew she was going to jump, leaving them sitting there in a fifteen-hundred-dollar bag . . . that seems stupid. And she was by all accounts a pretty smart girl. Wouldn't she be afraid somebody would steal them? Hell, I'm shocked nobody did."

"That part of the lakeshore is pretty swanky." Graham sounded less sure.

I pounced on the uncertainty. "But the bag wasn't down on the sand. It was up at the top of the dam. Where anybody could've picked it up and taken off with it. That section of the road might be closed, but the park is popular with runners."

"That is true." Graham's hands drummed on his knees.

"So why would she do that?" I put the blinker on and moved into the right lane to exit onto Twelfth Street.

"I'm not sure. Let's go see what she's got left to tell us."

Score. Graham was about as black and white as a person could get, and stone set in his opinions. If I had him wondering what had happened to Tenley, I was onto something. I stayed quiet as we parked outside the ME's office, then walked next to him to the door and shrugged out of my holster for the metal detectors inside.

Just inside security, a tall man in a rumpled black suit sat slumped on a bench, head cradled in his hands, eyes pointed at the bright-white floor tile.

"Mr. Andre?" Graham asked, stopping next to him.

A ravaged version of the man from the canvas over Erica's fireplace sat up and blinked red-rimmed eyes at Graham, putting out a hand.

Brent Andre looked flat-ass destroyed. No other words for it.

Graham shook the offered hand and pulled Brent to his feet in one smooth move, gesturing in the direction of the morgue. I fell into step beside them, waiting for a window to introduce myself. Graham opened it for me, ticking his head in my direction. "This is Faith McClellan from the Texas Rangers. She's assisting with our investigation of Tenley's death."

"I'm so sorry for your loss, Mr. Andre." I kept my voice low. "Are you sure you want to do this? It's not necessary for identification, and I can't imagine it'll be easy."

Brent Andre's chiseled chin quivered as he nodded. "I keep thinking I'm going to wake up soon, you know?" The rasp in his voice rivaled Louis

Armstrong's. Poor guy. It takes a whole lot of tears to do that to a person's throat.

We turned the corner, and I patted Mr. Andre's shoulder. "I understand."

He shuffled along, giving no sign that he'd heard me.

I opened my mouth to explain how the identification would go as Skye Morrow stepped out of the alcove in front of the doors to the morgue. "Good morning, Detective." She smirked at me. "Ranger."

My eyes rolled back before I could stop them, but I managed to bite down on the *Who let you back here?* before I was outright rude. Skye had been around the Austin cops scene for longer than she'd admit under military torture. She knew everyone, and people owed her more favors than a mafia don.

I loathed her right down to her Louboutin stilettos. But I couldn't deny that she was good at her job.

"Morning, Ms. Morrow." Graham nodded, putting a hand on the small of my back and propelling me forward.

"Skye." I managed it without choking on the word, which could be called an accomplishment.

"Little Faith McClellan has made it all the way to the Texas Rangers." Skye reached one perfectly manicured crimson talon toward the silver star on my shirt, clicking her tongue. "I wonder what your mother has to say about that?"

"I'm sure you've spoken to her more recently than I have." My tone was cool, but not unprofessional.

Graham landed a light elbow to my ribs, and I slid my eyes sideways. Mr. Andre's vacant stare hit me like a whole tidal wave of ice water. He didn't need to watch a cop–reporter catfight in the middle of the worst week of his life. I nodded to the doors. "If you'll excuse us. Police business. I know you understand."

Skye eyed Mr. Andre, her most charming smile lighting her face as she started to extend one hand.

"This way, sir." I stepped between them, not-so-gently knocking Skye's arm aside with my elbow, and pulled the door open.

I kept my eyes on Skye as Graham ushered the victim's father into the sterile, frigid room. "Leave them alone. It's only been a day." I kept my voice low, but every word could've sliced a tin can.

"That's about five thousand Twitter cycles," Skye said. "Why are you here? What interest could the Rangers possibly have in this girl?"

"I'm afraid that pertains to a pending investigation. Sorry. No comment." I flashed a half smile that said I wasn't sorry at all.

"I'm sure I can call up my old friend Billy Boone in Waco and find out what you're doing here," Skye said, her lips curling into a smile when my eyes widened.

Witch. She really did know everyone.

"Dig all you want." I kept my voice even, stepping into the room. "Just leave the family be."

Skye tipped her head to one side. "Promise me a sit-down with them first," she said. "That's all I want from them, anyway."

Ratings. Money. Did anybody really give one damn about anything else? I swear it was hard to tell some days.

I nodded as the door slipped closed, and blew out a breath I didn't realize I'd been holding as Skye turned on her heel and strode away. I didn't say when she could sit down with the Andres, and I did get her off their back.

The problem I'd invited was that Skye was smart. Just my being there would make the case more interesting than the parents, which is why she gave up so easily.

It also left me racing two clocks instead of just one. Fan-goddamn-tastic.

18

By the time I'd gotten rid of the Hill Country's nosiest reporter, Brent Andre was a puddle of tears. Tenley's father leaned on Graham's shoulder, his raw sobs punching me in the gut. I pulled in a slow breath, the formalin in the air stinging my nose and making my eyes burn.

Jim resettled a thick white sheet over Tenley's waxen face, nodding a somber hello to me as Graham led Mr. Andre from the room.

"That part of this shit never gets easier," Jim said when the door shut behind them. "You see Skye out there?"

"You the one who let her back here?"

Jim shrugged. "I owed her a favor from way back. Now I don't anymore. And why does she care about a rich kid who leapt off the dam, anyway? She doing some sort of after-school special on the dangers of pushing your kids too hard?"

My teeth closed over my bottom lip. "I don't know." Rather, I knew Skye would want to have the story first, but that train left yesterday. Her early-morning trip to the morgue still made no sense.

The only logical conclusion was that she knew something.

But was it something we already had, or something I needed to know, too?

Damn. I tapped one foot as Jim prepped tools next to the drain table.

"You okay?" he asked, cocking one unruly eyebrow. "I know you have a strong stomach, but she's—" He paused, laying a hand on the sheet over Tenley's arm. "Are you absolutely sure you want to be in here for this?"

Nope. But I just nodded. Tenley needed me. "I have to get this one right, Jim."

"I'm happy to slip you an unredacted report if you'd rather go find Graham. You know, out there . . . away from the smell."

Tempting. No matter how many times I did this, that part never got easier to take—I was practiced enough to know better than to eat beforehand.

"I want to stay." I couldn't say I thought I might see something he didn't, but I knew it was possible, even as good as Jim was.

He nodded and clicked on a little silver stick voice recorder. "Today is Wednesday, April twenty-fifth. James Prescott, Travis County Deputy Medical Examiner. White female, positively identified by fingerprints and next of kin as Tenley Louise Andre, age seventeen, of Austin."

He continued with the description of the body discovery as he pulled the sheet back. "Examination attended by Faith McClellan, Texas Department of Public Safety, Rangers Division." I stepped closer to the table, my eyes on Tenley's beautiful face. A bluish undertone had developed since yesterday morning, but she was no less gorgeous.

"No bruising or marks on the face or neck," Jim noted.

There were no marks on the rest of Tenley's front, either, save the healing scrapes on her knees I'd noticed the day before.

Jim clicked the recorder off and crooked a *Come here* finger my way. "Any idea what could've done this?" He gestured to Tenley's knee.

"She was a runner, so my first guess is that she fell recently. But it's spring; maybe it's a razor mark."

He leaned over the scab, eyes scrunching up behind his glasses. "I don't think so," he murmured, waving me even closer to the table. "See the long, individual cuts here?"

I leaned over, linking my fingers behind my back so I wouldn't accidentally reach for anything. "I'll be damned."

Jim was good. I'd caught the wide rust-brown scab on Tenley's knee, but not what looked like a fresh set of wispy slices running through it. "It didn't even have time to clot," I breathed.

"Which means this happened days to maybe weeks ago"—Jim's finger hovered above the larger wound—"but these . . . they came right before her heart stopped beating."

"Could she have hit her leg on the way down?"

He shook his head. "The wall of the dam is too smooth. I can't see a way for just this knee to hit it hard enough to do this without leaving some other evidence of injury. This skin was dragged across something for several inches. The way she was lying, I'm not sure how she could've been contorted enough in the air for the concrete to do that with no other marks visible on her."

I met his eyes. "So, she fell. Before she fell."

"Sure as hell looks that way. Which could mean she was running, especially in those shoes." He shrugged. "But you're the cop. I'm just the body guy."

I nodded, a tingle starting in the pit of my stomach and spreading to my toenails and the roots of my hair. I knew it: whatever happened out there, this girl didn't intend to die yesterday. "Any evidence of sexual assault?"

"You have reason for me to pull a kit?"

"Not one I want to share?" I hitched the last word up at the end and offered a sweet smile.

Jim snorted. "Keep your secrets. I probably don't want to know anyway."

He moved to the end of the table and arranged Tenley's legs before he flicked on an overhead lamp and positioned it for proper lighting. After retrieving a sealed kit from the cabinet to his left, he opened it and laid out a small plastic comb, a long cotton swab, and a sterile baggie.

I turned my back. The girl was dead. Privacy wasn't really a concern anymore. But it still felt intrusive to watch.

Jim cleared his throat after ten of the longest minutes in history ticked by. "Sex, probably. Assault, I can't say for sure."

I turned back as he sealed the comb and swab inside the bag, straightened Tenley's legs, and prepared to roll her over. "Care to elaborate?" I asked.

"There's some bruising and swelling in her vaginal tissue, and *slight*"—

he hit that word hard—"tearing. That's all common in sexual assault. But when you're dealing with a rapist who's also a killer, I might expect the injuries to be more pronounced. Doesn't mean she didn't have rough sex with someone within twenty-four hours or so of time of death, though. Also doesn't mean she didn't decide to jump if she was assaulted."

Damn. "Why does every answer bring three new questions along for the ride?" I shoved my hands into my snug pockets. "You got a good swab?"

"Of course. I might be an older old man before it gets processed, but it's there." He nodded to the tray.

I flashed a half smile. "Thanks."

"Just doing my job." He reached into his pocket, turned the recorder back on, and listed the findings from the pelvic exam, then turned it off again and rolled Tenley to her stomach.

Jesus. "Good thing Graham went out," I whispered, my eyes stuck on Tenley's head, my brain not wanting to process what I saw.

The gold hair was purple black with dried blood across the misshapen back of Tenley's skull, globs of sand and bits of tissue I didn't care to dwell on caught in the bloody mess that had been a waterfall of flaxen waves less than forty-eight hours ago.

"Massive trauma to the posterior skull," Jim said into his recorder. "Observed are possibly fatal blood loss, congealed-in sand and dirt, and sections of scalp attached to fragmented bits of skull in her hair. No visible brain matter." He moved the light. "Bruising along the back of the neck suggests trauma to the C-3 and C-4. X-rays should confirm. Shoulders show expected levels of lividity, as does the victim's lower back and—" He stopped on a sharp breath, pulling my eyes from the gruesome mess at the top of the table.

"Victim has a slash over her right buttock, approximately"—Jim fumbled with a tape measure—"eight centimeters in length, down at an inward forty-degree angle."

I stepped closer, the wound holding my full attention.

"No evidence of clotting or bleeding." Jim clicked the recorder off and turned away from the table.

"Faith."

I didn't answer at first, my eyes fixed on the gash.

"Yeah?" It came out mangled. I cleared my throat and tried again. "Sorry. Uh. What the hell is that?"

"I've been at this longer than I care to remember most of the time. A blade did that to her skin."

I nodded. "It looks like it, yes."

"After she was dead."

I pulled in a slow breath, the chemical sting in the air bringing tears to my eyes. "How sure are you?"

"I'm sure," Jim said, shaking his head. "The head injury fits with a jump. But this . . . does not."

He pulled out the recorder. Didn't touch the "Record" button. Stuck it back in his pocket and paced four lengths of the floor before he inspected Tenley's legs and resettled the sheet over her.

"You okay, Jim?"

"I admit, I thought I knew what we had here before we started. But you wouldn't be here unless you thought this wasn't a suicide. So, Ranger McClellan, tell me: What the hell happened to this young woman?"

19

Graham jumped, sloshing freshly refilled coffee over the back of his hand, when I tapped his shoulder. "Damn, woman. Make some noise when you walk," he snapped, grabbing a handful of napkins and blotting the hot liquid. "I liked that layer of skin where it was."

"Sorry, I wasn't trying for stealth." I took the cup so he could run his hand under cold water.

He reached into his pocket with his good hand, pulled out a bright-yellow paper square, and laid it on the counter. I leaned over. Neon-purple and turquoise ink lines scrolled into an almost-psychedelic jumble of numbers and words. Smack in the center was yesterday's date decorated with tiny flowers and butterflies.

"What's that?" I asked.

"Dad found it on the desk in their study last night next to his mostly unconscious wife. Says it's Tenley's handwriting." Graham leaned one hip against the counter, ribbons of water sluicing over his scalded skin. "Secrets. Freedom. Fly. Kinda sounds like a kid who was planning to, oh, I don't know . . . jump off the dam, maybe?"

I reached for the note and held it up to the light. Long, sure, loopy lines. Bold strokes.

"This doesn't look like the work of a girl who was depressed or afraid to me," I said. "People in Tenley's world seem to tell a story of two girls: one who was impossibly hard on herself and desperate to make her mother proud, and one who was popular, smart, and confident. I'm going to say this was done by the latter."

"Dammit, you're stubborn." He sighed. "You miss the part about flying?"

"Did you miss the one about joy?" I shot back. "I'm only as stubborn as you are."

He shut off the water and wrapped his burned hand in a paper towel. "It makes sense, Faith. And under the circumstances, finding a note is enough to call this a suicide and move the hell on."

I pulled air in through my nose for a ten count, my fingers curling into a fist at my side. *Don't yell. He hates yelling, and you need his help, Faith.*

"We seem to have a few more things that don't add up." The words slid, one by one, through my teeth.

"Such as?"

"She's got little bitty cuts on her knee that hadn't scabbed over," I said. "They were too new."

"What kind of cuts?"

"Jim is going to swab them when he's done. I decided my time would be better used out here in light of what we found. But they look like gravel to me. Pretty fine gravel."

"Like the kind of fine gravel you might find on a high school track?" Graham raised one eyebrow.

Smart-ass.

I shrugged. "I guess we'll see what the swab finds. But no high school track made the three-inch gash somebody carved into her right hip after she was dead."

"Define gash."

"Looked like she was cut with a blade. Deep enough to bleed. No blood. Downward and inward line at about a forty-degree angle."

Graham drummed his fingers on the countertop, looking behind me. "That, I don't like the sound of."

"Oh good, then we don't have to stop to have you sent up for a psych eval." I rolled my eyes. "Who would like the sound of that? But it means whatever happened to this girl, she didn't jump off that wall."

I tapped a toe, my teeth latching around the inside of my cheek. I was right about this, dammit. Graham used to trust me. Why didn't he just believe me?

"Who goes to so much trouble to make something look like a suicide and then carves up the corpse after the fact?" Graham shook his head. "This makes no goddamn sense at all."

I didn't answer, something floating around the back of my brain that I couldn't quite grab ahold of. He was right. None of it made any sense. It was our job to see the twisted logic in an illogical situation.

"Let's say you're right, and this wasn't some random sicko who found her and started to chop her up and thought better of it," Graham began, and I raised one hand.

"Are you even listening to yourself? She was cut postmortem, under her replaced clothes, and then turned over and arranged. For the love of God, Graham. Tenley Andre was murdered."

He pinched his lips together, his eyes darting from one corner of the room to the other. "Yeah." It floated out with a long sigh, so low I almost didn't catch the word.

My forehead drew down, my voice dropping as I stepped closer to him. "This isn't you at all, is it?"

He shook his head so slightly a blink would've made anyone miss it and put a hand on the small of my back, propelling me toward the door.

We were halfway down the block before he spoke, the sun warming the back of my neck even as a chill stole through me at the creepy-solemn set to Graham's jaw.

"This is complicated."

"Murders usually are." I shoved my hands in my pockets, turning to face him. "Explain. Now."

"Tenley Andre will make the second young woman from a well-to-do family murdered in Travis County in eight months."

Jessa DuGray. "And?"

"There are people who are afraid the press will start hollering 'Serial killer,' and you and I both know ratings would encourage that even without a shred of evidence the murders were related. People stop letting their kids go out at night, parents decide not to let their daughters come to the university . . ." He raised both hands, palms out, when my eyes narrowed. "Just the messenger."

"You can tell whoever's writing the script that your message fucking sucks." I stomped one foot, wishing for something I could kick. "Money? They want to let this go, leave this family with no answers, and actually leave a killer out there walking free, over money?"

"You know just as well as I do that everything is always about the money. Hell, I'd wager you know it better than most of us."

Blood rushed to my head, roaring in my ears, drowning out Graham and the rest of the world with him. I closed my eyes, no longer in the sunshine with cars whizzing by, but back in the frigid hallway outside the governor's private study, low voices filtering through the wall. Talking about my sister. My hero. My biggest champion. Like Charity's death was a goddamn political situation to be handled. Headlines. Polls. And donors. Always all about the money. Money and power, where Chuck McClellan was concerned.

A hand closed over my shoulder and I jumped, pulling my right fist back for a jab before I opened my eyes.

"Faith!" Graham ducked anyway, but I stopped my arm before the punch actually flew.

"Sorry." I let the hand fall back to my side.

"You okay?"

I shook my head. "I am going to get to the bottom of this, with your help or without it."

"You didn't actually have to tell me that. I've met you." He bumped my shoulder with his own. "You're going to piss off some powerful people."

"I have a bit of experience with that. But I get it if you don't want to join the fun. It can suck sometimes."

He sighed. "I thought I wanted this promotion. Youngest commander in the history of the department."

I smiled, opening my mouth to congratulate him. He shook his head. "Then they called me in, gave me this case. Told me to 'handle it.'" He wiggled his fingers in air quotes around the last two words, disgust creeping into his tone. "Keep it quiet, that's what they meant. As long as I could convince myself there was a reasonable chance she jumped, that's one thing. But covering up a murder . . . that's not me. I'm a cop first. And what's the use in doing this job if you're not proud of it? If you're not serving a greater good? Nobody gets into police work for the money or the glory, that's for damned sure."

I snorted. "I have a Costco package of ramen in my pantry and a couple of .22-shell-sized scars that will testify to that."

He started walking again. "So what now?"

I shook my head. "There are so many geese zipping around this I haven't one damn clue which to chase first."

Graham pointed to a coffee shop. "Shall we caffeinate while we make a plan?"

I nodded, grabbing the door and holding it open for him. "I've missed you, partner," I whispered to his back as I followed him inside.

He ordered our coffees and paid before I could object, handing me a cup with a smile. "I missed you, too. Why do you think I'm still going this alone? Nobody is as good as you at catching the little things, at unraveling the webs around shit like this." He waved his cup at a round table along the back wall. "Let's get to work."

I sipped my coffee as I took a seat, my jangled nerves practically screaming for a nicotine fix. No time, and besides, Graham hated the smell. I pulled out a notebook and started ticking off what we knew.

"Tenley was seeing someone, but so far nobody I've talked to is saying who," I said. "She was involved in an accident two years ago and befriended the woman she crippled when she ran a stop sign. Spent time tutoring at the gymnastics school the lady runs. One of the students completely flipped yesterday when she saw me, but I couldn't find her to figure out why."

"Flipped how?"

"Took right the hell off. Hollering about how she didn't know anything, nothing was her fault. Really bizarre."

Graham tipped his head to one side. "And the gymnastics coach said?"

"Not much. Gave me a home address. I went by there last night, waited for a while. Kid never showed up."

"Let's go see if she's there now." Graham stood.

I waved him ahead of me and tossed my cup in the trash on the way to the door.

We were halfway to Lena's house when the tinkling started.

"You need to take that?" Graham asked as I flipped the blinker on to turn onto Lexington.

"It's—" the "not mine" died on my lips as I remembered putting Erica Andre's cell in the glove box yesterday. I stayed quiet as I pulled the phone out and stared at the screen.

Brent.

"That the mom's phone?" Graham didn't miss a trick.

"Possibly. Call coming in from Mr. Andre."

"I imagine they need to arrange a funeral." Graham paused. Tapped the dash. "You know you have to give this woman her phone back, right? You can't search it without a warrant, and what judge is going to grant that?"

"I can too. I just can't tell anybody I did," I grumbled, dropping the device back into the glove compartment when it stopped ringing.

Graham turned when I stopped at the light at Barton Springs and Dawson. "You're way in on this one. I get it. But it won't do anybody any good for you to get to the bottom of it if the guy walks because we were in a hurry."

"But I'm not looking to book the girl's mother. I just want to know how cozy she really is with the track coach."

"I thought you thought the track coach was sleeping with the victim. Or the pregnant girl." Graham shook his head as I laid on the gas when the light changed. "Husband seems like a decent guy, and pretty fit for his age, too."

"Billionaires cheat on supermodels every day." I rolled my eyes. "Women can't have wandering eyes, too? Wait'll you get a look at this one and then you tell me."

"Rich people. Never happy. I guess the thing about money not buying it is really true, huh?"

I snorted. "In my experience, the relationship is inverse. The trick is to want what you have."

"How very insightful of you."

"I saw it on a Facebook meme."

"Beautiful and honest, too, ladies and gentlemen."

My cheeks heated and I cleared my throat. "So, this guy, Jake Simpson. Maybe he was doing the mom. Maybe he was the new guy in Tenley's life that her friends mentioned. What if he's both?"

"Sleeping with the mom and the daughter?" Graham grimaced. "There's a D-list porn director somewhere in this city who wants to talk to him."

And Graham didn't know the half of it. Yet.

I wanted to tell him Archie and I thought the coach might be caught up in Jessa DuGray's death, too, but that wasn't my case, and the last thing I needed was to step on the toes of the one guy in the Rangers' service who didn't treat me like I had some sort of contagious incompetence.

Tenley gave me an easy in on Simpson. I could talk to people about him —even talk to him—and nobody would wonder if I was digging for darker secrets than maybe him having inappropriate relations with a student.

I just had to be careful how my questions were phrased. And if growing up in Chuck McClellan's house taught me a single useful skill, it was how to extract information from people before they realized what I was up to. As much as I loathed the governor on any given day, I had him to thank for much of what made me a good cop. I just didn't like to admit it.

I flexed my fingers around the wheel until my skin pulled tight, the mere notion of my father setting off a nic fit.

I'd started smoking at fifteen, powering through layers of disgust (and there were so many) because I knew it would irk my father and drive my mother bugshit crazy.

I still woke up every Monday determined to quit twenty-plus years later because the damned things steadied my nerves when I had a big case, or when I let Charity wriggle too far into my thoughts.

My big sister was walking energy, with a massive, infectious laugh that could make the darkest day bright. Brilliant, talented, Charity was everything I was not, and our parents made sure nobody ever forgot it. But Char always had just the right words to convince me that I was special in my own way. *"You're so smart, Faithy-bear,"* she used to say. *"You see things other people don't notice. Someday, you're going to change their world, and they'll never see it coming."*

Some days, I missed her easy confidence in me so much I flat-ass couldn't breathe. On balance, nicotine was easier to juggle with police work than Valium. Or Scotch.

"Twenty-five thirty-nine?" Graham's voice pulled my attention back to the world outside the window. A neat row of postwar Sears-kit houses lined the street, long oak branches reaching overhead, drought-droopy green leaves fluttering in the breeze.

I nodded, pulling the truck alongside the curb and shifting into park.

Graham kicked his door open. "It's almost nine. We should hurry if you want to talk to this kid."

"I don't think she goes to public school," I said. "Pretty sure the gymnastics place is some sort of charter academy. Tenley was helping the girls there with their grades, probably so it wouldn't lose its accreditation."

We walked up the cracked concrete driveway and across three flagstones set in the sun-baked Bermuda between it and the front steps.

Graham raised a fist and rapped on the brown metal edge of the storm door.

"She was freaked out by my badge yesterday," I whispered. "Smile and be cool."

The flat-gray-painted plywood front door didn't have a peephole, but a bay window jutted out behind the shrub to my left, overlooking to the porch. The curtain fluttered. Feet shuffled.

"Who is it?" The voice on the other side of the door was female, but not teenaged.

"Graham Hardin, Travis County Sheriff's Office." Graham kept his voice low and soothing.

The door cracked open. "You got a warrant?" asked a scratchy alto that matched the button nose and single almond-shaped hazel eye I could see.

"We're not here to search anything, ma'am."

"What do you want?" She pulled the door wide enough to stick her hot-roller-covered head out and give me a shrewd once-over through the screen. "That a Rangers badge? I didn't even know we still had those."

"I'm hoping Lena might be able to give us some insight into what's been going on with Tenley Andre lately." I smiled as I talked, keeping my voice light. Every word true. I simply omitted the part where the kid flipped out and bolted, because who would go home and tell her mom she'd run from a cop?

The door opened a little wider, a shoulder appearing as Hot Rollers leaned forward. "The tutor? Seems like a straight arrow. Real stand-up of that kid, going to Stella trying to make amends for that accident. What're you bothering her for?"

Did they not own a TV? Tenley's picture had been half of the local news cycle for at least the past eighteen hours, every station in town hosting child psychologists who postulated about the dangers of pressure and perfection. Front page of this morning's *Statesman*, too.

"Tenley's dead, ma'am," Graham said gently.

Hot Rollers's face went slack, her gaze drifting in the direction of the tree behind Graham.

I folded my arms across my chest.

"What happened to her?" Hot Rollers finally asked.

"That's what we're trying to figure out," I said. "Stella told me she'd seemed troubled lately, and that she was closer with Lena than the other girls at Lone Star. I'm hoping she confided something in her that will help us find an answer."

"Really seemed like that girl had her shit together." Hot Rollers shook her head, opening both doors and waving us inside. "Smart. Pretty. Lena said she was going off to college in California on a scholarship. You never know when your number's gonna be up, I guess."

I kept quiet, nodding as I stepped onto the linoleum in the shoebox entryway. The woman was petite—shorter than my five-ten by a good six inches—and rail-thin, the pink-and-white diner-style waitress uniform hanging on her frame at least three sizes too big. The plastic tag pinned under her left collarbone read *Rachel* in white block letters.

"Lena's still in bed. She doesn't have to be at the gym until ten, so she's seldom awake before nine thirty. I'll get her."

"Mom or sister?" Graham whispered when Rachel disappeared through the doorway in front of us.

I shrugged. "She's going to let us talk to the kid, which is all I really care about right now."

A groan issued from the other side of the wall. A door slammed. Muffled shouting.

"Still doesn't want to talk. Are we sure she's not a suspect?" Graham was still whispering.

"I'm not sure of a damned thing. Every time I—" I clamped my lips down on the rest of that sentence when Lena appeared in the doorway, marshaled by Rachel's death grip on her arm.

"What do you want?" she muttered, her eyes on the round black ears jutting from the top of her worn Mickey Mouse slippers.

I pulled out the cocktail-party smile again. "To talk with you about Tenley." I glanced at Rachel, who nodded that she'd broken the news.

"It's not like we were friends," Lena snapped. "She was just this snotty rich bitch who was trying to play teacher because she hurt Stella."

Rachel's pointy elbow had to jab like a razor, and Lena's breath hissed in so fast I thought for a second she might choke.

"Manners. Momma raised you better than this." So, sister then.

Lena narrowed her eyes at Rachel, then shrugged. "She wasn't even doing that right anymore. I think she got over her guilt. That or she was just too into herself and her own stuff."

"When did you notice a difference?" I asked.

Lena rolled her narrowed eyes back so far I could only see white. "Like I have nothing better to do than remember when other people have shit going on in their lives." She didn't bother to mutter.

I blinked, pretty sure she was deflecting with her assessment of Tenley's character.

"I don't expect you marked it on a calendar, but if you can give us any sort of estimate, we'd sure appreciate it." My voice stayed calm thanks to years of practice.

Lena folded her thick arms across her more-muscular-than-normal chest, biceps visible even through her sleep shirt. "Three weeks? Five? Seems like she was real happy right after Christmas, and then something changed her a few weeks ago."

"Changed how?"

"She got quieter, for starters. Thank God. All the peppy rah-rah school crap she gave off can wear you out. And she started getting phone calls.

Kept tripping over her tongue saying she was sorry and going outside to talk. Too important to not take it, she'd say."

"But you never asked her who it was? Never wondered what was so important?"

"She wasn't my friend, okay? None of my concern, and I really couldn't bring myself to care. Maybe she started smoking dope. Shooting up. She did seem skinnier the last couple weeks than she was before."

Still didn't fit with Tenley's school and sports performance.

"Did she seem like she was afraid of anything?"

"Like, somebody was out to get her?" Lena's eyebrows went up. "What happened to her, anyway?"

"That's what we're trying to figure out." My words had a knife edge that made Graham lay a hand on my arm. I shook him off. I knew how to question a witness. But did this girl have to be so damned hateful? What kind of teenager doesn't care when they hear somebody they knew is dead?

Maybe the kind who had something to do with it?

Coach Smarmy was still my favorite suspect. But he wasn't the only one by a long shot. And every road has to be followed in a good murder investigation. No matter how crazy a theory seems, it's never wasting time to chase it because at worst, proving it wrong eliminates a card from the mystery's hand.

Deep breath. Smile back in place.

Lena's pointy face looked interested for the first time since her sister dragged her out of bed. "I figured she was in another car crash or something."

I shook my head. "She was not." I didn't elaborate. "Do you remember her seeming afraid recently?"

"I wouldn't say she was afraid. She was off somehow, sure, but not looking over her shoulder or nothing."

"And you didn't overhear anything? She didn't talk to you about anything but school?"

Lena scuffed one toe over the threadbare carpet.

Rachel poked her with the elbow again. "Tell them."

The gymnast shot her sister a glare. "It's not my place. I even told her to knock it off."

I flexed my fingers, nails biting into my palm.

Rachel shook her head. "The girl is dead, Lena. I know you know what her family is going through. Tell. Them."

Lena shuffled the foot again. Sighed. "She was bugging Stella for money," she said to the carpet. "Threatening her and stuff."

Zayne's disgusted *"She kept emailing that lady she ran over"* floated through my head.

But . . . why? That didn't sound like the Tenley people had practically waxed poetic about since yesterday. Didn't fit with the rich girl who stopped to chat up the gardener. Or the shock and concern I'd gotten from Stella herself.

I slid a glance at Graham. Still good at covering shock—his eyes were a little wide, but other than that a passerby would've thought Lena had just told him the trees needed water.

"Threatening her how?" I asked.

"Blackmail? She knew something, I guess." Lena looked up. "I don't know what, I swear. I just saw one of the emails over her shoulder one day because I went hunting for her to ask about a math problem. She clicked it right off when I asked what it was, and she wouldn't say anything about it no matter how hard I pressed. I told her it was horrible, that Stella had forgiven her and everything, and I asked her how could she, but she just sat there and shook her head."

"And you've never asked Stella about it?"

"I was afraid it'd upset her if she knew I knew, and I don't really know anything except what I just told you."

"Tenley didn't give any indication why she was doing this?"

Lena shook her head. "Sorry." Her eyes said she wasn't. Not even a little bit.

I nodded, pinching my lips together. "Thanks for your time."

Graham handed Rachel a card. "If she remembers anything else, please have her give me a call? My cell number is on the back."

Graham and I were quiet for several blocks, I suspected turning over very different takeaways from that conversation. I liked the silence, though. Easier to think, and I didn't have to pretend to entertain his theory that Tenley had started using, gotten so desperate for money she was blackmailing the wheelchair-bound gymnastics coach, and decided she could fly. Until Graham had an explanation for somebody hacking at the poor girl after she jumped, I wasn't listening.

Someone else was with Tenley when she died. Someone who knew her pretty well. And if she was really blackmailing Stella, I couldn't trust a word of the story Stella had given me the day before.

"This is getting more complicated the further we dig." Graham ran one hand through his close-cropped hair. "This girl was into secrets. If she had something on the gymnastics coach, and the woman was tired of paying her to keep her mouth shut . . ."

"It's sure got me wondering about the accident the two of them were in." I stopped in the parking lot behind Graham's cruiser. "Any idea if Tenley's phone was found at the scene?"

"I can find out. You take the accident report, I'll check evidence?"

I nodded, the same creeping dread I'd felt walking out of the gym yesterday sending my skin crawling right up my arms. Was Stella Connolly's secret the kind worth killing for, too?

20

It happened at 2:33 on a Thursday morning.

That was the first thing that jumped off the accident report at me.

I grabbed a pen and pulled my notebook from my back pocket.

Where was a teenage girl going in the middle of a school night? I put a star by the question and kept scrolling, wondering about my chances of talking to the Richardson boy again. I remembered high school pretty well, and I'd bet my last smoke Tenley hadn't told her parents where she'd really been. The BFF was definitely a better source for that kind of truth.

I kept scrolling. No evidence of intoxication on the part of driver A, according to the officer's narrative. Driver A said she glanced at her GPS screen and ran the stop sign at the southwest corner of Westlake and Redbud. Driver B was transported to University Medical Center with severe trauma to her lower extremities. Driver A admitted fault at scene, could not produce license. Called father from accident scene.

GPS screen. I scribbled that, too, then saved the document to my laptop in case I needed it again.

So. Two years ago, Tenley Andre, who only had a learner's permit, was going somewhere she didn't know how to get to in the middle of the night on a Wednesday. By herself.

So many things weird about that I didn't know how to list them all. But my gut said there'd been big stuff going on with Tenley. Maybe stuff that got her killed. It was the which thing and the how that my gut lacked a bead on just yet.

I clicked over to the county court site and searched for the case. A crash like that was more than enough grounds for a reckless-driving charge, but I had a hard time with the idea that Stanford was taking a golden girl with a record on a full sports scholarship. That only seems to happen in football.

The computer flashed a *No results found* for Tenley's name. I clicked the report back up on my screen and copied the date, moving back to the court search box. Before my hand stopped.

Wait.

Permit. Because Tenley wasn't sixteen yet.

Fifteen. Tenley was fifteen two years ago. Did Jim say she was seventeen when he started the postmortem this morning? I closed my eyes.

Yep. He did.

Which meant I subtracted my way to the wrong birth year when I'd tried to crack Erica's phone.

I stood to go fetch the thing from the truck, and mine buzzed on the desk next to my laptop. I flipped it over. Austin area code, number I didn't recognize.

"Faith McClellan," I said, putting the phone to my ear.

"Hi Miss—Officer—um. Ranger McClellan? This is Erica Andre. We met at Marshall High yesterday?"

"Of course, Mrs. Andre." I knew better than to ask how the woman was doing. I had come to despise that question after Charity died. *How the fuck do you think I'm doing? Don't you know somebody killed my big sister?* That's what I'd wanted to scream. Every time. But of course that would never do. The governor would've had me locked up for the rest of forever over such an outburst.

"What can I help you with today?" I asked Erica.

"I seem to have misplaced my handbag yesterday, of all the stupid things, and I'm hoping I left it in your truck, because I'm down to my last place to look for it." Erica's voice was bright on the surface, but I caught the frailty in the depths. Sunshine and normalcy two breaths from shattering into a million tiny pieces.

"I do have it," I said. "I was planning to bring it by to you today, but I didn't want to call so early." True. I just didn't say it was because I wanted a look into her phone.

Erica sighed. "Thank God. Can I meet you somewhere and pick it up? It feels a bit like missing an arm, not having my phone."

"Of course. Or I can drop it by to you if that's better."

"We're not home right now," Erica said. "We're getting coffee and discussing . . ." She paused so long I thought the call had dropped. I pulled the phone away from my head and the screen lit up. Still connected. "Arrangements," Erica said finally.

Ah.

"Whatever is convenient for you, ma'am."

"Could you hold for one moment?"

"Sure."

I stood, closing the laptop, and shoved the notebook back in my pocket before I grabbed my keys. I wanted a last crack at the phone before I had to give it back. Didn't want to let the magic rock slip through my fingers because of policy.

"Can you meet us at Lola Savannah? Anytime in the next half hour or so would be fine," Erica said in my ear.

That was ten minutes away, tops, which gave me at least a few to try my new passcode theory. Perfect. "Of course."

"Thank you so much. You're a lifesaver."

I shook my head at her word choice. Not usually, but I tried to make up for it by getting justice for the ones that had needed saving.

"See you soon, Mrs. Andre." Touching the "End" circle on the screen, I tossed a five on the dresser for the maid on my way out the door.

My phone buzzed again as I punched the elevator button. Graham: *Phone is in the evidence locker at TCSO. It's fingerprint locked. Photo of her and the wrestler kid on the wallpaper.*

Outstanding.

I stepped into the elevator, typing. *Can you check it out? 12 hours?*

Buzz. *Why?*

I just want a crack at it. What if the answer is sitting in your evidence room in a little electronic box?

The elevator doors opened onto the lobby as his reply came through.

Buzz. *There are rules about this stuff. And they change all the time.*

I'll be careful, I tapped. Really, why did it matter to anyone whether I got into the phone's data today or the cyber guys did it three weeks from now? It didn't as far as I could see, except the trail was a whole lot hotter today. Well. Trails. But that was exactly why I needed the phone. Maybe it would help me figure out which was the hottest.

By the time I made it to the truck, the computer search I hadn't gotten to finish had gone completely out of my head.

21

Erica's phone screen popped right to life when I typed in Tenley's birthday with the correct year.

"Come on," I muttered. "Give me something."

I clicked the contacts first, looking for the track coach. Found him. Selected the text icon and followed that to the thread.

Nine messages in twelve months, all of them about Tenley's training.

So maybe the weird vibe between Simpson and Erica did mean the coach was involved with the girl. Might be a good idea to mention the guy to dad and see what kind of reaction I got.

Email? I touched the blue button and scrolled. Lots of messages. Lots of names on the return addresses I recognized.

Including my mother's.

I stared at my last name on Erica's screen for way longer than I should have.

Why was Erica Andre getting emails from my mother? And for the love of God, why did I care so much?

I kept scrolling. I might not be sure what was going on with Tenley and her family, but I knew that I knew Ruth McClellan had nothing to do with it. She despised drama. Wouldn't even get within field-goal range of a production this big. Which meant reading that was nothing but an invasion of privacy. I couldn't.

A dozen messages down, I found a thread from Stella Connolly.

That one, I was happy to click on.

"'Tenley has more than repaid you, and God knows we've given you enough money,'" I muttered as my eyes skimmed the newest message. "'I'm not sure you understand who you're screwing with here, so let me make it clear: I'm not what I appear to be, and I will do anything for my daughter. Leave my family alone, or sit by and watch your life become an utter dumpster fire.'"

Holy shit.

I'm not what I appear to be. I stared at those letters until they were seared onto my retinas. Maybe Erica was bluffing, talking big to jettison a blackmailer.

I clicked one message up. From Stella.Connolly@gmail.com, three weeks ago yesterday: *If you want your perfect golden child to keep her perfect golden crown, you will transfer another 2500 to the account on file by midnight Friday.*

The blazing pink-purple crepe myrtle on the other side of my windshield went fuzzy; my eyes unfocused as the variables of this fragmented equation shifted yet again: Stella didn't drop the charges against Tenley out of the goodness of her heart, or to give a "broken" kid a new friend. She did it because the Andres paid her off.

And it looked like she got greedy.

Of course. I should've gotten there faster. Second rule of a homicide investigation: always find and follow the money. But how much money? And what could Stella possibly do to hurt Tenley? I looked back at the message. Ticked back through a day and a half of random witness interviews. Everyone knew Tenley hit Stella and paralyzed her; that wasn't a secret.

So what else did Stella know? And how did this trail work, exactly—was Tenley blackmailing Stella because she knew Stella was shaking her parents down? Why wouldn't she just blackmail her into leaving Erica and Brent alone? It didn't fit. There had to be another variable at play here that I couldn't see yet.

Bank records. But that would require a warrant. To be legal, anyway.

Later.

Right now my time with this phone was ticking away. I had to take it back to Erica.

So I kept scrolling through emails.

Nothing else jumped. Back to texts.

Found a thread with Tenley. I pulled it up and scrolled, but there wasn't much. Five fashion memes, a link to a news story about Governor Holdsthwaite's new child bride redoing the mansion that made my nose wrinkle regardless of how I felt about my parents, and a few *When are you coming home?* type messages.

I started to touch the return arrow, then paused. The *When are you coming home?* texts weren't in blue bubbles. It wasn't Erica asking when her kid was coming home.

It was Tenley looking for her mom.

Huh.

Clock check. Drop dead for meeting Erica's half-hour window was in three minutes.

Back to the list of message threads, this time with a mission. Where was dad?

I had to scroll pretty far: Erica hadn't texted her husband in more than five months. And the last one had been deleted; the most recent date on the thread I pulled up was September twenty-ninth, but iPhones have this funny quirk where if a text is deleted, it goes out of the conversation screen, but the time stamp on the main messages preview window stays with the last message, even after it's gone. Deleting a whole exchange is the only way to get rid of that.

So what did Erica and Brent text about on November twelfth that she didn't want to look at anymore? Maybe nothing important. A Christmas gift for Tenley. A holiday card proof. But still—so many questions with these folks.

I pulled out my notebook and scribbled a few big ones, still wishing for just one answer.

Double-clicking the home button to put the windows back the way I found them, I noticed another familiar name on the text screen.

Nicky.

Clock.

Time to go.

Damn.

I touched the messages once more, hit Nicky's name, and crossed my fingers and toes.

November eighteenth: *Something's wrong with T.*

Erica never replied.

What the hell?

I tossed the phone onto the passenger seat, cranked the key, and pointed the truck toward Sixth Street.

Deleted texts, an unanswered alert, under-the-table payoffs. Mrs. Andre was not all sweetness and Botox and perfect hair.

Supermom had some secrets of her own.

Time to see if I could pry a few of them loose.

22

Erica and Brent Andre were fighting.

Not the sort of chilly-voiced, barb-filled fight my parents excelled at, either—these people were cage-matching it up in the middle of Tarrytown's hippest coffeehouse, oblivious to the gawkers catching every screech on their smartphone cameras.

Shit.

I stopped in the doorway as Erica jumped to her feet, knocking her chair over backward. "For fuck's sake, Brent, you'd have people think I'm advocating tossing my baby in a hole in the backyard!" Her stomping foot rattled the cups lining the top of the copper espresso maker behind her. "Tenley despised the dark, and you know it. Given the choice between ashes and darkness, she'd take the ashes."

"It's barbaric," Brent Andre's half shout was rough. "You can't burn her. I won't have it."

I puffed a short breath out toward my hairline. Without knowing how long they'd been like this, I wasn't sure I could stop the video footage from going viral. But I could give it my best shot. That was something I could do to help them today.

Two long strides put me at Erica's trembling elbow. I laid two fingers on her arm, holding up her purse when she swung furious eyes on me. "Mrs. Andre," I said, keeping my voice even and light. "Can I get you anything?"

"A less fucking pigheaded man to deal with as I try to lay my child to rest would be great," she snapped, the words flying out like daggers before her eyes widened. I felt her sharp breath in, even through the light contact with her forearm.

Her "oh," was much softer, her back and shoulders straightening. "Officer. Thank you so much for coming."

Just like that, she was back in control, the mask I'd seen when she first stepped into the office at Marshall the day before settling over her features.

The crowd shifted. Phones returned to pockets and purses and tabletops. A barista watched for thirty seconds or so and decided the cease-fire would hold, then scuttled around the counter to right Erica's seat.

Mr. Andre didn't look up, his frame folded into a chair, face buried in his hands. Erica took her purse and tried to smile. I gestured to the counter and repeated my offer. "Can I get you anything?" I asked.

She shook her head, sinking back into the black plastic chair. "Thank you."

I took the seat between them, leaning back and relaxing my posture to invite ease. Body language sounded like hogwash to me once upon a time, until I'd noticed it was the governor's single most powerful personal weapon. He wielded it like a master, plying everyone around him to his will. I wasn't into the whole puppeteer thing, but it had turned out to be damned handy when I wanted folks to talk to me.

"I'm not going to ask how you're doing," I said, shifting my eyes between them as Brent sat up. Jesus. His swollen, scarlet-rimmed, and bloodshot eyes and lengthening scruff would have convinced me he was on the fourth day of a three-day bender if I didn't know better.

"Have you found any leads?" he croaked.

I seesawed one hand back and forth. "Nothing that will get us a warrant yet, but we are pursuing a few different avenues," I said. "If you're up for it, I'd like to ask you some questions."

"Anything we can do to help." Erica sounded rushed, but her shoulders and hands stayed relaxed. "Thank you for coming to return my bag. It might make today slightly easier."

I nodded like that was actually true. It wasn't. Nothing would make these people have an easy day for a while yet. Which was why it was best for me to swan dive right in.

"I hate that I have to sit here and ask you questions today," I said. "But the most difficult thing about my job is that I'm flying blind most of the time. I didn't know Tenley, but I need to learn her deepest secrets in short order if I'm going to be of any help to y'all."

"We understand, Officer," Brent said. "Of course. Anything you want to know."

Erica murmured agreement, her gaze dropping to the pale hands she folded on the table in front of her.

I kept my tone easy, though her posture change said she wasn't as comfortable talking as she would have me believe.

"Had you noticed anything different about Tenley in the past few weeks?" I asked.

Brent shook his head, his eyes bright with new tears. "I honestly can't say if that's because there wasn't anything or because I wasn't looking hard enough, but I did not. I've been . . . preoccupied lately."

I jotted that down. Erica coughed over a snort on the other side of the table.

"When was the last time you saw your daughter, Mr. Andre?"

"Monday at lunch. I left for the airport early yesterday, and I got ready in her bathroom, but I assumed she was still sleeping."

He got ready in Tenley's bathroom? I glanced at Erica, whose face plainly said she didn't know that, and was thinking the same thing I was. If Erica didn't hear Tenley in the bathroom at all Tuesday morning, that left a bigger span of time unaccounted for. I made another note.

"Did Tenley have a credit card?" I asked.

Brent nodded. "She's got a card for my AmEx account. Uses it for gas and online stuff mostly. Food too."

"Can you tell me if there are any unusual charges to it in the past couple of months?"

"I haven't gotten any alerts, but let's have a look." He picked up his phone and poked at the screen.

I rolled the pen back and forth between my fingers, the tension crackling between Tenley's parents making me squirm in my seat.

Brent's eyes narrowed. "There's a charge from Uber. Pending, dated yesterday."

I wanted to whoop and pump a fist in the air. The driver was likely one of the last people to see Tenley Andre alive. And might remember if anyone else was at the dam with her. I scribbled a big star and a note.

"That's how she got out there," Erica blurted. "If Nicky dropped her at home, and then she called a car, she must've been going to meet someone. Someone she trusted enough to bring to her special spot."

Brent nodded along.

Was that the story behind the cryptic Post-it? Tenley meeting someone?

I pulled it from my pocket. "Graham told me you gave this to him this morning, Mr. Andre," I said. "What can the two of you tell me about it?"

"I found it last night, next to Erica in the study. She was . . . asleep," he said, shifting in his chair. His tone said she was more passed out than asleep—but given all the hints about alcoholism people kept throwing around, I hoped I was reading it wrong.

I turned to her. "Mrs. Andre?"

"It was with her doll." The words came out automatically, her eyes staying on Brent. She looked . . . odd. I couldn't tell if she was mad or hurt, but she sure didn't seem to want me to know about this note.

"Doll?" I prodded.

Erica seemed to snap back to the present. "I got it for her when she was a little girl. Her guardian angel. I worried over her driving around in that death trap convertible, so she hung it from her rearview mirror. Flipped my own trick against me." She shook her head. "So smart.

"The note was tucked up inside the doll's dress. I knocked it loose last night, sitting in her car." Her chin dropped to her chest, shoulders heaving with deep breaths.

Brent reached across the table and picked the note up. "Why in God's name would she hide it with her doll?" he murmured.

"It had to be important to her," Erica said. "I'd give anything to be able to ask her to explain."

"You're sure it's Tenley's handwriting?" I asked. Because if someone was setting up a suicide story, this would be a brilliant play.

They both nodded. "Her writing was so crazy. Loopy, but still kind of hard to read. Like a personal code," Erica said.

"Any idea what any of these words mean?" I asked. "Did yesterday hold special significance for Tenley or your family?"

"I've been trying to think all day of anything that happened on that date, and this is all I can come up with," Brent said. "It was never notable to me until Officer Hardin called me yesterday." He glanced at Erica. "You?"

She shook her head, taking the note from him. Her eyes welled as she stared at the letters, but she didn't offer any more words.

So, something, but nothing definite.

Next up: those emails. How much money had Tenley pilfered from Stella? "Can you see recent activity on her checking account?" I asked.

Brent shook his head. "She didn't have one. Probably should, but I've never gotten around to it. We do everything on the cards, anyway."

The Wells Fargo envelope in Tenley's desk was for what, then? I circled a question mark, but didn't press. Maybe there was a reason she hadn't told them about it. Better to find out before tipping my hand.

"Any new people in her life?" I asked. "Nicky Richardson said she was seeing someone, but wouldn't tell him who."

Erica's face tried to scrunch, the Botox fighting back. "She wasn't seeing anyone."

"Her friend says otherwise." I kept my voice low and neutral.

"I would know." Erica's voice assumed a steel edge, her fingernail beds going white as she gripped the edge of the tabletop. "She told me everything."

I didn't reply. I didn't know Tenley. Maybe she did tell her mother everything.

But if she didn't, maybe it was the thing she kept quiet that got her killed.

Dammit.

"It's not uncommon for teenagers to have secrets . . . ," I began.

"He. Is. Wrong." Erica's tone left no more room for debate. Unless I wanted this discussion to be over.

I let it go and turned to Brent. "I take it you haven't heard anything about this, either?"

"Not a word. You think she met someone who could've hurt her?"

"It's one possibility of many. Just on my mind because Nicky mentioned it, and we also heard she'd been getting frequent urgent phone calls. That's all."

"Phone calls?" Brent sighed. "What the hell was going on with her? And why were we too busy to notice?" The last words were half mumbled at the table as he dropped his forehead onto one hand.

"What 'we'? There's only been me, trying to juggle my job and the house and Tenley since . . . Christmas, at least." Erica's razor-sharp shout turned heads all around them and snapped Brent's back up.

Uh-oh. Round two. I sat up, putting one hand toward each of them.

"Maybe if you acted like you ever fucking wanted me around, that wouldn't be the case." His tone was icy, his voice low.

Erica sat back in her seat. "What do you mean act like I want you around? When have I ever not wanted you around?" The bewilderment rang clear in her voice, anger still snapping in the air around her.

I let my hands drop—to them, they were the only two people in the world right that second. The best I could do was hope my badge would offer a measure of damage control—with me sitting between them, people were watching, but I didn't see any obvious displays of recording. And I couldn't blame folks for looking. The whole thing was morbidly fascinating, in a reality-show sort of way: From the outside, everything was perfect. They were good-looking, successful, had a fantastic kid.

But behind the toothpaste-commercial grins and pretty pictures, things had gone about as wrong as wrong gets. Tenley had to know that. Did it have something to do with why she was out in the middle of nowhere alone in the dead of night?

"You name a time you were genuinely glad to see me in the past three months, and I'll eat my sneakers." Brent locked eyes with his wife. "I try and I try and I try to make you feel special, and you don't want me."

"You try to make yourself feel less guilty for fucking around on me, that's what you try to do." Erica spit the words like they were soaked in vinegar.

Brent's jaw went slack. "I what?"

"Don't you dare sit there and try to act insulted. I know you're sleeping with that stewardess. I saw her texts. No woman texts a man she's not intimate with as much or as familiarly as that one texts you. And you talk to her on the phone all the time, too."

Brent's head started shaking the instant she started talking, moving faster as she went on.

Erica's hands trembled, her voice following suit. "Deny it all you want, but do not sit there and make me the bad guy in this. You found someone else. You gave up on us. And Tenley knew it, too."

Brent jumped to his feet, flipping the table and sending the whole room into chaos. I shoved my chair back, but coffee had already splashed over my boots and the hem of my jeans.

Erica screamed. At least four customers called 911. The manager crept close enough to us to register in my left peripheral, stopping when I held up one finger. I wanted to see where this would go.

"Have you lost your mind?" Erica sputtered, bending to tug on the table. I moved to help her, but Brent's cold, flat glare stopped me before I got my hands to the tabletop.

"My wife just accused me of having an affair, my daughter is in a locker at the morgue, and I'm pretty sure this woman is here because she's at least curious if one of us is somehow responsible for the latter." Brent's arm swung toward me, his voice booming. "Let me assure you on the record, Officer, that I would give anything—anything you can name—to have my little girl sitting here with me this morning. I suggest you look elsewhere if you really want answers about what happened to her."

Anyone in the room could've heard a flea sneeze. I'm not sure a single soul even dared to breathe, every eye in the place on us, cameras forgotten in the commotion.

Erica's face twisted into a horrified mask. "Shut up, Brent," she hissed.

"I haven't accused anyone of anything, Mr. Andre." I stood up straight, the table still on its side.

Should I? How deep did the imperfection seeping through their cracked façade run, exactly?

"Shut up, Brent." Erica tried again, a layer of calm almost covering the tremor in her voice. Almost. "She has been nothing but helpful since this nightmare started. If you want to yell at someone, yell at me."

Brent's shoulders dropped, a sigh escaping his chest. "I don't want to yell at you, Erica. I just want to be left alone. No more wondering, no more fighting, no more bullshit. Let's bury our baby and just be done with this."

Erica raised her chin. "Fine." The look she shot her husband would've wilted the hardiest cactus. "Can you take me to get my car?" she asked me, looping her purse over her forearm.

I nodded. "Of course, ma'am."

She grabbed her bag and started for the door without another word or a backward glance.

I watched Brent Andre pick up the table and the pieces of the broken coffee mug, a soft "Son of a bitch" sliding through his teeth when blood welled on his thumb. "Nothing's ever going to be easy again, is it?" He let his head fall back. I couldn't tell if he was asking me or God or the universe in general.

All around us, murmurs floated in a sort of incredulous empathy before the coffeehouse came back to life, the staff and patrons resuming their normal, un-murder-interrupted Wednesdays with croissants and espresso and easy conversation.

"Not for a while, no," I whispered.

Brent didn't move. I turned to see Erica waiting on the sidewalk. "I'm so sorry, again, sir," I said. "Please let me know if you think of anything that could help."

Tenley's father nodded without looking at me, fresh tears disappearing into his short silvered sideburns as he clenched his eyes shut. Just for half a second, I tried to remember if the governor cried when Charity died.

I knew better than to wonder such things. I patted Brent's hand and strode after his wife.

Erica's face was tipped back toward the sun, her eyes closed, her breaths slow and even. I stopped next to her, giving her another moment to collect herself. She blinked, and I peered at her eyes from behind my sunglasses. Slightly bloodshot, but I couldn't say it was more from drinking than crying.

Just over her shoulder, my gaze landed on a slight man with graying, greasy hair cinched into a short ponytail against his neck. Almost-translucently pale skin hung on a thin frame covered by a dirty white T-shirt and jeans that had probably seen better days when Reagan was president. I scanned reflexively for a gun bulge under his ill-fitting clothes. Didn't see one.

The first minute of the first day at the academy, they start preaching about being observant, because not everyone is, and it's that important. A good cop's personal radar can pick up a scumbag at thirty paces, and this guy had mine pinging like a pinball machine in bonus. It wasn't just the hair or the clothes or the scruffy face: some of the best people I've ever met are homeless folks who frequent Austin's parks and shelters. I didn't like something about him. I just couldn't tell what from so far back.

I took a small step to the side when he moved past Erica, my gaze staying with him. He turned our way. Took a step back. Scrubbed at his eyes with both fists and blinked. Rushed forward.

I lunged for Erica. He was more agile than he looked, skipping to his left to brush right past my shoulder and put a hand on her forearm. "Sammy Jo?" a three-packs-a-day growl asked, red-rimmed, rheumy blue eyes searching Erica's face. "You done real well for yourself, now didn't you? Your momma, she—"

I watched his eyes stray from her profile, to the streetlamp, to the stop sign on the corner, feeling my muscles uncoil. He wasn't menacing, he was just on something. But today was not the day to indulge drug-addled rambling where Tenley's mother was concerned.

My eyes on the distance from his hand to her purse, I moved to slide between them and tell him to move along, but Erica's face stopped me cold.

It was the eyes. Botox-frozen eyes don't move. Don't emote. They just see, smooth and clear and line-free. But Erica's had gone wide enough for me to see white all around the blue, her nostrils flaring with deep breaths as she tried to extricate her arm. "I'm afraid you have me confused with someone else," she said. "My parents died a long time ago. Good day."

I stepped in. She was grieving, anxious, and now shaken. Women like Erica Andre don't get themselves accosted by the unwashed masses every day. I put one palm on his shoulder, keeping my voice calm, but firm. "You heard the lady. I'm going to have to ask you to step back now."

He complied, shaking his head as he dropped her arm. "I could've swore . . . ," he mumbled as he half stumbled back. "You got her eyes."

Erica scooted behind me as he disappeared down the street. When we couldn't see him anymore, I turned back. "You're having a bitch of a week, ma'am," I said.

"Almost makes you wonder what anyone could do to deserve this." I couldn't tell if she was talking to me or herself.

"I've seen enough to know that's not the way the world works," I answered anyway.

Erica flinched, then dropped her purple Prada sunglasses over her eyes, covering half her face. "I wish I had your confidence on that." She started for my truck.

I followed her, watching. Squared shoulders. Set jaw. Uneven breathing. Barely managing to balance the weight of the world on her thin shoulders. That she was upright was flat-ass astonishing. I slid behind the wheel and started the truck, leaving the radio off. Pressure to fill silence can be a good detective's best asset.

But not today: Erica didn't say a word the entire ride to Marshall High, keeping her face turned to the window and her hands clenched in her lap. I let her out behind her Jaguar SUV in the parking lot and drummed my fingers on the wheel as she climbed into the car.

Something wasn't right with these people. Brent and Erica's issues only mattered to me if they had something to do with why Tenley was dead, though. I wriggled my phone out of my pocket and sent Graham a text before I pulled away: *Pretty sure Tenley had an account at Wells Fargo her folks don't know about. We need a warrant.*

Dropping the phone in the cup holder, I sped through the red light at the parking lot exit. It was only nine-forty. I could still make it.

Buzz. Graham: *Finally, something easy. On it.*

Thanks, I tapped after I hit my brakes in front of a wide midcentury ranch with gray brick facing and a dozen different kinds of plants trailing from iron hanging baskets lining the porch.

"Officer, I didn't expect to see you again so soon." Stella Connolly looked up from watering a potted aloe as I ambled up her sidewalk. "Is everything okay with Lena? She never came back to the gym last night."

"Lena's fine." I walked up a wooden ramp to the porch, shoving my hands into my pockets. "I didn't catch up with her until this morning, and she told me something I'd like to ask you about, actually."

Stella's brows flashed above the plastic rims of her glasses. "What's that?"

"Why was Tenley blackmailing you, Mrs. Connolly?" I watched Stella's face carefully. Sometimes shock makes people blurt answers they might otherwise hide. "And is that why you were trying to gouge more money out of her parents?"

Stella tipped her head to one side. "Tenley was what?" She set the watering can on the concrete floor of the porch, stray droplets darkening the smooth gray finish. "I was gouging who? I haven't the first clue what you're talking about. Did Lena tell you something that made you think this?"

"What if I told you Lena saw the emails Tenley was sending you? And the boy she went out with Monday night, he said he saw her emailing you hours before she died."

Stella shook her head. "I can't recall ever having gotten an email from Tenley. And I haven't had any contact with her parents in more than a year."

"Mrs. Connolly, this is not a difficult thing to check." I skipped telling her I'd seen the emails to Erica with my own eyes, since I wasn't technically allowed to know that. "With two witnesses, I can have a warrant in half an hour." That was true. I leaned on the post at the top of the steps. "This will be easier on both of us if you just tell me the truth."

"But I am telling you the truth." Stella pulled her phone from her pocket and held a finger over the home button, then tapped the screen before she handed it over. "Look for yourself. I have nothing to hide."

I took the phone, my forehead scrunching as I scrolled through Stella's inbox. Generally, people who say they have nothing to hide are liars. Most everyone has something to hide, when you get right down to it. But if Stella Connolly was lying about this, it wouldn't be smart to hand over her phone.

I made it through a week's worth of ads, notices from parents, and other miscellany before I handed the phone back. "I appreciate that, ma'am, but how do I know you didn't just delete them?"

"You want to look in my computer, too?" Stella asked.

I stayed quiet, watching her. Breathing even, eyes staring straight on. No fidgeting. If she was lying, she was damned good at it.

"Why would the kids have both said . . ." I stopped.

Hang on. What exactly did Lena say?

"Tenley just kept shaking her head . . . ," I murmured. I stuck my hand out. "Can I see that again for a moment, please?"

Stella obliged, and I clicked into her Mail app and scrolled down to look at the accounts.

Yahoo.

"Is this the only email account you have, ma'am?" I asked, the letters on the screen blurring in front of my eyes as my brain waded through the muck around this case.

"That thing bings so many times a day I can't keep up with it as it is," Stella said. "Why would I need another?"

I nodded slowly, my fingers tapping the edges of the phone. I opened the browser. Navigated to Gmail.

Create an account flashed on the screen.

But the return address in Erica's phone was Stella.Connolly@gmail.com.

I handed the phone back. "She didn't ask you for money."

Stella shook her head. "Her folks spoiled her rotten. Have you seen her car? Why would she have to ask anyone for anything?"

I bit my lip. It was a damned good question. More to the point, my gut said Lena and Zayne assumed when they saw Stella's name on the screen that Tenley was talking to Stella. But what if she was talking *as* Stella?

"Are you okay, Officer?" Stella peered up at me. "What in the world was going on with that girl?"

"Something she was good at hiding, it seems." I backed down the ramp. "Thanks for your time. Please call me if you remember anything else."

Back in my truck, I made it almost to the corner before my phone rang. Archie.

"Tell me you got something on your case we can call an answer. Every time I think I've found one on Tenley, it brings two more questions to the party," I said by way of hello.

"I've got a high school track coach in my interrogation room I thought you might like to have a go at." The smile on his face practically leapt from the receiver.

My everything went slack, my fingers slipping right off the wheel as I rounded the corner off of Stella's street.

23

He missed.

Plunging the blade toward his thigh, he flinched when it went through his jeans and sank into the leather upholstery.

Dammit. There was something . . . something he needed to know. It danced around the corners of his brain, moving away every time he got close, drowned out by the monster when he tried to focus.

So he kept watching her.

She was luscious.

Tempting.

Everything he'd worked for. Bled for. Ever wanted.

But he couldn't let the monster win. Wouldn't give in.

Not until he could be sure.

God, the pressure. It built in huge waves until he couldn't even blink.

He fumbled with his zipper, desperate to relieve it, a soothing voice drifting through his head.

You believe God has a plan for you, don't you? You believe He and He alone can bestow blessings. Favor.

Of course.

You are special. God himself has seen fit to elevate you above lesser mortals. You believe that? You are better. Stronger. Faster. You can take what you want. Be what you want.

It made such perfect sense. Erased the fear.

Go ahead then. Take her.

The voice faded when the angel moved.

She stood and turned to the side, his divine reward for so much hard work. Linking her hands behind her back and rolling her shoulders heavenward, she pulled in a long, slow breath, her perfect tits straining against the thin fabric of her top.

His angel was cold, it seemed.

His universe narrowed to two pebbles under fluttering linen.

Get up, *the monster howled.*

His left hand clamped down on the door handle, his right finding his fevered skin.

She bent one knee, catching her foot behind her and leaning forward, her balance so immaculate she had to be floating. Reaching her free hand toward the horizon, she stretched her long leg until her shoe nearly brushed the crown of her head.

His grip tightened, his breath shallow, every nerve ending alive with the possibility of her.

She pivoted toward him as she let go, gently rocking her hips side to side before she arched back to grab the other ankle.

The monster clawed for control.

He was lost.

24

"Which judge are you blackmailing?" I was only half kidding as I tugged the steering wheel and swerved back onto the road, missing a tree by inches.

"No judge necessary. Thought about what we found last night. Decided to go by and see if he'd talk. He agreed to come with me."

"I'd wager you didn't make it sound like he had much of a choice."

"Is it my fault people don't read enough to know their rights?"

I rolled my eyes. "Seems like we've had this discussion before."

"And I imagine we'll continue to have it periodically until you decide I'm right."

I made a U-turn at the next light. "Today, I'm grateful for your stubborn streak. I'd like to see what else he doesn't know he's supposed to keep to himself."

"So far, I think you might like where our little chat is going. Room C."

I laid on the gas. If we could tie the coach to either of the girls, we'd have enough for a search warrant.

I grabbed the phone at the next light and texted Graham. *Something came up, call you when I'm done.*

A block later it buzzed a reply: *Waiting on warrant. Plenty here to keep me busy.*

I shot a thumbs-up emoji back before I moved into the right lane to park. I pulled into the first space I saw, then jogged up the sidewalk and steps, pausing with my hand on the door.

Look like you belong.

Because you do.

Repeating the mantra in my head, I swung the door back and turned toward the interrogation rooms off the back hall. I made it three steps before I walked smack into Lieutenant Boone.

Papers flew, coffee splashed. I yelped when it soaked through my jeans, scalding my thigh. What the hell was with the spilled coffee today?

Tears bit at the backs of my eyes and I fluttered my lids. Not like I could wriggle out of the jeans in the middle of the office.

"New Girl? I thought you were on vacation," Boone said, bending to reach for the folder he'd dropped.

"I was. I am." The pain radiating from my leg made me sniffle. "Just meeting a friend. For coffee."

He stood up straight, his irises rolling in to look down his nose from under fleshy hoods. "You have friends here?"

I flashed a smile so fake it would've made my father proud. "I do spend an awful lot of time running down here to drop off files." The words could've cut glass, and Boone raised a brow and backed up a step.

"I suppose you have, at that." He nodded. "Well. I have a meeting to get to. You enjoy your time off. Nice day to be outside."

I didn't even bother to nod, stepping around him and barreling for the interrogation rooms. Found C.

Breathe. Calm. Collected. Couldn't have the coach mistaking my annoyance with Boone for suspicion about him—it'd shut him right up, and Archie would never let me help with anything again.

Pushing the door open, I slipped inside.

The room was smaller than my childhood closet, with a flat steel table and three metal chairs in the middle of the floor. Simpson was in the one facing the mirror on the opposite wall, but he didn't see me step into the room because his eyes were fixed on the table. I raised a brow at Archie, who had the chair opposite, and he gestured for me to sit next to him.

"I believe you met Coach Simpson yesterday, didn't you?" Archie's booming voice was pleasant, so I followed his lead.

"I did. I'm sorry again about the circumstances of that."

Simpson nodded without raising his head. "Tenley was a special girl. I still can't believe she's gone." The words dropped to the table devoid of emotion, and Archie cleared his throat, leaning forward.

"Can you describe your relationship with Tenley Andre for us, Mr. Simpson? Were you close?"

Simpson raised his head just far enough to roll his eyes up and see us. "I wasn't fucking her, if that's what you're asking me."

"I don't think anyone mentioned that," Archie said in the same easy tone. "But thank you for clearing it up."

I knew Archie didn't believe the guy, because I didn't, either. Why would that be the first thing out of his mouth? Because he was guilty of it. Nine and a half out of ten times, anyway.

"I saw her every day for the last four years. She was an incredible athlete. So yeah, I guess I was as close to her as anyone."

His voice caught for the first time since I'd walked into the room, and I laid my hands on the table. "Tenley was beautiful and accomplished," I said. "So she had a lot of friends, I imagine. Girls like her can inspire jealousy in some. Can you think of anyone who'd want to hurt her?"

Simpson's head shook slowly. "Tenley was beautiful. She was smart. But she was . . . different. People flocked to her, but she kept most of them at a distance."

"Different how?" Archie asked.

"Quiet. Really hard on herself." Simpson shifted in the chair, sitting up but not looking at us, his eyes on his reflection behind us. "The, like, three times she didn't finish first in a race—once because she was coming back from a broken ankle—she didn't get over it for weeks. She lived on the track. Training harder, talking to herself."

Archie scribbled on the yellow legal pad in front of him and pushed it toward me.

Anxiety?

I tapped a finger on the paper and nodded. It fit everything I'd seen.

High-functioning anxiety disorder is common in gifted teenaged girls. Charity had struggled with it for years, so I knew how debilitating it could be. Our parents used to whisper fears that it would cost my sister her shot at a political career. What they didn't know was that Charity's stubborn streak was the biggest obstacle to that: she knew politics inside out, and loathed every twisted principle and half truth required for success at it.

"Did Tenley seem upset about anything lately?" I asked.

Simpson shook his head again. "Quite the opposite, really. She was so excited about college, she had called and asked for a meeting with the coaches from Stanford. That's what they wanted yesterday. I was glad to see her back up there. She got really down at the end of cross-country season last fall. Really down. Worried me. I even tried to tell her mother something wasn't right."

He wasn't alone there—the text from Nicky that Erica didn't answer. He'd tried, too.

"She didn't believe you?" Archie asked.

"I'm not sure she didn't believe me. She just seemed like she was . . ." He threw his hands up. "Not all there? Like she couldn't handle the idea."

Archie made another note. He didn't slide this one over.

Didn't have to. I remembered that all too well.

"How well do you know Mrs. Andre, Coach?" I asked.

"She's my star runner's mom." He spoke to the table.

That wasn't a real answer.

I started to open my mouth again, but Archie held up his phone and pushed his chair back before I got a word out.

"If you'll excuse us for just a moment, I have a phone call holding that I have to take," he said, tugging lightly at my sleeve as he stood.

"And I have another matter that needs a bit of my attention." I stumbled over the lie like I always did, swallowing hard when my starched jeans slid over my burned thigh as I rose.

"When can I go home?" Simpson asked.

Whenever he wanted. But I knew Archie didn't want him to know that, so I smiled and waited for Arch to answer.

"Just a few more questions?" Archie added the inflection at the end so slightly I almost didn't hear it, but I knew if anyone reviewed the recording they'd be able to argue it was a request and not an order. I hated semantics, but too often they made the difference between catching the bad guy and missing him by a breath.

Simpson nodded, dropping his forehead to his folded arms. I paused in the doorway and stared. He wasn't that upset over Tenley unless he was lying about sleeping with her. He was young and fit. Why was he so exhausted?

I followed Archie into the middle room, a half-closet-sized space where the two-way glass let me and Archie watch Simpson without him watching us. Along the other wall, the window looked into room D.

I shut the door and leaned on the table next to the digital recorder that pulled audio from the interrogation rooms. "Did you get anything out of him about Jessa?"

Archie shook his head. "He claims he's only been to that bar once, and says he doesn't remember seeing her. I'm going to pull more video and see if he's lying about the place. But you were right. I don't like him, either."

"Excellent. But agreement on his shitty personality doesn't get us a warrant."

Archie turned to the glass. "He seems awfully beat for not even noon yet, doesn't he? I wonder what could be keeping him from sleeping?"

"I had the same thought, but being tired isn't a crime." I fell quiet. Archie and I were world-champion people-readers, and both of us getting a lousy vibe from Simpson meant something was off. But we needed every duck from here to San Antonio in lockstep—if we rushed and let him walk and another young woman ended up dead, neither of us would ever get over it.

"Can we tail him?" I pushed off the table and paced the tiny room. "If we try to hold him, he's going to ask for a lawyer. And so far every shred of anything we have on him is circumstantial. A lawyer will have him out in an hour, and if he's our guy, he'll be looking to show us who's smarter."

Archie nodded. "I like it. I'll grab a patrol car from APD and set them on it. How about you?"

"I need to go catch up with Graham. Still trying to unravel this web. For somebody with a life that looked so perfect, this girl's whole existence was pretty damned sad. New this morning, it seems she might've been posing online as a woman she paralyzed in an accident, demanding money from her own parents. Who are a dozen kinds of hot mess behind their Crest-commercial smiles."

Archie's brows floated up. "Blackmail? Did she get anything?"

"I couldn't think of a way to ask her folks without upsetting them, and I'd like to know I'm right before I tread there."

"Bank records?"

"Graham is working on the warrant." I threw up my hands. "I just—the dad got her a Porsche for Christmas. The mom designed her a bedchamber fit for blue blood. Why would she bother with the lies? Why not just ask them? Or just buy whatever she wanted—she has a card on dad's AmEx account, too."

"Drugs?"

"Ordinarily, I'd already be there, but the best friend says no way, and her race times have been stellar. I don't see how she could be using."

Archie touched his chin, turning back to Simpson, who still had his head down on the other side of the glass. "Was she pregnant? Maybe wanting an abortion?"

"Or maybe had one?" I bit my lip, nodding. That fit. She'd written about the other girl on her track team being pregnant. Maybe she knew because she was, too. Secret relationship, family's social status, Tenley's obsession with being the best . . . A pregnancy would bring it all crashing down. "Shit. I should've gotten there sooner. Thanks, Arch—I'll text Jim."

I gestured to the still form on the other side of the glass. "The thing he said about her behavior was . . ." I swallowed hard. "Enlightening. Could help us. It's good you got him to come in."

Archie's lips turned up in a sad half smile. "I know you miss your sister. I also know it seems like every day with the Andre girl, there's something that reminds you of Charity. But promise me you'll watch yourself. Emotions are no good to you in this job, kiddo. They'll screw you every time."

I nodded, my eyes still on Jake Simpson. How could anyone be responsible for the death of either of these young women—let alone both of them—and still sit in that room, breathing so slowly and evenly?

Maybe he didn't do it.

Or maybe he thought he was getting away with it.

Not on my watch, asshole.

25

Lieutenant Boone stood just inside the door, pushing away from the wall when he saw me coming.

What now? I didn't see him that much in a normal day at my own office.

I tried to smile. "Hello again, sir."

"Coffee okay?" He kept his face carefully neutral, but something in his tone told me being crafty with my answer was the only way to avoid a beeline for deep shit.

"Not sure any cop is qualified to judge coffee," I said, putting a hand out to open the door.

"Where're you off to now?" He stepped in front of the door, and I withdrew my hand.

"Lunch with an old friend," I said. Every word true.

"The kind of old friend who might work for the Travis County Sheriff's Office, and might be investigating the death of one Tenley Andre, fallen teenage track star?"

Dammit. I kept my face unsurprised and pleasant as I twisted my lips to one side. "I think Graham is handling that case, yes, sir."

Who snitched? Not that I could ask. Hazard of working in a room full of cops: secrets mostly don't stay secret for long.

"Any idea why Skye Morrow was just on the TV saying the Rangers' newest hotshot, former governor McClellan's only daughter, is assisting him?"

My cheeks burned. Damn Skye Morrow and her ratings-grabbing bullshit to hell and back. "I'm not aware of any assignment to that case, sir." I kept my voice flat and my face smooth.

"Me either. And it sure as shit better stay that way." He pushed the door open and waved me through ahead of him. "I understand this is a rough time of year for your family. You have a nice *vacation*." He hit the word hard. "Monday morning, we'll have a talk about your future with this organization."

I nodded at the not-so-subtle threat to my job and took long, quick strides toward my truck. Boone could take his threats and stick them right up his ass—I couldn't bail on Tenley now. Hopefully, it wouldn't come to losing my job, but if it did, so be it. Good cops aren't exactly in oversupply. I'd find something else. And if Simpson turned out to be Archie's guy in the DuGray case, all my hard work to make it as a Ranger wouldn't be a total loss.

I tapped out a text to Jim, asking about pregnancy or recent abortion, and got back an almost-immediate *Not there yet. I'll let you know.*

Starting the truck, I dialed Graham. He picked up on the first ring. "Tell me you got that warrant," I said.

"In my hot little hands as we speak. You get anything else?"

"A couple things, and I'm not sure where they'll go." I clicked the turn signal down and made a left onto Fifteenth. "I know why her car was still at home yesterday morning—she called an Uber in the wee hours."

"You don't say. Want me to call them and ask who drove her?"

"I've used their service a couple times. She should have emails in her inbox with information about the vehicle. If we can get into her phone, we'll get to the driver faster than messing with corporate red tape."

"Have I ever told you how smart you are? Damn, I've missed you."

I couldn't tell if he meant to push so much emotion behind that, but it was nice to think about. "Back at you," I half whispered.

Graham cleared his throat. "You headed this way?"

"Being seen there could be detrimental to my career, since Skye went on the air with the fact that she saw us this morning and my boss wasn't excited about it. Meet me at the hotel?"

"On my way. What was the other thing you found?"

"That's why I'm curious about the checking account. I think Tenley was blackmailing her folks," I said. "She needed money for something she didn't want to just ask them for, when they gave her everything."

"Christ, these people have more skeletons than the fucking catacombs. I don't suppose we have any idea what she was trying to pay for?"

"Not yet. Hoping Jim might move that along for us in the next little while, though." I turned into the hotel parking lot. "I'm here. Come on up when you get here."

"See you in a few."

I grabbed my notebook and loped to the doors, taking the stairs two at a time with the chaos that was the last months of Tenley Andre's life whirling through my thoughts. Secrets and lies, everywhere this girl turned. The notes she left for her nearest and dearest were about outing them, clearing the air.

I shoved my key card into my door a couple minutes later and barreled into my room muttering, "Everything comes back to who didn't want to be discovered. Who had the most to lose, then?" The question died on my lips when I stepped past the closet.

"Do not talk to yourself, Faith. It's common, and no matter how determined you are to prove me wrong, you are not a common woman." Not a single drop of emotion behind the words.

It worked for her. Matched the face.

"Mother." I shoved my hands into my pockets. "What are you doing here?"

26

I didn't bother asking who let her in.

Ruth McClellan wasn't the sort of woman who requested things. She gave orders. And something about her made people—most people—follow them. Like Mussolini with better skin and designer heels.

I walked to the window, staring at the federal building across from the hotel and trying not to wonder if my mother's black pantsuit was a nod to my sister's memory or a testament to how little color Mother kept in her massive wardrobe. Could be either, and really, it didn't matter much.

"What do you want?" I dragged the heavy blue drapes back and forth a quarter inch, my attention on the *scritch-scratch* the plastic made in the metal track.

Anything to distract from the disappointment radiating from the other side of the room.

"Nice to see you too, dear," she said.

"No, it's not." I didn't shout. Didn't even move. "You wouldn't be here unless you needed something. We both know it. Why pretend? Better for you to say it and let us both get back to our days. I'm sure you have a million things on your schedule, and I'm . . . tied up with something."

"You're poking around in Tenley Andre's death, according to the TV."

The emails in Erica's phone. Shit.

"I thought you didn't watch Skye Morrow?" I sidestepped the question like only a politician's daughter could.

"I don't. I happened to hear an ad for her piece during my program."

Her program? No way. Did Ruth McClellan really still turn on *The Price Is Right* while she sprinted to nowhere on her treadmill every morning? Memories of loitering in the sunroom doorway with Charity, calling out guesses for the showcases and giggling when Mother told us we needed better shopping skills and reeled off amounts that were often within a few dollars of the actual total, tugged the corners of my lips up. For a second.

"So? Why do you suddenly care what I'm doing?" I didn't turn to her, counting the windows in the front of the federal building across the street to keep any sneaky emotions at bay. There were seventy-eight.

"Erica Andre has done work for me for several years." Ruth's voice sounded softer than I had heard it in . . . maybe ever. That got the best of my curiosity. I turned from the window and studied my mother. "She's a good decorator. Better than good. Gifted. And her daughter is—was—a lovely girl. What's going on, Faith?"

Holy shit. Did her lip just quiver?

Ruth McClellan. Former first lady of Texas. Always the iciest heart in any room.

Was sad.

Or worried. Or something else that made her blue eyes shine a little more than she would normally deem appropriate.

Tenley Andre had gone and done what nothing and nobody had ever managed: she broke through Ruth's shell.

But how? And why?

"Mother?" I couldn't keep the question mark out of my voice. I didn't remember her looking that upset when Charity died.

Ruth waited a beat. "Yes?"

"Why do you—" I paused. Not the time for ghosts or guilt. I wanted Ruth long gone before Graham arrived. "I'm trying to understand your question. You've never taken an interest in anything like this before."

Ruth stood, pacing the little strip of navy-and-forest carpet between the bed and the wall. "I know your father and I weren't exactly supportive of your decision to enter this profession," she said. "Criminals and junkies and all manner of lowlife people you've surrounded yourself with. On purpose."

I felt my eyes start to roll. She made it sound like I was working a street corner in South Austin, not managing to successfully navigate an almost entirely male world and make my own mark in it. Well. I would someday. If I didn't get fired trying to figure this mess out.

"Which tiara I'd win next and which overinflated ego to marry hardly seemed like a life's pursuit after Charity . . ." I let the sentence trail, my hands floating up. "I never have understood how you didn't get it."

Ruth sighed, her blue eyes flashing. "And I've never understood why you didn't see that the best response to your sister's death wasn't for you to dive headlong into a life that puts you in mortal danger every single day."

I snorted. "Yeah. Playing errand girl Friday is super dangerous."

Oops. I snapped my teeth down over my lips, sealing them tight. I didn't mean to spill that. I groped for another subject. Any subject.

Mother's eyes went to the carpet and stayed there. She looked . . . guilty.

Surely not.

"You're kidding." I let the words fall heavy.

"It wasn't me," Ruth said to her shoes. "But I didn't stop him."

Words bubbled up my throat, rolling off my tongue before I could swallow them. "Are you goddamn serious? More than half my life I've chased this job, and they're treating me like a fucking secretary because Daddy said so?"

"Language, dear." Ruth still wouldn't look at me. "What did you expect, going to work at a place where he had political pull he could use? Really, I'd have thought you were smart enough to know that." She shook her head. "You've always been a little too smart for your own good. Your father . . . When you got shot on that traffic stop at the DPS two summers ago, I thought he'd lose his mind. He wanted you in a place where he felt like he could keep you safe."

What?

I plunked onto the corner of the bed.

"Wanted me in a place?"

Of course. I'd been so thrilled the day the call came.

The call came from Archie's boss. The governor's personal bodyguard, once upon a time.

"They only hired me because he said to." It wasn't a question.

How could I have been so stupid?

I'd spent months feeling like I wasn't good enough. Obsessing over every conversation, every action, anything that might have given Boone the impression I couldn't be an asset to his team. When there wasn't much to analyze, I'd decided he was a sexist troll and set my sights on proving him wrong.

And it turned out it was neither? That my father had been meddling behind the scenes the entire time?

"I should've known he was in this up to his perfectly waxed eyebrows," I said. "He always is."

"He was only trying to keep you safe." There was the Ruth McClellan I knew. Sharp. Cold.

"I do all right at that myself." I stood. "If there's nothing else, I'd like to get back to this case I'm not supposed to be investigating."

Mother followed me to the door, her chilly fingers closing around my arm as I moved to open it. "Nothing ever fills the hole that's left when a mother has to bury her child." She cleared her throat. "But not knowing . . . that's a special kind of hell. Find Erica an answer. I don't want her to wonder forever what happened to her daughter."

The flat arctic tundra behind her stare made me pretty sure I didn't want to ask if that was personal experience talking, or something she'd heard from her shrink. "Done. It'd be helpful to that end if you could tell the governor to back off. I'm using up my vacation time to work on this case and I still might get fired."

"You're familiar with his stubborn streak."

Quite. I also knew that was as close to a promise as I would get from her. Better than nothing.

"Thank you." I pulled the door open, and Graham's knuckles landed on my right temple.

"Oh shit, I'm sorry! Are you okay?" Graham reached for me, moving to cradle my chin in his long fingers. I stepped away and his brow furrowed, his eyes going to my mother and narrowing for a moment before they popped wide with recognition.

"Deputy Hardin." Ruth McClellan put out a hand. "Nice to finally meet you."

I watched as Graham took my mother's hand, the wheels turning in his head practically visible as he tried to decide what to do with it.

Mother flashed a quick smile and shook his hand before she pulled hers back. "Nice to see you, dear," she said to me, stepping around Graham and turning for the elevator.

I yanked Graham into the room before drooping against the closed door, breathing like Freddy Krueger lurked in the hallway.

"That was . . . ," Graham sputtered.

I nodded.

"How did . . . ?"

I shrugged. "She's Ruth McClellan. People do what she tells them to."

"Wow." Graham dropped onto the foot of the bed. "So. You okay?"

I walked to the desk, plopping into the rolling chair. "She came because she knows the Andres. Asked me to get them an answer."

"Like you weren't dug in enough already." Graham shook his head. "So what's next?" He held up an evidence bag. Inside was a glitter-encased iPhone.

"My hero." I clasped my hands under my chin and batted my lashes before I snatched the bag from him. "Let's see what we've got."

I grabbed gloves from my bag and popped them onto my hands, then pulled the device out carefully and touched the home button. Nearly dead. I grabbed my charger and plugged it into the base of the thing, then set to work cracking the code. Tenley's correct birthday.

Strike one.

Erica and Brent's wedding anniversary.

Swing and a miss.

I tapped one finger on the desk. Flipped open my laptop.

"Did you get it already?" Graham asked.

I shook my head, opening LexisNexis and typing in Nicholas Richardson's name.

Date of birth, May 14, 2000.

I moved back to the phone. Tapped out all six digits.

Locked out. Try again in one minute.

I sat back in the chair and sighed.

"I thought I had it. Now I'm out of ideas."

"Mind if I take a shot?" Graham winked when I laughed.

"Sergeant Rule Book? Am I a bad influence on you?"

"I have a shot of pragmatic in amongst my rule loving. I'd say the good we can do with the information is more important than how we got it."

"Welcome to my world." I pushed the phone across the desk, offering him my gloves.

"I have some, thanks. Yours are what, kiddie sized?"

I rolled my eyes. "Shut up."

Graham pulled a little black pouch from his pocket and set it on the desk. From inside he fetched a tiny brush, a plastic tub of magnesium powder, and a roll of tape and lined them up next to the phone.

"You think the killer touched her phone?" I tried to hide my skepticism. Didn't manage to.

"Don't know, but I'm pretty sure Tenley touched it plenty," Graham murmured as he swept the powder down the side of the case, watching for the dull silver whorls to show up under the desk lamp.

I leaned over, careful not to block the light. "The case is the same color as the powder. I can't see a damned thing."

"Nothing about this has been easy yet," he said, flipping the phone over and trailing the brush slowly over the screen.

I held my breath for five beats.

A shiny swirled circle appeared, nearly totally intact. Graham opened another jar, this one a different kind of silvery powder, and brushed it over the top of the print, gently blowing away the excess.

"What's that?"

"Shaved steel," he said, pulling off a piece of tape and lifting the print from the screen. "It conducts heat and electricity just enough to . . ."

He pressed the print down carefully over the shiny circle surrounding the home button, holding his thumb there for a moment. A yelp escaped my throat when the screen lit up and flashed past the passcode entry.

"How did you figure that out?" I took the phone back when he offered it, touching the emails first.

"I saw it on the Discovery Channel. First time I've had a chance to try it out." He winked. "Leave the tape there in case we need to open it again."

I nodded while the emails loaded, then clicked up the one from Uber and copied the vehicle description. "Received at 3:27. Got it."

"You don't think the driver is our guy?" Graham sounded skeptical and I shook my head.

"Too cliché. Besides, we have his information right here. If you were going to murder someone, wouldn't you want it to be harder than opening an email for the cops to find you?" I winked. "I just want to know what this guy saw. And what else this little magic box can tell us about Tenley."

Scrolling down a bit didn't get me anywhere. Apple, Nordstrom, Tory Burch. Marketing people love email addresses.

I clicked back out and brought up the texts. Nicky.

Five sent back and forth Sunday and Monday, about a Spurs game that was on and a history test.

Until early Tuesday.

Really early.

Graham moved behind me, looking over my shoulder. "'I'm sorry'? At three in the morning?" His fingers landed on my shoulder. "Who is Nicky with a teddy bear emoji?"

"Her BFF. Darren Richardson's kid."

"Why was she apologizing to him?"

"I don't know." I stared at the screen like it could magically reveal more than was already there. "Wasn't there a gift for Nicky in her bag?" I backed out to the main text screen, looking for the other people on Tenley's spring Santa list. Did they all get a weird text in the middle of the night?

Mom? No. Dad? No. Simpson? No.

"So it wasn't anything to do with why she was at the dam, or the gifts she had with her." Graham stood up. "Which means maybe we need to have a little chat with Mr. Nicky?"

I nodded, turning back to my laptop. "Let's find this driver first, see if she said why she was going, or if the driver saw anyone else. Then with any luck, we can find the kid without his asshole father and maybe get him to tell us something useful."

Graham nodded. "There's a Wells Fargo on the corner. I'm going to deliver this warrant and I'll meet you at the car."

I murmured acknowledgment, already punching the Uber driver's plate number into the DPS site, one finger tapping Tenley's screen to the beat of "Eye of the Tiger," keeping the phone awake. Tenley and Nicky smiled from behind the app squares, their grins as flawless as a Barbie and her Ken.

The computer screen filled. The car was registered to one Sergey Valysnikov, by way of Bluebonnet Transport, LLC. A car service. Of course. Because a plain old regular answer just wasn't on the menu this week.

Phone calls. I touched "Recents" and scrolled.

Mom. Dad. Mom. Dad. Dad. Coach?

I clicked that one. Five thirty Monday evening. Two minutes and change, received call.

Nicky, an hour before that: outgoing call that lasted two seconds.

And a local number not saved to a name, at two forty-eight Monday afternoon. I clicked the information circle. Four minutes on that call, but there were more than a dozen others to and from the same number over the past few weeks. I scrolled faster, my brain spinning right along with the numbers on Tenley's screen. Pulling out my own phone, I snapped a photo of the call detail.

Every call except one came in or went out during the day. Could this be the mystery guy?

That would rule out Simpson, because Tenley had his number saved. Didn't mean he was in the clear, but added a dash more doubt.

"What else were you hiding, Tenley?" I half whispered, touching the email icon again and clicking to the accounts list.

Just one, with Tenley's name serving as the address.

Damn.

I laid the phone down.

Picked it back up.

Scrolled left to search for an app: Gmail.

Yep. I touched the white-and-red square.

And found a single long conversation thread. From Erica Andre.

Tapping the screen, I watched the same snarky-yet-threatening message I'd read on Erica's phone earlier materialize on Tenley's screen. I picked up my phone again and fired off another photo just as it buzzed a text arrival. Graham was ready to go.

Sliding Tenley's phone back into the evidence sleeve, I finally had one solid fact: whatever the blue hell she had been up to, Tenley Andre had been in way over her head.

27

Sergey was pretty easy to talk information out of, thanks to about ten OSHA violations Graham and I spotted on the way into his shop.

After crossing his thick arms over his chest in his best *Goodfellas* pose when he got a load of our badges, he folded easier than a pair of old jeans when Graham pointed to a guy running a welder with no safety gear and I remarked on my father's good friend the small-business commissioner.

"Why you bothering me? Aren't there bad people out there"—Sergey swept one arm toward the door, his Russian accent still thick after seven years of running this company in Austin, according to the business license Graham pulled up on the ride over—"who need to be in a jail?"

"We didn't come here to bother you, Mr. Valisnykov, and I don't want to bother the commissioner with issues I'm sure you can clean up yourself now that we've pointed them out for you. Right?" I raised one eyebrow.

"Of course, of course." Sergey crossed his arms again, but he nodded. "Perhaps if you told me why you are here . . ."

"We're looking for one of those bad people you mentioned." I didn't get the rest of the sentence out before Sergey started shaking his head. He didn't stop for a good thirty seconds.

"Sir," I said. "If I could . . . There was a passenger in one of your cars

Monday night. She called through Uber. We'd like to talk to the driver. That's all."

"This woman, did she say one of my drivers is bad person?" Sergey's brow furrowed. "Because my guys are all solid. I do the hiring myself."

"She did not say anything of the sort." To us, anyway. "We just have a few questions for him."

"Which driver? Only sedans we run through Uber. It's easy extra money."

I pulled my phone out and touched the image of Tenley's screen. "Dimitri, according to the email she got." Sergey waved for us to follow as he turned for a glass-walled office in the back of the shop.

He plucked a folder from a stack on the desk and flipped it open. "Monday night?"

"Correct."

"*Da.* Dimitri." Sergey put the folder down, his forehead bunching again.

"Is he here?" I turned back to the windows overlooking the shop.

"Dimitri!" Sergey shouted, cupping his hands around his mouth. "Come here!"

A stocky man with graying hair laid a magazine on the dash of a black Lincoln Continental and climbed from behind the wheel, ambling belly-first toward the office.

He was definitely big enough to throw Tenley off the dam.

Graham and I exchanged a Look. The kind that said we both knew what the other was thinking but couldn't say it right then.

"Hello." Dimitri's voice was deep, his tone unsure.

"These police officers have questions about a pickup from Monday night. Uber call," Sergey said.

I fixed Sergey with a polite smile that waited for him to leave the room.

He sat down and put his feet on the desk. Okay, then.

I pulled out the photo from the Marshall yearbook. "You would've picked her up—"

"Dammit, I knew I shouldn't have left her up there." Dimitri smacked himself in the forehead. "Stupid! I knew it."

Graham glanced at me. I gave a tiny shrug. On a list of reactions I'd expected, this didn't make the top one hundred.

I bent my head and caught Dimitri's gaze, my voice smooth and untroubled. "If you could give us a little more detail, we'd really appreciate it."

I watched his face. He'd gone paler, but his hands were loose at his sides, his bright-blue eyes staring straight ahead. He looked like he was shaken, not like he was lying. I took a slow breath, not wasting a smidgen of attention on anything but the large, bothered man in front of me.

"She wanted to go to Mansfield Dam. Insisted I leave her on the side of the old road by the park. The one that's closed."

"Did you see anyone else up there when you dropped her off? In the park, maybe?"

"I knew I should've stayed." Dimitri shook his head. "She said she was meeting someone, and I thought she'd be okay."

I stood up straighter. "Meeting someone?" Too high. I cleared my throat. "Did she happen to say who?"

"A boyfriend her folks didn't like. She was plum anxious to get away from her house."

He had no way to know that unless Tenley told him. She could've lied to scare him off if she got a bad vibe from him, of course, but my gut said he wasn't our guy. I went with it, for the moment, pulling out a pad and jotting a note. "Did you notice anything else about her? How did she seem? Scared, sad?"

Dimitri nodded. "She was nervous. Or excited. Bounced in her seat the whole way up there. And she reeked of booze."

Really, now? That was new. Nicky said Tenley didn't drink. Like, not ever.

I snuck a sideways glance at Graham. "You're sure?" I asked Dimitri.

"Hard liquor. On her breath. I could smell it every time she spoke. Which wasn't much until she started trying to talk me into leaving her on the side of the road in the middle of the night. Please, is she okay?" He raised wide eyes to meet mine.

"I'm sorry to say she's not. We're investigating the circumstances surrounding her death." I stretched my lips into the sympathy line most cops practice in the mirror until it's a bad-news delivery reflex. My phone buzzed against my hip. I kept my eyes on Dimitri. "You're sure you didn't see anything else we might need to know about?"

He shook his head, his hands clutching at his unruly hair, a single word sliding through his teeth on repeat. "Stupid, stupid, stupid."

I turned to Sergey, handing him a card. "Call me if he remembers anything at all."

He nodded, his face blank. "Thank you, Officer."

Graham leaned forward as we stepped back into the shop. "There's one more for the mystery boyfriend. You still think that's Coach Simpson?"

I wobbled one flat hand. "There was a number in her phone. Someone she talked to twice a day, just about, for the past few weeks, but she didn't save them as a contact. I'd like to figure out who that was before I settle on Simpson."

I pulled my phone from my pocket and looked up at him with my finger on the home button. "You get anything from the bank yet?"

Graham checked his email, shook his head. "They told me they want their lawyers to look it over. But it'll come."

I clicked my browser open and logged in to DPS. Tapped the digits from Tenley's call log. Crossed my fingers.

"Damn." I flipped the screen around to show Graham. "Prepaid cell."

His eyes rolled. "We can't catch even a little break."

I stared at my screen until the numbers blurred. "I wonder if Tenley's secret friend is around today."

He leaned against the side of the truck and watched with raised eyebrows as I tapped my screen and put the phone to my ear.

Six rings.

"Come on," I whispered.

Seven.

The tiniest *click*.

And nothing.

My eyes popped wide. I checked the screen.

The call timer ticked off two more seconds.

"Hello?" My voice rang clear. Sure. Authoritative.

Beep. Beep. Beep.

Call ended, the screen advised.

"Well?" Graham snatched my phone.

"Thirty-five seconds of silence, and they hung up when I spoke," I said.

Graham clicked my recent calls up and saved the number into his phone before he handed mine back.

"Weird," I said.

I pressed the home button just as the thing buzzed again. Graham's fingers closed around my wrist. "Did you just give a murderer your number, McClellan?"

Honest answer? Maybe. Creating a break in a stubborn case often requires risk.

I watched the dark screen.

Archie's name flashed up.

I shook my head, raising the phone to my ear. "Hey, we were talking to the driver who took Tenley up to the dam. Says she told him she was meeting a boyfriend her parents didn't like. Did you let Simpson go?"

"Yeah, but the APD is on him. If he farts in the direction of an underage girl, I'll hear about it before he smells it."

I covered my mouth to muffle a snort. "You and your metaphors."

"He had an alibi for the night Jessa disappeared, though. Says he spent the night with someone he met at the bar. I got a number, left a message."

"Damn." I bit my lip.

"Listen, I have something else I'm not sure what to make of, and I'm hamstrung by the damn media at the moment."

"How can I help?"

"That website Skye put all over the TV last night? APD took a dozen calls before midnight from women claiming their actual assault was filmed and put on the internet."

"Good?" I winced at the ludicrous use of the word as it came out.

"Our cyber guys woke up a judge and got a warrant at one thirty. They went to the building she showed on TV and took the servers. One of them called me about an hour ago. There was a backdoor section of the site—invitation only, not traceable anywhere online, dark web stuff—with the most graphic of the videos, all proclaimed one hundred percent authentic."

I froze with my hand on the truck door. "And?"

"The video in that section with the heaviest traffic is of a directed sexual assault. Multiple perpetrators. And the victim is Jessa DuGray. Faith, she—it looks like she's wearing the top she had on the night she disappeared."

"Christ almighty." My eyes fell shut as I slid into the truck.

"Mr. Wooley seems to have vanished, but I'd sure like to know where he got that clip. Is Hardin with you? And do you have time to go by this scumbag's apartment? His last known is 1253 Rollins Road, but we can't find any trace of him since before her piece aired yesterday. No credit card use, no traffic cameras, nothing."

I scribbled the address down, nodding. "We're not far from there now. I'll let you know what we find."

"Thanks. Be careful."

"Yes, Dad." I shook my head as I touched the "End" button and started the truck.

"Why do I think I don't want to know?" Graham buckled his seat belt.

"Because you don't." I gunned the engine. "Get me directions to Rollins Road, would you? Archie needs a favor." I sped to the corner while he checked Google Maps.

"Nine blocks west of here, then four north." Graham let out a low whistle. "That's not a great neighborhood."

"Then it suits the guy we're hunting."

"Why're we hunting a guy?"

"Because it seems he's making money off a video of Jessa DuGray being gang-raped, probably right before she died."

Graham's breath went in on a sharp hiss. "You got a cherry in this thing?"

I pointed to the glove box, and he reached out the window and put the portable light on the roof of the truck. I turned north at the next corner and stomped on the gas.

I nearly missed the turn on Rollins, jerking the wheel to the right when I caught the street sign with the corner of one eye. I slammed the brakes in front of what looked like it used to be a townhouse before it became a slum, threw the gearshift in park, and jerked the keys free, itching for a few minutes alone with the kind of asshole who could profit off a young woman's assault and death. I'm not generally a believer in the use of force when it's not strictly necessary, but excuses can be found in special cases.

"Ready?" Graham unlatched the safety strap on his holster when he stepped out of the car, and I reached under my arm and did the same thing, nodding as I started up the sidewalk. "Kinda like old times."

Graham stepped around me when I stopped at the door to the building, one hand on the butt of his 9-millimeter.

I nodded and he flattened one boot against the door and pushed, freeing a hodgepodge of stench that made my stomach recoil into my spine. Sharp urine, sickly-sweet decay, and some kind of spice I didn't recognize.

"On three." Graham gulped a deep breath and turned back for the open door. "One."

"Two." I concentrated on shallow breaths.

"Three." He plunged into the mail foyer.

I followed on his heels, a small scream escaping my throat when my eyes fell on the carcass in the corner.

28

"Who the hell leaves that in the hallway?" I swallowed hard, my grip on my Sig tightening as I moved into the building behind Graham.

"Is that a . . ." Graham squinted. "Chicken?"

I nodded, not wanting to risk another look. The thing's head was missing, but the blood-soaked feathers looked very chicken-like under cursory inspection.

"Could somebody be planning to eat it?"

"Would you eat something that smelled like that? No way it's been there less than forty-eight hours. Even the rats know better."

"I wasn't aware rats had a discriminating palette. Maybe there just aren't any in here."

I inspected the dismal alcove. Spray-painted graffiti on three walls, a layer of grime we were leaving actual footprints in on the cracked linoleum floor, and peeling stick-on labels with handwritten names marking the tiny mailboxes. "If there's a rat in three miles that doesn't frequent this place, I'll shine your boots." I nodded to the stairs. "The mailbox says Wooley is in 2A."

"The boots will need it after today." Graham prodded the dead chicken with the toe of one ostrich roper and jumped back when he sent up a cloud of tiny flies. "Seriously, who would do that? And why the hell wouldn't the neighbors complain?" He followed me to the stairs.

I shook my head, a stomping sound overhead making me pull my weapon and slow my pace.

"Somebody's up there." Graham's whisper was so low I almost didn't hear him.

I chambered a round and took another step. Graham was so close behind me I could feel the heat coming off his skin. Hear his breathing.

What the hell was I about to drag him into?

I wasn't afraid of anything. Hadn't been in a long, long time. But standing in that stairwell, for just a minute, I was fourteen again, hiding in the closet, listening to men shouting over my sister's screams. I swallowed hard.

Breathe. Focus.

That scared little girl was long gone. I was strong. I was fast. And I was a damned good shot. I had devoted every minute of my life since that night to becoming the hero I wished I could've been for Charity. Whatever was going on upstairs, I could handle it.

Two more steps and I crested the landing, the musty-smelling plaster wall warm against my back in the sticky, unconditioned air. I edged along, then whipped around the corner, elbows locked and Sig straight in front of me, index fingers resting lightly on the trigger guard.

Ten empty steps stretched into darkness. I nodded to Graham and he crept up to the landing, careful not to point his weapon at me.

I put one boot on the bottom stair. Steady and quiet, we climbed to the hallway above. Cops on TV always shout a warning when they're entering a space, and truth be told it wasn't a terrible idea in a situation like this—except I didn't want to give the porn dealer a head start. Graham was on the same page, his lips pinched into a fine line, rapid breaths going in and out through his nose the only noise in the still, stale air.

The hallway split the second floor in half, one door on each wall. Ray's apartment was to my right. I looked at Graham. He jerked his head to the door and nodded a *Go-ahead*, keeping his weapon lowered but still out. I holstered mine, raised one fist, and rapped my knuckles on the once-white-painted wood.

We didn't breathe too loudly, both listening for any sign of movement behind the door.

Nothing.

I gave it a full minute before I knocked again. "Mr. Wooley? Open up."

More silence.

I glanced at Graham. He nodded a *Knock again.*

Raising my fist for a third time, I added an edge of urgency to my voice. "Texas Rangers, Ray. We need to make sure you're all right. Please open the door if you're able."

Graham winked when I turned back to him, mouthing, *Nice.*

It was an old trick Archie taught me before I graduated high school. We couldn't legally enter the apartment as part of a criminal investigation without a warrant. But a welfare check was a perfectly reasonable and above-board excuse to try the door, and Archie did say the guy was off the grid today. Now if the neighbors were home, we had established that we went in to check on the occupant. What we happened to see while we were in there that might aid an investigation . . . well, that was fair game.

I counted to sixty. Three times. "Sir, we're coming inside to check on you now," I called, putting a hand on the doorknob.

It turned. I pushed, and the door swung inward.

The smell hit me first.

Sweet and acrid at the same time, it was the thing about this line of work I would never get used to. Twelve years after my first body dump, the smell of rotting flesh still flipped my gut smooth inside out. I'd been a vegetarian since my second week at the sheriff's office.

There was no mistaking it once a person knew it, either: someone was dead in this space. Who it was and whether the killer was still there were the only things I wasn't sure of.

I jerked the gun back up and moved into the shoebox-sized living room. "Ray? Police. If you're in here, please come out slowly with your hands where we can see them."

Graham on my heels, I moved through the apartment, my freakish brain cataloging everything along the way. The tiny kitchen held a cooktop, a microwave, and a small refrigerator with both doors hanging open. A hallway ran past it, and I could see a bathroom sink through a barely open door at the end.

Still no Ray. Still no corpse.

I moved toward the bathroom, my stomach folding in on itself as the warm air thickened, decay overlaid with the metallic tang of blood and the stench of loose bowels.

Jesus.

Nobody in the bitty bedroom off the hallway, one queen-sized mattress and an open, messy trunk filling the space end to end.

Whatever was wrong here—and something was very wrong here—it was in that bathroom.

I caught a deep breath and held it, moving my finger to the trigger and shoving the door with the sole of my boot. The knob crashed into the tile wall, but I didn't hear it over the blood pounding in my ears.

I'd found Ray.

And the rats.

29

I managed to both hold on to the gun and avoid shooting at the gnawing rodents.

I did not manage to hold on to my breakfast, leaning forward as regurgitated latte and banana spewed across the black-and-white checkerboard linoleum floor. Graham's footfalls were heavy behind me, sending shockwaves through the water in the tub.

The rats turned blood-soaked, beady-eyed faces in unison, a few of them screeching and the rest hissing in chorus.

Graham's arm roped around my waist and yanked me straight backward, depositing me in the hall behind him so he could grab the door and jerk it closed.

My eyes fell shut, but I forced them open when the rats' feast began playing on a loop on the backs of the lids.

I leaned forward, resting my hands on bent knees as I braced against the wall, sucking air in deep gulps before I realized the putrid smell wasn't settling my stomach.

"What. The actual. Fuck?" Graham's words came out on short breaths.

I shook my head. "Christ almighty, Graham. Odds that was our porn peddler?"

"That was definitely a man. At some point recently, anyway." He fumbled for his phone and poked at the screen.

"Dispatch, this is one-three-five-two requesting backup and crime scene to . . ." He put his hand over the phone. "You still have the address?"

I nodded and dug my phone from my pocket, unlocking it so the map came up.

Graham read the address off to the dispatcher. "We have a deceased male, indeterminate causes, in the bathroom in the back of the unit," he said before he hung up.

"They're coming." Graham stepped toward me. "You okay?"

I straightened, nodding. "I told you there were rats. Seriously, brain bleach needs to be a thing. Somebody in the lab should get on that."

He smiled, putting an arm around my shoulders. "Jokes mean you're not in shock. I think we can wait farther from the vermin, if it's all the same to you."

"It's vastly preferable, as a matter of fact." We couldn't do anything to help that guy, and the scene behind that door would rattle anybody. I shuffled my feet next to Graham until I was sure my watery knees would hold me up.

We reached the living room, the hallway much shorter on the return trip, and exchanged a look. "So." Graham took his arm back. I missed the warmth. "My days haven't been this interesting since you left. I'll say that."

"I'm not sure I'm all that happy to know I bring the disgusting and alarming to this relationship." I took in the threadbare little room. The walls were the kind of variegated rust-on-white that meant the roof leaked, the floor covered mostly with the same linoleum I'd puked on in the bathroom, but bare all the way to the plywood subfloor in three places. There was no couch, only a loveseat worn clean through to the Styrofoam padding across most of the cockeyed right cushion and a card table next to it topped with a neat stack of envelopes and papers.

The only thing in the room made in this century was the TV, a massive flat-screen anchored to the wall opposite the loveseat. I walked over and checked the brand. Sony. In the floor at my feet lay a sound bar, a Blu-ray player, and a PlayStation.

"What's missing?" I asked.

Graham pulled a pen from his pocket and used it to flip through the mail on the table as I turned my head to the sound of sirens in the distance.

I should duck out. Graham would get it. But I still had a few blocks' worth of looking around before my being here would cause him a headache.

I turned to him when I noticed he hadn't answered me. "You okay, Hardin? What've you got over there?"

I stepped closer when his only reply was a furrowed brow.

The mail pushed to one side, Graham was using the pen to scatter thin papers across the tabletop. I leaned over his shoulder, my mouth going dry when I saw what had him so fascinated.

Newspaper clippings. More than a dozen.

Every one with a photo of Tenley.

Graham shook his head. "What the hell was this girl into?"

I couldn't answer, pulling my phone from my back pocket and snapping photos of the table, getting two close ones of the clippings. Clicking back to the home screen, I spotted an unread text.

Jim.

Please, God, something. Anything. I touched the little green square.

No sign of current or past pregnancy. BAC of point one nine, though.

Dimitri was right: That wasn't just a little tipsy. Tenley was wasted. I sent back a *Thanks* as the sirens got louder, and turned back to Graham with an apologetic half frown. "They're only a couple blocks out. I should—"

He nodded. "I'll get them going and meet you down the block in twenty?"

I kept one hand on my holster as I descended the steps, checking both sides of the lobby and the sidewalk before climbing into my truck. I rounded the southern corner of the street as the first patrol car appeared in my rearview.

In four minutes, Ray's apartment would be taped off, lit by spots, and full of cops and coroners doing their thing, the stench obfuscated by the VapoRub slathered on everyone's top lip.

I let my head fall back against the seat, the stomping we'd heard as we climbed the stairs rattling around my thoughts. Clearly, whoever that guy was had been in that bathroom a while. We couldn't have just missed the killer. But then where did the steps come from? And where the hell did they go? There wasn't a back door, or a fire exit.

And how in God's name did Tenley Andre fit into this? Why would a girl like her end up the center of a porn peddler's fantasies?

Money? She was posing as Stella to blackmail her folks, but by the looks of those emails, her mom had cut that off.

I wriggled my phone free and opened a text to Archie, pasting in the photos I'd taken of the table.

Pretty sure we found Ray. Unfortunately for him, it looks like somebody else found him first. And look what was on the table in his living room. Send.

But if Ray had something to do with Tenley's death, why was he rat food?

Not the first fucking clue.

I pulled a crumpled pack and a purple Bic lighter from the glove box, plopped a cigarette on my lower lip, and lit it with shaking fingers. Smoking in the car was usually a no-go for me, but rats eating a dead guy meant normal rules didn't apply. Inhaling, I closed my eyes and let the calm spread outward from my lungs.

This whole thing just kept getting murkier. Every time I thought we might get somewhere, a new kind of crazy popped up.

And Jesus, the secrets. There was a new one under every rock we turned.

Maybe someone wanted to make sure Ray didn't spill any. Someone who was in that video with Jessa? And what, if anything, did Tenley have to do with any of it?

I wrapped my arms tight around myself, chilled in the stifling, sun-drenched car.

The horror scene in that bathroom added a whole new level of disturbing to this case: Now, we had a murderer running scared. A murderer who had no issues with killing to cover his tracks.

A murderer I might've inadvertently handed my cell number to an hour ago.

Tick-tock.

* * *

Graham slid into his seat without a word, his blank face staring straight out the windshield until I couldn't stand it anymore.

"Everything squared away?" I asked.

"Coroners are on their way." His voice sounded hollow. "Forensics is working the bathroom now." I put a hand on his arm. Our line of work wasn't known for a tendency to boredom, but that scene was enough to give Dirty Harry himself nightmares. How was anyone working in that bathroom?

"Um. The rats?"

"Gassed. Sent to the lab in case they ate some important evidence." Graham's tone dripped with as much disgust as I felt. Important bits of the dead guy, that's what he meant. Ick.

"And the guy . . ." I couldn't finish that one.

"Ray Wooley, online porn king to the sick and twisted. Once the rats were dead, we got a look at his face. Well. At enough of it to ID him. Kinda poetic, in a way, given what you said on the way over about the video of the DuGray girl. The lead tech said it looked like he was castrated. Probably severed his femoral artery and he bled out." Graham's voice faded on the last words as I started the engine and turned on the radio.

"Damn Skye Morrow," I muttered. "Always the ratings above everything else."

"She didn't make the guy post disgusting videos of women being assaulted, Faith," Graham said in his best *Now be fair* voice.

"No, but she put it on TV instead of calling the police. Hell, Archie said they were already looking into his site. Less than twenty-four hours after she put his name and face on the TV, he's rat food, and because somebody cut off his—"

Before I could finish, a tap at my window made Graham reach for his gun. I jumped such that I whacked my sore leg on the steering wheel, and my face twisted into a scowl when I saw the microphone on the other side of the glass.

"Speak of the devil . . ."

"And the devil appears," Graham murmured. "That's creepy timing even to me."

"Haven't we seen enough of you for one day?" I asked as I lowered the window.

"Ranger McClellan, Detective Hardin—fancy meeting you here. Does Ray Wooley have something to do with Tenley Andre's death? Was she making pornographic videos?" Skye didn't even bother to hide the glee under the curiosity in her voice.

I would've had a smart-ass comeback for that on a normal day, but today was turning out to be anything but.

Tenley. Making videos for Ray?

Surely not.

Skye's eyebrows went up when I didn't bite her head off. "Is that a yes, Officer?"

Not a chance. I shook my head.

"We could ask him, if he wasn't dead," I said. "Proud of yourself today, Skye?"

She pursed her lips, jagged wrinkles rippling unevenly through the collagen. "I was doing my job, Ranger. Perhaps if y'all were a little better at yours, we wouldn't have a murderer on the loose for me to warn folks about."

My temper bubbled. "Your job? Channel two is in the business of creating vigilantes these days? Ad revenue must be down farther than we thought."

"That's a skosh dramatic, don't you think? Do you have proof this man's death was in any way related to our exclusive *News2* investigation?" Skye stuck the mic out again and it took everything in me not to snatch it from her hand and bop her over the head with it.

"No comment." I smiled straight into the yellow rose lapel pin I knew held a camera and rolled the window up. Skye shook her head and marched toward Wooley's building. I watched in the rearview, poking Graham when she got turned away by the APD sentries in the mail foyer. "She knows she's not just walking into a crime scene," I said. "What is she up to?"

We turned in the seat for a better view as Skye made a show of walking back out to the street before she doubled back and ducked into the alley between that building and the next one over.

"Tenacious, isn't she?" Graham asked.

"Reckless. Stubborn," I said.

"Why do you hate her so much?" Graham asked. "You've never said in all the time we've known each other."

I shook my head. "She's just . . . sleazy. That's all."

Graham shook his head. "Sure." He drew out the middle vowel.

I pulled out my phone and opened another text to Archie before I put the car in gear. *You at the office?*

I waited. Got a dotty bubble. *Always. My icy trail on Jessa DuGray is suddenly hotter than a whole peck of ghost peppers. You coming by?*

We need to dig deeper on this Wooley guy. Can I bring Graham with me?

Buzz. *I already have a jacket on Wooley. Hoping something would lead me to the sick bastard who did this to Jessa. Nothing too serious, though, and all his known associates are small-time crooks and dealers.*

I frowned, typing again. *Damn. And we're sure it wasn't him? On the tape?*

Buzz. *I'm not sure of anything. Cyber is analyzing it. One guy swears he recognizes the voice.*

Be right there.

I turned to Graham. "Want to see the best this state has to offer in action, maybe figure this out as a bonus?"

"I'll skip right past being insulted that you're not talking about me and say for the love of God, if you know someone who can make sense of this, lead on."

The first half of the drive was quiet, each of us lost in our own thoughts.

"So, if this guy got off on watching sexual assaults and he'd fixated on Tenley . . ." Graham let the sentence trail.

I nodded. "Maybe he's our guy?"

"Was she raped?"

"Can't say for sure. But Jim took swabs this morning and we have all the DNA we could ever need from Captain Porn. So we can find out as soon as someone has time to test it."

"I have a new friend at the lab. Let me see if I can ask a favor." Something in the way Graham said that pulled my eyes his way.

"Woman friend?"

"It's nothing serious." He said it too quickly, and the lurch in my gut caught me off guard. I didn't care. Much.

But why did I care at all? That's the part that irked me. Graham was just Graham. So I hadn't seen him in a while. So I hadn't had so much as a casual hookup in more than a while.

We had work to do.

"No big deal if it is, you know." I went for nonchalant, but neutral was the closest I could get.

"I know. Just wanted to be clear."

"A favor would be helpful," I said.

He unlocked his phone. "No promises, but I'll give it my best shot."

"Be extra charming."

"Always."

I focused on the road while he tapped at his screen. Maybe this was it. Ray was the big bad, and now he was dead, and the whole city could sleep a little easier. I would call Rebecca Stuart at channel four and tip her off as soon as we had it nailed down—the best way to punish Skye was to offer a scoop to someone else. She loved her exclusives more than her shoe collection.

Like Ray. He was yesterday's scoop.

Except Ray was dead.

Damn.

I thumped the steering wheel with one fist.

"What's wrong?" Graham looked up from his phone.

"It looks like Ray Wooley was obsessed with Tenley. He had that vile video of Jessa. If he killed them both, we have a nice little gift-wrapped case to deliver to the DA. But then who killed Ray?" I shook my head. "The web here just keeps spreading and tangling around itself."

"I'm sure we'll have no shortage of suspects. But we'll get him, Faith."

Sure we would. But we were up to three corpses and counting.

So the trick would be to manage that before he got somebody else.

30

"Just when you think you've been on this job long enough to see every damn thing." Archie grimaced at my rundown of the scene at Ray's apartment. "Any idea how long till you'll have anything concrete?"

"Hopefully the rats didn't eat his prints, but Graham said forensics was sure on the ID from his license photo even if they did, and there was no other name on the lease," I said, leaning my head against the wall. We were back in the conference room, photos and reports spread across the table. "This story fits with what we've already got, at least on Jessa." I pointed to the report I'd dropped off the day before. "The paint thinner on her clothes—I could buy that coming off any of the furniture in that apartment. And Graham has a friend at the lab who might be able to get us a DNA comparison on Ray and our victims sooner than the normal slow to never." Even with the modified rapid-analysis system, a person had to study the profile and interpret the results for them to be of any use. There weren't enough hours in the day or techs in the lab.

"I appreciate all the help I can get this week." Archie pointed at me. "Speaking of help, I called the sheriff up in Ardmore this afternoon about our friend Jake. He got good and busted, caught in the act in a no-tell motel with his star runner. Real headache for them, and quite the scandal in town—back then, our guy was the boys' track coach."

"Did his alibi from the bar return your call?"

Archie shook his head. "But I'm thinking if he's into teenage boys, perhaps he didn't have anything to do with Jessa's death in light of this video. And that blows our theory that he was sleeping with Tenley."

I offered a slow nod, a tickle in the back of my brain.

I let my eyes go unfocused, trying to let whatever was bothering me float up. *Into teenage boys.*

Nicky didn't have a note.

I shot to my feet, turning to Graham. "You said all the gifts in Tenley's bag had notes."

"Except Nick Richardson's. His envelope was empty." Graham snapped his fingers. "We never got around to finding him today."

"But Simpson's note said he was sleeping with a student," I said. "What if the student was Nicky? What if Simpson took Nicky's note and left his because you can't put that together without both letters?"

"And taking his own would make him more suspect." Archie nodded. "It's certainly not the worst theory we have."

Thoughtful silence stretched until Archie slammed a hand onto the table, nearly sending me out of my skin. He didn't lose his cool. Ever.

"Arch?" I ventured after three beats of silence.

He shook his head, his shoulders drooping behind a long sigh. "The problem isn't a shortage of plausible theories, it's that we can't discern the right ones. How can we have two cases so similar, brushing up against each other a dozen different ways, and not be able to find where and how they intersect? Did the girls know each other? Did they date the same sicko on the sly? Did they both go to the same gas station every Friday morning?" Archie stood.

I stayed quiet. Nobody could say. Yet. Those were the kinds of connections that looked easy once the bad guy was caught but were nearly impossible to see while we tracked him.

Archie picked up the photo of Jessa entering the bar the night she went missing. "The track coach looked like an easy bridge. He was there in the last place anyone saw Jessa alive. He was too involved with Tenley and her family. The scenes were different, but the story made sense. I was even arrogant enough to think we had the bastard before we left here last night.

Today, he doesn't look so good. But okay, because we've got this porn site jackass, and not only does he have video of what looks like Jessa's last moments, he has some sort of goddamned stalker dossier on Tenley. It's perfect. Except for the part where he's dead." He hurled an empty Dr Pepper can at the far wall. "What the fuck is going on here?"

Wow. Things were getting dicey when I had to be the voice of reason for Archie.

"There are too many possibilities," I said. "And too many uncertainties. Jim said Tenley might have been assaulted, but he couldn't swear to it. Given the video and the news clippings, I'm going to assume she was until we have proof otherwise. I think that's what we have to do—start ruling out the least likely possibilities and narrow our field."

Graham clapped his hands. "Yes. We are smarter than this asshole, y'all. So if we can't get to the end of whichever road we don't know to follow, let's work backward."

"Exactly. Jim took DNA swabs from Tenley this morning," I said. "Now, you said there was no match for what they managed to get from Jessa in CODIS, Arch—but did they check LDIS?" There are rules about which DNA profiles can be uploaded to the national databases, but local systems are becoming catchalls in the age of rapid profiling. "I'm betting our friend Ray has a file from a recent arrest." I snapped my fingers. Of course. "And if we can get Graham's friend to compare samples from Jessa's remains to samples from Tenley's—that would tell us if there's really a link here."

I glanced at Graham, who reached for Archie's laptop and poked a few keys. "Wooley, Raymond Herbert, age thirty-nine. Fifteen-loci profile from an arrest last year." He pulled his phone from his pocket. "She didn't answer me yet." The wrinkle in his forehead said that bothered him. "I'll try again."

I ignored Graham's irritation, smiling at Archie. "See? We're getting somewhere already."

Archie resumed his seat, lacing his fingers behind his head. "Cyber is going through Ray's computers with a microscope. We got one guy taking apart the DuGray video bit by bit, trying to see if they can catch a face on camera, another trying to hit a vocal match."

"Excellent." I dropped into a chair on the side of the table nearest the door. "That's another thing that was weird at Ray's place, though: He had a massive entertainment setup, but I didn't see a single computer. Not even a laptop. Why would a guy who runs a website not own a computer?"

"Afraid of being traced?" Graham asked, putting his phone on the table.

"Forgive me for being more concerned about the dead women than the porn king," Archie began, and I raised one hand.

"I didn't say I was concerned about him. But while we're eliminating geese from our chase, is this one too easy to catch? The video of Jessa, the clips of Tenley, the dead porn peddler—if you look at it right, it almost seems designed to make us pat ourselves on the back and go have a nice weekend." I glanced at Graham. "This vile little man with connections to both girls is the perfect bow. Who's going to care that he's dead?"

"And people can still bring their money to town." Graham nodded. "It does seem a little convenient all the way around."

"So what are we missing?" Archie asked.

I turned back to the whiteboard, my list from last night still there. "Jessa didn't run track. She wasn't from Austin." She picked up the marker again. "But I agree, they're too close to not be tangled up somehow. So what do they have in common?"

"Simpson?" Archie offered.

"Maybe, but why? And were they his type?" I tapped the marker against the board.

"Did you say Jessa was in the same bar he was the night she disappeared?" Graham asked. "What if he did go home with someone—like, maybe Nick Richardson? What if she saw it?"

Archie hauled the fattest folder from his box, pulling out the surveillance stills. "But how would Simpson know that? And why would he care?"

I grabbed a couple of the photos and scanned for Nicky's face or unruly hair. "Coach Richardson already knows his son is gay. So a student from the university knowing wouldn't be a big deal."

"Plus, I bet Darren Richardson had no idea who Jessa was until she went missing. She was just going into her sophomore year."

"Why was she on campus in July?" Graham asked, looking up from the missing person's report.

"Soccer camp. She was on a partial athletic scholarship," Archie said.

"Tenley was a star athlete, too," Graham said.

I scribbled that next to another bullet.

"But Jessa was burned, and Tenley wasn't," Archie said. "Why?"

"Evidence?" I paused, the slash on Tenley's hip snaking through my thoughts. "Or . . . something darker." I popped the marker cap in and out of place. "Sacrifice. Ceremony. Respect . . ."

I reached for Archie's DuGray file. Flipping pages, I found the picture I wanted: a full-length shot of the remains. Poking my nose a millimeter from the paper, I squinted. Huffed. "You have a magnifier?" I asked Archie.

He disappeared from my peripheral, and a glass materialized a few seconds later. I took it, running it first around the outline ringing Jessa's body, then wider, across the surrounding grass until I reached the edges of the frame.

"You have any idea what she thinks she sees?" Archie's voice sounded far away, even though he was inches from my elbow.

"This is a leap too big for me to follow yet." Tension and curiosity tinged Graham's reply. "Give her a minute. She likes to talk."

Hush, boys. I'm thinking.

I moved the glass back to Jessa.

Arms folded over her ribs. Skull facing the sunrise.

Like she'd lain down to take a nap and fallen into hell.

I sat straight up, dropping the photo and the magnifier to the table and turning a triumphant grin on Archie and then Graham. "He knows them."

Archie moved his reading glasses down the wide bridge of his nose. "Um. What?"

I stood, pacing as I talked. "Follow me here."

"Can't. We'll get dizzy." Graham leaned his chair back. "Why haven't you learned to think and sit still at the same time?"

I waved a hand at him, focused on Archie. "Were there any unusual marks on Jessa's remains?"

He picked at the edge of the manila folder, shaking his head. "It was difficult to discern anything. The autopsy showed she was dead before the fire started, but the burns obscured tie marks of any kind on her wrists or ankles."

"What about tissue damage?" I spun and retraced my steps again. "Lacerations, specifically?"

"You think someone tortured her?"

I shook my head. "Jessa was burned after she was killed. Tenley was cut after she was killed. But they were both laid out with care. Placed, not dumped. We're looking for someone strong enough to move deadweight and agile enough to avoid leaving usable footprints. Someone who thought enough of them to care how they were found. Someone. They. Knew." I hit the last three words hard.

Graham cleared his throat. "I hate to argue, but all evidence suggests that Tenley Andre was found where she fell. The blood on the ground and the damage to the back of her skull are consistent with one another."

Archie's eyes went from me to the photos of Jessa. "And I'd stake my badge Jessa had a stroke. The screams on that video . . ." A shudder rippled through his torso. "Nineteen years old, and whatever they did to her terrified her to death. But Jim hasn't examined Tenley's brain yet, right?"

I shook my head. "It's too soon." Brain tissue has to cure in formalin for hours, or the coroner risks losing possible evidence to a mushy mess. I resumed my seat, foot bouncing as I pulled Archie's laptop back across the table. "I'm telling you. I haven't had a feeling this strong since I laid eyes on Tenley. He knows them, guys. There's our narrowed field: I bet the answer was hiding right in plain sight this whole time."

Archie's forehead wrinkled. "Hiding where?"

"Everything teenagers do is on the internet." I opened two browser windows and pulled up both girls' Instagram feeds. "We need to find the people they had in common."

Strong.

Agile.

Smart.

Like, say, Zayne Davenport?

I clicked Tenley's followers list.

"If nobody objects, I'll take a look at these files and see if there's anything lurking in them that might jump-start my train of thought," Graham said.

Archie nodded. "Be my guest. I'm going down to check in with cyber on those servers. See if Mr. Wooley can shed any more light on this."

I scrolled, stopping on a familiar face in Jessa's followers list.

Shit.

Agile.

Strong.

Troubled.

But . . . the video. The tearing Jim found during Tenley's autopsy. Nicky Richardson loved Tenley. Nicky Richardson was gay. He couldn't seriously have anything to do with this.

Could he?

31

I spent an hour poring over followers and friends lists. Seven guys were common online acquaintances of Jessa and Tenley.

Including, as it turned out, one young Mr. Zayne Davenport.

List in hand, I clicked over to the IAFIS system search to run a criminal background check on each.

A long breath escaped my chest when the *No results found* came up on Nicholas Richardson. Good. I liked that kid.

And he had the only clean record in the bunch.

Three of the boys had moving violations, two had at-fault accidents—and Zayne had an assault charge.

"Fuck. Tell me I didn't miss this," I whispered.

I clicked back to the FBI page and found a date. County courts system. Case located. Judgment: three hundred hours of community service. For a high school kid? What the hell did he do?

I clicked the plus sign next to the case number.

Sealed. Damn.

Graham looked up from his file when I jumped out of the chair again. "What now?"

"I got one guy who knew both girls, and he's got a sealed juvenile court remand that carried three hundred hours of community service, charge listed as assault."

He leaned back in his chair, stretching his arms over his head. "That sounds promising. But we can't get a judge to grant us access to the records until morning at least. It's after dark already."

I walked to the end of the table. Turned and retraced my steps. Damn, damn. I hadn't liked that kid on sight. Why hadn't I checked his background yesterday?

Because the plate check showed he wasn't near the dam Tuesday morning, and what kind of seventeen-year-old rich kid has a criminal record?

More than I'd have thought, in this part of town. I spun back again.

"They're going to make you buy new carpet if you keep that up," Graham said.

I ignored him, biting off the end of my right pinkie nail. I wanted a cigarette. But that would necessitate pausing. We didn't have time to pause.

I stomped one foot, spat the nail into my hand, and dropped it into the wastebasket behind me. "I missed it."

"What?"

"This kid. Zayne. He was at a party with Tenley Monday night. Her friend Nicky said he walked out on the porch to find this guy pawing her."

"Zayne Davenport? That's the boy you were talking about yesterday?"

Every hair on the back of my neck stood up. Didn't I tell him that last night?

I must not have.

"Why? Do you know him?"

Graham didn't reply, just spun the laptop around and pecked at the keys with two fingers.

"What're you doing?" I asked.

"Checking LDIS for a DNA record on your kid."

"Who takes routine samples from juveniles?"

"I do when they're accused of sexual assault."

"Son of a bitch. I knew it!" I slammed one hand onto the tabletop.

I resumed pacing as Graham went on.

"There's a good chance your guy is left-handed: this lab report shows a higher concentration of accelerant on Jessa's right side, and didn't you say Tenley was cut on her right hip?"

I nodded, not pausing.

Graham folded his lips between his teeth, then pulled them apart with a *pop*. "The Davenport kid is a southpaw. That's why Marshall is so hard to defend against on the football field."

My eyes fell shut, Zayne's privileged-little-prick smirk waiting on the backs of both lids. He was right the hell in front of me, and I'd watched him walk away.

I kept moving. "The car wasn't out there, though. I ran his plate and the last camera pickup was near his home before two on Tuesday morning." So I'd blown him off as a narcissistic brat and focused on Simpson.

Wrong move.

What else did I know about Zayne?

"The animals," I muttered, my foot hanging in midair as the gardener's words filtered back to me: *"High pH in the soil."* I pressed one fist to my lips. Jesus, what if Jessa spent last fall in Bethany Davenport's rose garden? The hikers found her remains in February, which was just about when the landscapers would've come to turn the beds for the new season. My foot hit the floor with a *thump* and I charged for the far end of the room. Spun back. Stomped again.

"He was literally in front of my nose, sweaty BO and all," I fumed. "He could've gone home and gotten another car. I'm sure they have half a dozen. Hell, he lives across the street—he could've followed her. Dammit!"

"I'd hardly say right in front of you," Graham drawled, rolling his eyes up to watch me. "And this still offers nothing on how that porn site dude ended up in a tub full of rats."

I waved one hand. "He was afraid Wooley would talk. Maybe he didn't want anyone telling where that video of Jessa came from?" My eyes squeezed shut. "I talked to that kid twenty-four hours and one dead guy ago. Why did I let it go?"

"Stop it, Faith. It's not your fault Ray Wooley is dead." Graham resumed pecking at the keyboard.

"Prove it," I muttered.

"Got him." He flipped the screen back around.

I leaned on the edge of the table with two hands, scanning the police report. "And they sent him straight back to school." I shook my head. "What is going on with our system, Graham? We get these assholes away from decent people so daddy can chat up a judge on the golf course and he can send them right back out?"

Graham's chest puffed out with a slow, deep breath. "Oh, it's not just dad. The mother actually sat in front of me and said, 'My son doesn't have to rape girls to get laid. Look at him.'"

"And of course she wouldn't hear that rape is about power, not sex."

"Nope. Said she had a Stickley dining set in her workshop that needed her full attention and she was in no mood to entertain my slandering her boy." Graham shook his head. "Girl was a nobody by Westlake Hills standards. Goes to Marshall because she lives in an apartment complex on the eastern attendance boundary. She was at school working on a calculus project, went to the bus stop at the corner about dark. Zayne pulls up in his Camaro, offers her a ride home . . ." He raised his eyebrows and let me finish the sentence in my own head.

His description of the victim filtered through Erica Andre's trembly, raw alto. *"My neighbor refinishes pieces for my studio."*

I turned to the list on the whiteboard. Paint thinner.

"Could it be Zayne's voice on the video?" I swallowed hard, not sure I wanted to think a teenager could ringlead something like Archie's description of what happened to Jessa.

"I suppose it could. But why would his voice be familiar to a cop?" Graham's forehead bunched. "What's eating you?"

I reached for my keys, nodding to the board. "Paint thinner. His mother refinishes furniture. I know where he lives. Let's go."

Graham shook his head. "You underestimate these people. The tiniest crack in our case, and they'll have it thrown out and sue the state for slander."

"We don't have time to fill in detail, dammit. What if it is this kid? What if another young woman dies while we're spackling cracks?" I shook my head, Tenley's waxen, bluish face flashing on the backs of my eyelids with every blink. "That's too much risk."

"So we spackle fast. How's your midnight-oil supply? And who owes you a favor?"

"We're out of time. He's getting braver."

"You're assuming it's all the same person, and we don't know that yet," Graham said.

I glared. I knew. Somehow, in my gut, I knew they were connected. They had to be. It was the how I had an issue with.

"It's here, Faith. You know it is just as well as I do. Just slow down and let's find it first." Graham used his best soothe-the-victim voice.

I stared at him for five heartbeats. His lips tipped up at the corners, crinkling the edges of his moss-green eyes.

I could do this.

We could do this.

"Just tonight. Tomorrow morning, cracks or no, I'm picking him up."

Graham tapped the edge of the computer keyboard. "I know the family. Let's call Jim, study the files, and get something stone-solid." His stomach gurgled and he laid a hand on it. "And maybe some food."

"Who says all-nighters are just for college kids?" I turned for the door to fill Archie in, dialing our favorite pizza place from my cell. "I'll get food."

"I'll call my friend at the lab. She didn't answer my texts yet."

He picked up his phone and tapped the screen twice before he put it to his ear. Speed dial.

I strode to the stairs like it didn't bother me.

Halfway down, the girl at the pizza place told me it would be two hours for them to deliver an extra-large pepperoni and a small veggie lover's. I told her I'd make the fifteen-minute trip to pick them up. She said they'd have them ready in twenty.

I paused on the landing as Archie opened the door at the bottom of the steps.

"I think we got him." I grinned around the words, leaning on the rail. "Graham picked up the Marshall High quarterback on a sexual assault last year that was made to very quietly go away. According to Tenley's friend, he was with her Monday night, and Instagram tells me he knew Jessa, too. Plus, his mom refinishes antiques."

"Paint thinner." He double-timed it up to meet me. "Which means he might've killed the porn king to keep him quiet. Holy shit. Nice work. Address?"

I raised one hand. "Graham says these people are very rich and even more callous. I'll spare you the nightmare interview with the mom and just say we need this nailed down, bolted, welded, airtight dead-to-rights before we go anywhere near him or we'll have to live with ourselves when he walks."

"Show me where the bolts are, kiddo."

"Can you check traffic cameras and security footage from both nights for any car registered to Zayne, Bethany, or Quentin Davenport? And maybe check the area the days the girls were discovered, too. He struck me as the type who might like to watch reactions to his handiwork."

Archie smiled. "Almost like you learned from the best or something."

"Almost." I winked.

"I'm on it."

"I'm going to run up to Mario's and grab pizza. I'll check on what Graham's friend at the coroner's office has for us on my way out." I pulled the door to the first floor open and waved him through. "We're going to get him, Arch."

Archie smiled. "You're going to get him, New Girl. I didn't do enough to take any credit, and this arrest will boost your status around here faster than any argument I could mount on your behalf."

I laid a hand on his shoulder. "Thank you. For believing in me."

He patted my fingers and reached for the phone on his desk. "You make it easy, Faith. You always have."

I smiled and squeezed his hand, hoping I could keep that up for at least a few more days.

32

Quiet helps my mind meander through things. And there wasn't a damned thing on the radio to keep my thoughts busy on the way to the pizza place.

Less than twenty-four hours after being exposed as a porn peddler of the vilest variety, Ray Wooley was dead. The press couldn't get enough of it; this was Texas, after all. Rebels and vigilantes aren't criminals to the masses here, they're goddamn folk heroes. I clicked through six radio stations to get to one that wasn't talking about whether Ray's murder was a sin or a public service. And the only station not talking about Ray was playing Florida Georgia Line. "Oh for the love of God." I poked at the knob to click the thing off, my thoughts running back through my day. Tenley's slashed skin. Ray's disgusting apartment.

Parked in front of the pizzeria, I started to turn off the truck and get out. But my hand stopped short of pulling the door handle.

Ray's apartment.

The couch, the trunk, the half-open fridge.

They didn't go with the neat stack of mail or the absolute lack of clutter.

Wooley was certainly a pig of some variety, but he was a computer geek. Structure. Organization. It fit the personality like a neat string of code. He didn't keep his house that messy.

Which meant our killer was hunting something in that dive apartment.

I hung a U-turn at the next intersection and laid on the gas, pointing the truck toward Ray's place.

Inching up his street a few minutes later, my eyes peeled for police cruisers and meat wagons, I was slightly surprised to find it dark and empty.

They'd gone. Already. Not impossible, but weird that they'd close a scene that gruesome so quickly.

I parked in front of the door, picked up my phone, and opened a text to Graham.

Food will be there shortly. I want another look inside Ray's place.

I sent it and slid the phone into my pocket, laying one hand on my sidearm as I nudged the front door open with my foot.

Thank God, someone had disposed of the chicken corpse.

I flattened my back against the wall and crept silently up the stairs, even breathing quietly in the still, heavy darkness. Not surprising for this part of town, an all-day police presence seemed to have cleared the building, so it was just me and the darkness and probably a few hundred roaches, given what Graham said they'd done with the rats.

Ray's door was still taped off, but one side had come loose from the peeling hallway paint, so a low strip hung across the bottom of the doorway while the higher one lay flaccid against the left side of the jamb.

I turned the knob. Stepped over the low-hanging tape. Reached for my phone and clicked on the flashlight.

The stench was mostly gone, the place quiet and relatively neat.

Which just made me more sure something was off.

There should've been a computer. Hell, there should've been a lot of computers. The servers Archie had were taken from his business address, not his home, but a guy who worked in shady websites still should've at least had a laptop in his house. And we didn't find Ray until well after Skye's piece aired, but he had been dead a while at that point. So if he'd hidden his hardware, it was somewhere nearby. Maybe there was a clue as to where.

I shone the light into the corner near the TV, looking for a hiding place. Nothing.

I tiptoed to the kitchen. Three cabinets, fridge, freezer, two drawers: all unremarkable. I checked every one for false bottoms, too. Nothing. Damn.

I turned for the hallway. Turned back. Paused.

My phone buzzed in my hand. I didn't bring the light down to look. It had been a good ten minutes, which meant Graham had put down the files and checked his phone and he was pissed. Understandably—I knew the rules, and going into a murder scene alone wasn't exactly smart. Today, it was necessary, at least to me. We had dead folks piling up, a well-insulated prime suspect, and zero hard evidence. If I'd gone back for Graham, he would've been obligated to call TCSO forensics and ask for permission to go into the apartment, and that would take hours we didn't have.

So I ignored his text, my feet shuffling toward the bathroom door. I didn't want to go in there. But if I was going to hide something, I'd put it in the toilet tank. A computer wouldn't fit, but a drive would.

I pushed the door inward slowly, holding my breath even though I knew the room had been sanitized.

The light bounced off the mirror and hit the tub. Plenty of black metal spots and rust stains, but not a drop of blood.

I scooted to the toilet and lifted the tank lid, set it across the sink, and shone the light down.

Just water and run-of-the-mill toilet innards. Strike two.

I examined the tiny room, but no other hiding places jumped out at me.

The bedroom? I crept back up the hall and peeked around the corner, but before I stepped inside, my eye fell on the cockeyed sofa cushions in the living room.

Light. Mail. Press clippings. Kitchen.

Everything here was orderly. Ray was a computer guy.

Those cushions should've driven him batshit crazy, and he lived alone.

I stepped past the bedroom and crossed the living room quickly and silently.

Pulling the crooked cushion free, I peered underneath.

The thing made out into a bed.

Huh.

I put the first cushion on the floor, added the second to the stack, and pulled on the bed-frame handle.

A full-sized sofa bed unfolded, springs squealing a soft protest. I lifted the foot of the thin, yellowed mattress. Nothing unusual. I moved to the top and lifted there. Still noth—

Wait. I moved the light, and it glinted off something in the dead middle of the head of the bed. Something shinier than the rust-speckled brown bedsprings.

Something that looked a whole lot like the business end of a USB plug. A thumb drive, by the pink plastic lodged in the springs behind it.

"Bingo." The word actually came out on a sigh. Finally, I'd made a good move. My gut wasn't totally dead.

I leaned, reaching for the bit of silvery metal.

My fingers closed around a sliver of the tip. Pinching until I couldn't feel my fingertips, I worked the back end of it through the crisscrossed metal of the sofa bed and twisted my lips to the side when it came loose. I raised it into the light.

A pink sneaker. The end of the little stick of data in my hand was a pink plastic sneaker.

Coincidence?

Not likely. I gripped the thing so tightly the plastic bit into my hand as I turned back for the bedroom. Ray was good at hiding things—and apparently, Tenley Andre was, too.

I took one step toward the hallway and the air shifted in the warm little room. It wasn't a sound so much as a feeling: my gut telling me I wasn't alone.

Shit. I shoved the thumb drive into my pocket and reached for my gun as I pivoted back toward the dark corner behind the sofa on one foot.

I was fast.

Someone else was faster.

I didn't even get my flashlight up high enough to make out a face before something hard and sharp connected with my skull just above my left ear. Darkness rushed in from every side. All I saw as I dropped to the dingy linoleum was a blurry red hoodie and Ray's rust-stained walls.

33

Sirens.

The high, ear-grating wail filtered through the darkness first. Somebody had hit me, and now the cavalry was nearby—so my best shot at seeing another sunrise was to get to them. I stiffened my abs, trying to sit up before I even managed to drag my eyes open.

A warm hand landed in the center of my chest, holding me down. I landed two quick jabs to the arm attached to it and tried to roll away, but my stupid body wouldn't catch up to my brain.

"Whoa. Easy there, partner."

Graham? I cracked my eyelids and squinted.

Even the dim light from Ray's single-bulb overhead fixture sent an ice pick clean through my temple, but I blinked and tried to focus anyway.

He was really there.

I slumped back to the floor, groaning when my head landed a little too hard. My fingers moved into a sticky pool around my ear. Blood.

"Ouch," I whispered.

Graham's long fingers smoothed a lock of wayward hair out of my face, his green eyes a stormy combination of anxious and pissed off when I could focus on them. "I found something," I said by way of a peace offering, reaching for my pocket. "He had it hidden well, too."

"Nothing is worth you almost getting yourself killed." He shook his head, his fingers closing around my hand. "Pairs, Faith. You know the rules are the rules for a reason. Did you get a look at whoever was here with you?"

I didn't dare try to move my head. "No. Red hoodie. About my height. That's all I got."

I swiped a finger through my pocket. Then two. Reached for the other one.

"What is it?"

"The thumb drive. It's not here."

His forehead wrinkled. "Thumb drive?"

"I found it. A pink sneaker. Like the kind of thing someone would give a runner."

I tried again to sit up, and again my head protested, this time by sending waves of roiling nausea surging through my middle. I locked my jaw, breathing through my nose. One upchuck was enough for today.

"It's not here." I patted my pockets, trying and failing to look around when moving my head just made a kaleidoscope of color explode in my left peripheral. "Did I drop it?"

Graham laid a restraining hand on my shoulder. "I'll look. You be still."

He stood as a team of paramedics rolled a gurney in the door. I tried to follow him with my eyes as they descended on me, but they cared more about my bleeding head wound than my missing piece of evidence.

I tucked my hands under a sore hip and closed my eyes as they poked and prodded and conferred. I needed stitches. Because my face was involved, they assumed I'd want a plastic surgeon—maybe it's vain, but I kind of did. A really good one. But not badly enough to consider calling my mother.

Nobody wanted to let me walk downstairs. Including Graham, who eyed me so sternly when I opened my mouth to argue that I snapped it shut.

I shouldn't have come alone. The odds were in my favor to walk in and out without incident, but fate also didn't seem to be my friend this week. Fine. I let the medics scoot me onto the gurney and settled my head against the pillow. The cool softness did feel nice.

"I'm sorry." I said the words to my twisting hands, fidgety in my lap, but Graham knew I was talking to him.

"Why didn't you just come back and get me?"

"I had a hunch. Figured what forensics didn't know wouldn't hurt anything, and I'd be in and out quick and then go get dinner and it wouldn't be a big deal."

"You have a way of turning the ordinary into a huge deal." He smiled when I glanced up at him. "I'm just glad you thought to text me—it was easy enough to find you when you took too long. I wish I'd been in time to get ahold of whoever did this, though."

He climbed into the back of the ambulance with me. "Scared the hell out of me, when I walked in there and saw all that blood and you weren't moving." His voice was low, hoarse. He blinked double-time.

I patted his hand without moving my head. "Thanks for coming to look for me."

I paused. How long was I out? "What time is it?"

He glanced at his watch. "Eleven fifteen. It took a bit for you to come to, even with me poking at you."

The paramedic picked up my arm to start an IV, and Graham dropped my fingers.

"We'll be at the hospital in no time, Officers," she said. "This is deep. You're lucky your friend came when he did—you might've bled to death in there otherwise. But they'll have you back out, good as new, in just a few days."

I smiled a thank-you at her, my eyes sliding to Graham. Could've bled to death. For what? "Did you find it?"

He shook his head, his lips pinched into a thin line between his teeth.

"What about your friend at the lab? Did you get ahold of her?"

"She never answered me. But I do have something." He held up his phone. "Bank records came in at four thirty. Damned spam filter."

I took the phone from him, squinting at the blinding white screen.

"Does that say a hundred grand?" My eyebrows tried to move and my cut protested. "Tenley scammed a hundred thousand dollars out of her own parents?" I paused. Ray. Simpson. Maybe all the money didn't come from her folks. "What the hell did she need that kind of cash for?"

"Something she was doing Monday, it seems." Graham pointed at the top line. "All but twenty dollars was withdrawn just before lunchtime."

I handed the phone back, shaking my head. "She was planning something big, this girl."

"And jumping off the dam is free. Time to call her folks?"

"I hate to bother them, but I don't see where we have a choice. It'll wait until morning, though, given my current situation."

I would give the Andres their answer, even if I had to burst their perfect-kid bubble to get there. In the long run, they'd find more peace knowing the truth. That was some tiny measure of comfort.

A bigger dose: if my gut was right, that little Davenport prick would rot in a cell for half his life. There wasn't a rug big enough for daddy's friends to sweep a double-murder rap under. And if he had a red hoodie, assaulting an officer doesn't get you much sympathy from your average Texas judge.

So I'd almost gotten myself killed, and maybe handed our big bad whatever got Ray killed as a bonus. But Graham had proof that Tenley was in possession of a whole lot of cash Monday night. Cash that wasn't on her or in her bag when she was found.

I closed my eyes, the fingers of my free hand tightening around the sheet.

I didn't have a few days to recuperate. The case was getting more urgent —and more personal—by the hour. Some stitches and a few Band-Aids were in order, because we had a killer to catch.

34

Staring smack into the sun when a freshly sewn head wound that's less than twelve hours old isn't any fun at all. I'd sooner be shot again, and that's saying something, because that bullshit hurts.

I pulled a ragged Astros cap from the glove box in my truck and tucked it low over my eyes, still wishing my sunglasses were darker. *Thud. Thud. Thud.* My stitches throbbed in time to the truck's engine, the Tylenol I'd swallowed on my way out of the DoubleTree not even slowing it down. The doctor had given me a small bottle of Vicodin on my way out of the ER, but I disliked pills as a general rule, and narcotics scared me. Besides, I needed everything firing on as many cylinders as I could muster if I was going to talk to Nicky Richardson.

He was the reason for the glaring brightness currently producing multicolored spots in my left peripheral. Sitting in his Mercedes convertible in the school parking lot, drumming two fingers on the steering wheel and looking for all the world like he'd never smile again.

Which made me smile more than I had in days.

Serials don't feel remorse for their crimes. They get a kick out of the chase, the defeat, the kill. They don't mourn their victims. So Nicky's soulful, sad gaze was the best evidence I could've hoped for that he hadn't done anything wrong.

But he did know both dead girls. Which meant I had to ask a few hard questions. The way to do that without causing myself a lot of grief was to catch him between home and school. Since I was all stocked up on grief and difficult situations this week, there I sat, staring into the sun.

He moved one hand toward his door, and mine followed. Finally. The bell rang twenty minutes ago.

He paused. Let his head drop to the top of the steering wheel. He was still for three blinks before his shoulders started heaving. Big, hollow breaths that don't feel like they're doing their job. The kind where you know your lungs are full, but you still can't breathe.

Poor kid. But . . . thank God.

I opened my door and crossed the lot, the sun mercifully disappearing behind a cloud. It took a few beats for him to notice me, his eyes popping wide when he looked up. The door opened and he scrambled to his feet. "Officer." He swallowed hard. "What can I do for you today?"

I nodded. "Can we just talk for a moment before you go to your first class?"

"Of course." He put out his hand, gesturing for me to lead the way to a shaded concrete bench. I obliged, patting the cool surface so he'd join me. No easy way around it, so I just asked.

"How did you know Jessa DuGray, Nicky?" I asked.

I watched his face for cues.

Not a twitch, not a flinch. He looked me dead in the eyes as the corners of his lips ghosted up before they fell again. "Tenley. She was the one who knew Jessa. Or I guess really, Tenley's mom did. But that's how I met her. She was sweet. Cute. A little quiet." His brow furrowed. "It's weird that T is gone less than a year later, isn't it?" His hands flew to his curls, palms obscuring his forehead. "My God. You don't think she knew something about what happened to Jessa, do you? I mean, they said she jumped, right?"

I tried to force words out over the throbbing above my left ear, but my mind was having trouble processing his sentence and forming a reply. "Ten . . . Tenley? Knew Jessa?" It even sounded half-addled to me.

He didn't seem to notice, his head shaking. "She had to have jumped," he repeated.

I blinked. Knew better than to shake my head. "Nicky, exactly how did Tenley come to know Jessa?"

He dropped his hands back to his lap. "She was an artist. Won some kind of contest Erica's firm sponsored for Texas high school seniors. So when she came here to go to school, Erica offered her a sort of internship where she helped out with stuff. T hung out at her mom's office sometimes, and they talked. They weren't best friends or anything, but Tenley liked her well enough. Said Jessa was into older guys and it worried her. She was too trusting, T said, and maybe she was right. She followed me on every site like the first time she ever met me, and I followed back because it's a dick move to not follow a sweet girl just because you don't want to screw her, you know? But then she disappeared."

I pinched the bridge of my nose between two fingers. "Jessa was a business major."

Nicky nodded. "She wasn't allowed to study art. Told us her dad said she couldn't waste her free ride on a useless degree. So she figured she'd learn business and be a designer, like Erica. Her dad sounded like a real douche. Maybe that's why we hit it off, me and her." That brought a twisted smile to his stubbly face.

Intern. Artist. Decorator. Learn the business.

I stood. "Nicky, do you know if Jessa ever spent any time with Zayne Davenport's mother?"

He nodded. "She liked helping out with the refinished furniture. Especially when people wanted funky stuff with bright colors."

Holy shit.

I patted his shoulder. "I'm so sorry for your loss. Again."

I cursed the morning traffic every inch of the way back to the hotel and flipped my computer open what seemed like a lifetime later. How could I have missed this? I pulled out my notes and ran back through every interview.

Erica didn't say they knew Jessa.

But I didn't ask her, either. She was mourning her daughter, and the chances they would know Archie's cold-case victim were too slim to even register. Days of looking for a way these girls were connected. "And they were friends," I muttered, plugging my phone into the laptop and pulling up Tenley's passwords. Instagram. Snapchat. Twitter. They were on each other's friends list everywhere. Even last night, I'd focused on looking for guys they both knew and just big fat not noticed.

Hiding in plain sight. Dammit.

The magic rock was at least in this field. I could feel it, a tiny electrical surge skating through my gut. I was finally close.

I grabbed a piece of paper and started a chart. Jessa knew Erica because of her career. She knew Tenley through Erica. She knew Nicky through Tenley.

Back to Erica. Then Bethany Davenport. Then Zayne. The paint thinner on her back. "Because she was in his mother's studio when he attacked her." I said it right out loud.

My gut said yes.

I just needed proof, and that was the tricky part. Bethany Davenport would lie through her caps till she went to her grave to keep her kid out of trouble, and her husband would make sure it worked.

Erica. She was the common denominator here, and if I've ever met a mother who loved a child, it was her. I clicked the pad to wake up my screen. How far back did she and Bethany go? Was there anything in a shared past we could leverage to make her tell the truth?

I googled Erica first.

More than a thousand hits. I scrolled.

Paused.

It was nothing. She was a decorator. Letting the work speak for itself.

Right?

There were no photos of her. Not one, on the whole internet. Rooms she'd done by the dozens, from every angle. I stopped, hovering the arrow over one of a peach-and-silver bedroom.

Charity's bedroom, one I remembered as gold and white.

Erica redecorated my sister's room at the mansion for Governor Holdswaithe and his ditzy little trophy wife. That shouldn't make me angry. I had no love for that endless tomb of a house—hell, I didn't like living there when I had to. But sacred spaces aren't supposed to be reimagined. I kept scrolling.

Not so much as a snapshot of Erica. My mother would have definitely told her that with her looks, that was bad business. Erica clearly took pride in her appearance. And my mother didn't take kindly to having advice ignored. Another place where two and two was some sideways exponential, theoretical version of four. An alternate-universe four.

An alternate-universe Erica Andre?

The guy. The one in the shabby clothes with the grease-laden hair who looked like he'd walked up on a ghost outside Lola's. What had he called her?

Sammy Jo.

What if he wasn't high or half-crazy?

I needed a maiden name. Tax records—I clicked to the Travis County property database and punched in the Andres' address.

The house was in Brent's name. Just his.

I tapped a finger on the edge of the keyboard. Maybe that's why she stayed even when she knew about his girlfriend—but why had a woman like Erica Andre agreed to that in the first place?

Because mortgage companies have a way of dragging skeletons out of the deepest closets, maybe?

I went to the marriage records next. Travis County had nothing. Bexar County had nothing. I searched half the state before I found them in the Harris County database. October wedding, twenty years ago this coming fall. Brent Ryan Andre and Erica Louise Tenley.

I clicked the search bar again. *Erica Tenley & Texas.*

Twenty-three hits.

All of them news articles from this week.

Not a single link more than five days old. Every one with Erica's name highlighted as Texas track phenom Tenley Andre's mother. No trace of Erica before she was Tenley's mother: no high school sports articles, one-off mentions in the small-town paper's list of honor roll students . . . nothing.

Damn. If I had a good old-fashioned print to run, it would be faster, but processing grieving parents is usually frowned upon. And unnecessary. So I'd have to do this the sneaky, time-consuming modern way.

I cleared the search field and typed *Sammy Jo & Texas.* Two hundred links came up. Nothing to do but start sifting.

I scrolled, reading, until my eyes were about ready to fall out of my face, then clicked to the images.

Nothing. Nothing for pages.

And all of a sudden, I found her.

Long hair. Frizzy, darker. Hollow cheeks. But the guy was right: those eyes. Erica's bright baby blues were hard to miss, and looking closely, the nose and the smile finished the picture. This girl was unmistakably Erica Andre. I'd stake my badge on that. I clicked the link to the article that accompanied the picture.

February, thirty years ago. Sammy Jo Felton died in a car accident when the SUV she was driving flipped over on a narrow road and exploded. I magnified the photo on the screen.

It was Erica. It had to be. I'd never seen relatives with a resemblance like this.

But Erica did say her mother died "a long time ago." In a car crash, maybe?

I double-checked the date. The math didn't work for the girl in this photo to be Erica's mother. The article said Sammy Jo was fifteen, and thirty years ago that would've been right about Erica's same age. I scanned the rest of the article. No other passengers mentioned.

It had to be her.

"She reinvented herself," I murmured to the desk lamp. "Just like she remade Charity's room, she remade her life."

But what had she run from? The news story in front of me didn't tell me anything about Sammy Jo other than that she was supposed to be dead.

I pulled out my phone and snapped a photo of the screen. Time for some of these skeletons to come out into the light.

35

I didn't call anyone on my way to the Andre house, mostly because I wanted time to think up the most inoffensive way I could muster to ask Erica if her entire life had been built around one massive lie.

Stopped under a tree on the Davenports' side of the road, I stared at the end of Erica's driveway. I couldn't seriously go up there and accuse this woman of knowing or even hiding something about her child's death, could I?

Three long blinks gave my eyes solace from the unrelenting sunshine, and I kicked the door of the truck open, adrenaline making quick work of masking my headache. Hard questions, and often being the person who asks them, are part of this job. I got over worrying about what people think of me years ago. I just needed her to tell me the truth.

The only question left concerned the best route to that: kindness or shock value?

I could be sweet and soft-spoken and ask her if there was anything she'd like to share with me to help Tenley—that sort of emotional plea is big with grieving relatives. Or I could go for shock. Wait for Erica to open the door, call her "Sammy Jo" or "Miss Felton" and watch her reaction.

I still hadn't decided when I rounded the pillar at the end of the driveway and spotted Erica. But she didn't see me.

She was too busy trying to cram a .22 into her tiny little eggplant Prada bag.

I scooted behind the pillar and stared, even pulling my sunglasses down the bridge of my nose to get a better view.

She wriggled the gun around, zipped the bag, and climbed into her Jag.

I made myself dizzy sprinting back to my truck, let her have half a block, and followed.

Granted, folks around here are about as likely to have a handgun as folks in Seattle are to have an umbrella. But Erica Andre had a place for everything. And that bag didn't have room for a handgun.

Where she was headed with it—and who she intended the bullets in it for—might just be Archie's elusive magic rock.

36

Two hours and about a hundred speeding violations later, Erica Andre got out of her car at a run-down beer joint at least ten exits past the ass end of nowhere.

I watched from the far side of the motel across the dusty two-lane road as she disappeared through a screen door holding on by a single hinge. Checking the clock, I shook my head. A Westover Hills decorator to the rich and powerful didn't belong in a wood-and-metal shack with a flashing neon sign out front that advertised OLD EER, thanks to a short circuit feeding the *C* and the *B*.

But the young woman from the news article—Sammy Jo, with her frizzy, unkempt hair and faded, ill-fitting clothing—she might.

Classy. Poised. Elegant. Erica Andre was everything Sammy Jo Felton never could've dreamed of being.

I'm not what I appear to be, she'd written in that email to Stella Connolly.

She wasn't there to drink, because she could drink on the quiet in a hundred places closer to home. Places she wouldn't need a handgun.

Which left two options I could see: She wanted to hire someone to avenge her daughter's death and knew this was where to find such people but wasn't stupid enough to go unarmed. Or she thought her past had caught up to Tenley and was looking to take a pound of someone's flesh in return.

I had to get in there. Preferably without Erica seeing me.

I stepped out of the truck and circled wide around the motel, crossing the road a good football field away from the bar. Skirting scattered yucca, I found the back door, and recoiled when my tug on the handle moved the entire wall. The whole damned building seemed in serious danger of crashing into a heap of rotted lumber any moment.

I twisted the knob harder. Locked.

Dammit.

I paced a short stretch of the dirt off the stoop.

The front door was open, of course, but my gut said it was more important to let this play out, for the moment, than to have Erica Andre in my line of sight.

I just needed to make sure she didn't leave.

I ambled halfway back to the front of the building, stopping when Erica's car came into view. Nothing to do but wait. If anybody'd tried to tell me yesterday I'd spend this afternoon staking out Tenley Andre's mother at a decrepit beer joint spitting distance from the Mexican border, I would've choked on one of Archie's peppermints laughing. There's no such thing as a typical homicide investigation, but this one was pulling levels of weird I'd scoff at TV writers over.

Shading my eyes against the glaring South Texas sunshine, I dug a handful of Tylenol from my pocket and swallowed it dry. My head throbbed harder in response, the stench of booze and cigarettes seeping from the wall next to me strong enough to make me step sideways.

If Erica was indeed an alcoholic, she had to be dying a little every minute she spent in there. Not much would make a person face those sorts of demons.

I'd seen the anxiety in her every jerky move when she climbed into her perfectly polished luxury car back in Austin. Erica thought she knew something.

I stared at the car. A little dusty, but otherwise spotless, not a hint of a scratch or dent. Like all those magazine spreads—room after gorgeous, flawless room—that had filled my screen this morning. Erica Andre had dedicated decades of meticulous care to building her daughter the kind of world where dreams don't get cut short by violence—they come true.

Tenley's world wasn't supposed to include the sort of people who murdered teenage girls.

But the longer I stood there, the surer I'd bet Sammy Jo's had.

So who or what was important enough to bring Sammy Jo home after all these years?

The screen around front slammed twice in quick succession, and Erica's SUV engine roared to life, tires spinning in the dirt lot as she slammed the gas in reverse.

The second she turned left out of the lot, I hurried to the front corner of the building. Spotted a skinny girl with bright-purple hair and a waitress's apron jiggling a key in the driver's door of an ancient Honda Civic.

"Excuse me, miss?" I smiled when she looked up.

"I don't want no trouble," she said, her eyes on my badge. "I just need another pen out of my bag."

"There was a blonde woman in the bar just now. She would've seemed out of place here." I kept the smile in place. Easy. Friendly. "I'm afraid she might be in over her head, though I'm not exactly sure how."

The girl snorted, rattling the tiny silver stud in her nose. "You can say that shit again. I never seen a classy broad like that in real life. What in hell she wants with Lenny Winchester is beyond me, but it ain't nothing good. Not when it concerns that lowlife jackass."

Damn. I turned to look back at the street.

Erica's car was gone.

"Where can I find him?"

She popped her gum. "He lives in the trailer park just back there." She pointed over my shoulder. "Other side of the field."

I was back at the end of the building before she stopped talking. Waving a thank-you, I took off across the field, my eyes on the taillights of Erica's Jag, three trailers in. This woman might have a whole figurative cemetery lurking in her closet, but I could sort that out later. Right now, I needed to make sure this Lenny person didn't end up in a literal one by way of Erica's .22.

37

Erica stopped at the mailboxes, and I ignored the ice pick piercing my head with every heavy footfall as I ran for a leaning telephone pole that would hide me while I kept an eye on her. She pulled something metal from her purse and stuck it into the front of the mailbox. I kept moving, hoping she'd stay busy with that long enough for me to get out of sight.

Erica came up with an envelope just as I flattened myself against the back side of the rusty-nail-ridden wood and pulled out my phone to text Graham. *Can you see what criminal records has on a Lenny or Leonard Winchester in Laredo and Austin?* Send.

I snuck a glance around the edge of the pole at Erica, who was wrestling with the envelope like she wasn't sure how to open it. Or didn't really want to, maybe.

What the hell business did she have with mail from a questionable-at-best collection of mobile homes in this dust bucket?

My phone buzzed in my hand. Graham: *Guy is a small-time dealer. Once meth, lately prescriptions from south of the border. Why do we care?*

I didn't know. Yet.

I stuffed the phone back in my pocket as Erica pulled a sheet of bright-white paper from the shredded envelope.

A gun. A drug dealer. And now a letter. Was Erica Andre dealing drugs?

There was no getting closer without being seen, so I ignored my protesting head and squinted. Erica was staring at the letter in her hand and mouthing something I couldn't make out.

She dropped the paper and the envelope in the dusty dirt before she ducked back into the car and kept moving. I gave her a ten-second head start, abandoned my hiding place, and sprinted low across the field, snatching up the paper as it began to flutter in a light breeze.

Dear Mr. Winchester, Thanks so much for your support of the Lady Cougar track team. Please find enclosed your tickets to the state championship meet. We look forward to seeing you there.

Signed by Sarah Bauer.

Oh shit.

I scanned the trailer park. Found Erica's Jag at the last dwelling on the right.

She opened the door and stood, pulling the pistol from her bag as she turned for the front steps.

* * *

The sky had started to lighten the barest bit, going just indigo at the horizon, when the angel stood. Teetering on the brink of disaster, she leaned forward. His breath stopped.

Yes. She was strong enough. Brave enough.

But was he? That was the never-quite-satisfied question.

Closing his eyes, he was sure. He was ready. He needed this.

He could do this.

Go time.

A small squeak, the barest hint of a noise, as he pushed the door open.

The angel spun on one heel.

Stepped forward.

He could see her. Already almost feel her warmth, her breath.

But she couldn't see him.

"I didn't know anyone else was out here," she called. "You're not an ax murderer or anything, right?"

He waited, standing fast in the shadows, no answer forming on his lips. He would never, ever lie. Not to her.

She spun back, sprinting all of two steps before panic sent her crashing into the gravel.

The monster roared, willing his feet to move before he was ready. He'd watched her run. She was fast. It wasn't sporting to chase when she wasn't on her game.

But the monster didn't care. It craved. Demanded.

And this time, it won.

The angel scrambled to her feet, turning to glance over her shoulder, her legs pumping hard. That was it. Strong. Fast. Run, angel, run. He wanted to say it out loud, but the monster wouldn't have it. His legs gobbled up the gravel between them, broad shoulders barely heaving with the effort.

He was so close, he could stretch a hand out and touch her.

His fingers brushed her silky hair, streaming behind her.

She screamed. Turned.

And stopped.

His hand dropped back to his side.

His angel blinked.

Turned around.

"How did you know I'd be here?"

38

I ran until I couldn't see, the pain in my head forcing me to slow down about halfway to Erica's car.

By the time I made it to the unstable near corner of a faded-green single-wide, Erica had used her pistol to force the greasy little man we'd seen outside the coffeehouse to let her inside.

Lenny and Sammy Jo, together again.

I caught my breath. Slid my back along the wall.

Thanked my God and my sister that they didn't shut the door.

"What the fuck is with you rich people?" Lenny had a whiny tenor to his voice. "No respect for anybody's time but your own. Richardson send you, too? Because that fucker owes me a thousand bucks, and no tickets to any sports bullshit are going to make up for it, neither, so you can tell him to pay up or forget it."

I scooted closer to the steps. Was there a single person in Tenley's life not up to their ass or eyeballs in secrets? What the hell would Coach Richardson want with a small-time South Texas smack dealer?

Shit. My fingers folded into a fist. Tenley wasn't taking drugs—but was she dealing them? A hundred thousand dollars: that was serious cash. What if we'd been looking under the wrong rocks altogether and this was just another dope deal gone bad?

"Unless of course you want to talk about working off his debt, maybe. I'm sure you and me, we could come to some terms."

"You are just as disgusting as you were thirty years ago." Erica's voice was cold. "You have one minute to tell me what the hell you did to my daughter and make your peace with Jesus, Lenny, so you'd better talk fast."

I scrambled to a window and stood on tiptoe to peer inside through a layer of grime. Lenny stumbled over a futon, sprawling onto the faded Navajo-print fabric, rubbing his eyes and snatching a pair of drugstore reading glasses off the nearby TV tray.

"I knew that was you, Sammy Jo," he crowed, his concern about the pistol seeming to dissipate for the moment. "We thought you was . . . Well, I mean, I guess you truly did die and get yourself reborn up there in the city. I had myself a feeling there wasn't no car wreck that could take out Lara Felton's little girl. Your momma walked straight up out the fires of hell itself, I swear it."

Erica's face stayed blank. "You would know, wouldn't you, Lenny?" was all she said before she shook the gun. "My daughter."

"Beautiful girl, just like her momma. My boy Ray, he went for the big time in Austin, got hisself in with the basketball coach at the college up there. Sent me a newspaper picture of this girl the coach said he was doing, and I thought I was looking back in time. She is carved straight out of you, that kid. But she's a runner, the paper said. Got me to wondering." Lenny's eyes darted around the room. Erica held the gun steady. I scooted as close to the steps as I could without losing my line of sight. "If she was, you know, mine or whatever."

We both stared at Erica from two different angles, my mouth popping into a disgusted little O.

She didn't even blink, her lip curling at one end. "I never met anyone else, even any of my mother's dealers, who could talk about fathering a child by way of raping a sleeping teenager like it was an everyday occurrence." Her finger twitched on the trigger. "She was mine. My supernova. Nothing about her ever had anything to do with you or this place, I made sure of that. And if you took her from me, so help me, I will send you to hell right here and now."

I moved for the door as Lenny's eyes went wide when he put that together and figured out she really meant to kill him.

"I ain't never laid eyes on your kid except in pictures, hand to God." Lenny raised his left hand, then his right. "I told Richardson I used to tear up the track . . . He said he'd get me tickets to watch his girl run. I ain't never seen any, though. Why don't you just have a seat and let's talk."

Her finger eased off. I paused.

I studied Lenny as Erica brandished the gun and shouted. He was half-wasted. Sleepy.

Not lying.

"You expect me to believe Darren Richardson would so much as speak to you?" Erica tightened her hands around the butt of the gun, moving to stand between my window and her target.

Lenny's voice got a little higher, his words a little faster.

"That prick speaks to me, all right. Me and Ray both. But he always wants something for nothing. Thinks his shit don't stink, that guy."

A fair assessment, when you got right down to it.

Erica waved the gun. "What would Darren Richardson want with home-cooked meth? And why would he need to get it from clear the hell out here?"

"I ain't made meth in years." Lenny rolled his eyes. "Shit blows people to kingdom come. One burner left on too long and Hustler was a crispy-fried redneck. You remember. I got my friends south of here. A lot more money these days in selling prescription shit from Mexico to people here who can't afford our pharmacies."

"Yeah. You look to be rolling in cash."

"I do all right." His tone got defensive and Erica took a step forward with the gun, forcing his hands higher. "Chill out, baby. Just saying I'm saving for retirement, not getting any younger or nothing, and the fucking Border Patrol gets greedier with their cut all the time."

Right then, I didn't give two shits what Lenny was selling or who he was paying to look the other way. Tenley was all I cared about. Tenley and what this guy might know about how she died.

"Richardson." Erica shook the pistol.

Yes, thank you.

"Quit swinging that thing around before you kill somebody," Lenny grumbled. "I don't fucking know. OxyContin and Zyprexa. Massive quantities of the painkiller and, like, normal prescription ones of the antidepressant. I figure he's giving his players the OC. Said he needed the other for his kid. Something about making the boy right in the head." His voice dropped to a whisper. "Apparently Mr. Macho Basketball Man has a homo for a son. Said he had to give the business to the kid's girlfriend because the boy couldn't even get it up for the hottest girl in school. I stay quiet. Not my place to judge other people's life choices, you know?"

There it was again.

Hottest girl in school.

Give the business.

Girl the coach was doing.

Surely.

Not.

I was so busy trying to turn that story right side up I didn't hear the Corvette stop behind me. Brent Andre charged right past me, his foot sending the rusty metal door flying and the interior of the trailer into chaos.

Erica's hands set to shaking even before the door crashed into the wall behind her.

"Whoa, whoa, brother, I didn't touch her." Lenny climbed to the back of the futon.

"Erica, what in the name of God are you doing?" Brent's voice boomed in the tiny space, and I opened my mouth to tell them all to stop, but it was too late. Erica jumped.

Her finger flexed on the trigger.

A flash of fire, a roar ripping through the afternoon, and Lenny disappeared behind the futon.

39

If only the damned headache would go away.

If he could find a way around the pounding, make everything slow down so he could think. Breathe. Remember.

It was like that more often than not these days. When he woke up.

Time lost. Foggy dreams floating around. So much clutter, so much noise, and he was always so tired, no matter how long he slept.

He fumbled on the night table for the remote. Clicked the TV to life. Watched the perky weather girl on channel two say another perfect Texas spring day was well underway and make a joke about sunscreen being easier to find than water.

Water. Sitting up, he reached into the night table and pulled out a bottle. He twisted the top free and gulped greedily, his eyes falling on the amber bottles on the table.

He needed his meds. Didn't want them. Hated feeling like a bystander watching his own life go by. But he was supposed to take them. He shook one out and swallowed it with the rest of the water. Plunked two more into an empty Altoids tin for later.

He knew they were supposed to make him better, but lately no matter how many he took, everything was just blurry. Like a bad dream, and too many of those danced just the other side of the noise already.

He dropped the bottle. Rubbed his temple with his free hand. Stood and stum-

bled toward the bathroom, trying to remember if the medicine cabinet had been restocked with Advil.

Nope.

Spinning from the sink, he turned the water on as hot as it would go and leaned both hands on the counter as the shower warmed up.

He stared into the mirror until it disappeared behind the steam, the scars criss-crossing his hips and thighs making a pattern from white to pink to angry red and new, the raised tissue far more prominent than his smooth skin. Opening the veins. Letting blood flow. Cleansing. Freeing. God's will.

Surely someday it would start to work like it did for the others. To heal his broken soul. His splintered brain.

Water spattered the tile, the gentle whisper drowning the never-ending noise in his head. If he could just think. If everything could just calm down for a minute.

Stepping into the shower, warmth sluicing across every fried nerve ending, he saw another angry red welt, this one wide and flat and streaking across his forearm.

He ran a hand over it, wincing.

That wasn't his knife.

Did somebody scratch him and he didn't notice?

At the party, maybe?

Guess so.

He leaned his forehead against the cool tile, the water heating his neck and shoulders. Everything was tight. Sore. Like his muscles had been overused, except they hadn't. He'd be sorry, come August, if he fell out of shape now.

He just needed the headaches to stop.

Slow, deep breaths. Don't chase the dreams. Don't fight the noise. *Just the sound of the shower spray and his own slow, even breathing.*

A hundred gallons of water later, he straightened, reaching for the shampoo and scrubbing his head, his face, the rest of him.

He stepped out and wiped steam from the mirror, flexing his biceps and pecs, studying the way his muscles moved as he brushed his teeth.

Back in the bedroom, he pulled a polo over his head and slipped his shorts on, then grabbed another water bottle and drained the contents.

Water always made everything better.

The shower, the lake, the tears—they delivered peace.

His clock said he was late. Again. The newscast was the lunchtime one, not the morning. Damn.

He stuffed two binders into his backpack and grabbed the remote to shut off the TV when the anchor's voice stopped him cold.

Turning up the volume, he sat down on the bed, his head shaking slowly as a photo took the announcer's place on the screen.

Bottomless eyes the color of a latte.

Skin that shimmered like moonbeams.

Flowing, perfectly golden hair.

"Remains discovered by a jogger at the foot of Mansfield Dam."

Darkness rushed both sides of his face, the TV disappearing into the void.

It couldn't be.

But the darkness receded and it was all still there, the perky weather girl shaking her head as the anchor said the sheriff's office would have more information soon and to download the News2 *app for breaking alerts.*

He hitched the bag over one shoulder, jogging down the stairs. Outside, he knelt and ran his fingertips across the fine white dust on his tires.

The drum in his head shattered into a thousand sharp, stabbing pieces, his heart taking off for the races this time, too.

Where had the car been, and why couldn't he remember how it got there and back?

40

I took all three rickety steps in one jump.

Brent Andre lunged for his wife.

Grabbing the barrel of the .22, he wrenched it from Erica's limp grip. Brent locked the safety before he stuck the gun in the back of his pants and strode to the other side of the futon, barely grunting in my direction as he leaned out the ripped window screen. Both of us eyed the greasy little man on the ground outside, still but not bleeding.

I glanced back at Erica.

"Did I kill him?" she whispered.

"You don't even sound too bothered about that." Brent rounded on his wife. "Who the hell is this person, and why do you know him?"

Scanning the wall, I spied a dime-sized hole in the glass.

"You appear to have killed the window, unless people shoot up this place on the regular." I cast an eye around the bare little room. A trunk served as a table at the far end of the futon. There was a TV that had probably shown first-run episodes of *Sanford and Son* on the opposite wall and a plastic folding lawn chair with a TV tray in front of it opposite the stove. A door next to the half-sized fridge led to what looked to be a bathroom.

"He said . . . he said Tenley . . ." Erica caught her breath in huge gulps, her shoulders shaking.

Brent stepped toward her, reaching a hand out but furrowing his brow over where to land it.

I cleared my throat. "Mr. Andre? What are you doing here, sir?"

"I needed to talk to her." He threw his hands up. "This morning, last night . . . I was thinking about what she said at Lola's. About me, you know, having an affair. And I needed to tell her some things. She wouldn't answer my calls, so I tracked her cell phone here."

Not bad detective work for a pilot. I nodded.

"What is she on about?" He cocked his head to one side. "Tenley didn't know places like this existed. I didn't think Erica did, either, for that matter."

I wasn't touching that one. His wife definitely wasn't what she seemed, but that story was not mine to tell.

Erica shook her head. "Darren. Drugs. Said Tenley was having sex . . ."

"With Nicky? I thought she said Nicky was gay?" Brent ran a hand through his hair.

"Darren. Darren was buying drugs. From Lenny." Erica waved a hand at the window. "Said Nicky wouldn't have sex with Tenley, so he had to."

Brent closed his eyes, balling his hands into fists at his sides. "Who had to what? Why the hell are you here, Erica?"

Erica's shoulders vibrated with a hitching breath. "I saw him, just yesterday." She gestured to the window as her eyes darted to me. "It got me thinking. About old scores and who might want to settle them. About why he would be in Austin. About how something like this could happen in our world. I thought . . . I thought he hurt Tenley. So I came here to kill him."

Brent eyed his wife like she'd lost her mind. "I don't feel like I'm any closer to understanding what's going on here."

Probably not, but I was pretty sure I had this part straight, at least. I turned back to the window. "Are you going to live?" I called.

"She broke my fucking ankle, man." Lenny's voice floated up.

"Consider it karma." My phone started buzzing and I backed toward the door, pulling it from my hip pocket. Austin number, but not one I recognized.

Brent pulled in a slow breath. "Officer? Can you possibly fill me in on what the hell has happened here?"

Erica raised her face, tears streaming a river down her cheeks and off her chin. "I'm so sorry, Brent. It's all my fault."

"While I'm not entirely sure of much right now, somehow I doubt that's true." Brent's voice softened.

"I was wrong, I was wrong every time. About all of it. And now our baby is gone and everything . . . The life I built so carefully. It's all trash. Dust." Erica stomped a foot, her stiletto punching right through the floor. "Broken."

They didn't need me for this part. I brandished the phone and smiled before I clicked the "Talk" button and stepped carefully back to the ground outside. Nothing here would tell me anything else useful about Tenley or Jessa or why they were dead. Which meant it would wait.

"McClellan," I said into the phone.

"Hi. I um . . ." The words were choked, but I was pretty sure it was a man. A relatively young one. "I need some help and you said I could call you and I didn't know who . . . I mean, I guess there's not . . . I don't have anyone else to ask. Can you help me, please?"

"I'm happy to help. Can you tell me who I'm talking to and what kind of help you need?"

"I'm sorry. Yeah. Sure." He cleared his throat. "This is Nicky Richardson. I'm in the emergency room at University and I can't go home and Tenley is gone and her mom isn't answering her phone." Words poured into my ear so fast I had to concentrate to keep up until he paused for a breath. "I found your card and I just dialed the number."

My fingers tightened around the phone. "What happened, Nicky? Why can't you go home?"

"Because I punched out my dad. He might need surgery to fix his nose."

Shit. Richardson probably had it coming, but the kid's timing sucked. I needed to catch Graham and Archie up, and we needed to figure out how to put Zayne Davenport in a cell. He was still our most promising lead—especially since Nicky had given me a direct link between Zayne and Jessa this morning.

An actual shit ton of work waited for me in Austin, complete with a ticking clock. But I couldn't turn away a kid who had nobody else to call.

"Stay put. I'm on my way."

"Thank you," he said. The line went dead.

The Andres came down the steps behind me. "Can I take you home?" Brent asked.

I opened my mouth to tell him I had my truck before I realized he wasn't talking to me.

Erica's face crumpled. "Why would you want to? Don't you have someone better to go see?"

He put his hand out, stepping toward her.

"I never did. I know you don't believe that, but it's a long ride home and it seems we both have some talking to do."

Erica stared at his hand. Turned for her car without touching it. "It seems."

They didn't appear to notice me as they climbed into the Jag and drove away, leaving Brent's Vette sitting there in the dust.

I started back for my truck, calling the local paramedics for Lenny before I dialed Graham.

"Where the blue hell did you take off to? And what part of 'Do not operate a vehicle while taking this medication' did you not understand?" He didn't yell, but I could tell he was good and worked up. "You're on speaker, by the way. Though Archie here might be too worried to talk to you."

"I didn't take any meds because I knew I needed to go out. Count the pills if you don't believe me, but you both know I hate how that shit makes me feel," I said. "I was just going to go talk to Nicky Richardson this morning, I swear, but then he told me Jessa and Tenley knew each other and I went to the Andre house, and now I'm walking out of a low-rent trailer park outside a dusty little border town."

I hit the highlights, talking without a breath until I opened the truck door.

"Now you have to go on speaker, because I can't hold this thing with the side of my head today," I said.

Silence.

"Graham?"

"So you left your hotel, with your severe head wound and no medication, and chased a grieving mother with a handgun all the way to the border? By yourself?" Archie had no problem yelling.

I pushed the button to turn down the volume on the phone.

"When you say it like that, I don't come off as the hero detective," I said.

"You're the stubborn detective. How does that suit you?" Graham half growled.

"It's accurate, if not terribly flattering," I said. "But did you guys hear me? The girls knew each other. That means it almost has to be one of those people they both knew. We need to start working on a warrant for Zayne Davenport. I met the gardener when I was there yesterday. It's too late tonight to find him, but I'll swing through the neighborhood in the morning and see if I can spot him. I want a soil sample from the Davenports' rose garden."

"What? Why?" Graham asked.

"She must think Jessa was buried there last fall," Archie said.

"I do. The gardener made a comment yesterday about the roses dying and finding animal remains," I said. "Since Jessa spent time in that house, I want to see if there's evidence that her body was hidden there."

"Good thinking," Graham said. "But Zayne didn't kill Ray Wooley."

"How do you know?" Archie and I asked in stereo.

"That's what I came here to talk to Archie about. Y'all aren't going to believe this, but the APD got lucky with the prints from Ray's apartment. And they got a confession, no attorney present. I got a courtesy call from a buddy there about a half hour ago."

"And?" I prodded when he got quiet. Graham likes his suspense buildups.

"Bobby Wayne Otis." Graham let the words drop one by one. "They're booking him as we speak."

"Senator Three First Names who won't shut up about gun rights?" Archie's voice sounded hollow.

I fumbled for words. That doesn't happen often. "But. What? How?"

"Apparently he's also Pastor Otis. He said he saw Ray on TV the other night and God told him to 'rid the earth of this scourge on mankind.' That's a quote." I could practically see Graham waggling his eyebrows. "Just put out his hands for the cuffs straightaway when he answered the door."

"You gotta give this job one thing: it's never boring," Archie said.

I tapped one finger on my thigh, turning the truck north. The vertigo-ish sensation that meant my brain was trying to pick apart a web was back, but I didn't have time to wait for my subconscious to catch up.

Next thing. "Did Ray know the Davenport kid?"

"Huh?" I wasn't sure which one of them grunted.

I flipped the visor down against the glare. "I'm trying to put all the variables here in order. What's the first thing we have?"

"Jessa's murder," Graham said.

"No. The video of Jessa's assault," I corrected. "And we know she had paint thinner on her clothes, but only on her back. And we think whoever poured the accelerant on her was left-handed. And now we know she knew Zayne Davenport via Erica Andre." I paused for a breath. "So, if Zayne sold Ray that video of Jessa, maybe he's the link between Ray and Tenley."

Silence ticked for more than a minute.

"Graham? Arch?" I didn't dare glance at my screen, accelerating on the freeway ramp.

"That's a pretty solid trail of evidence," Archie said finally. "And Tenley died either because she turned the Davenport kid down or because she figured him out."

"Or because he lied and he knew about the money?" Graham mused. "A hundred grand is a lot of motive for a high school kid. Even a rich one. I still think we shouldn't ignore that. Especially given that it's gone."

"What money?" Archie asked.

"Graham, can you fill him in?" I asked, eyeing the speedometer as it approached ninety, twilight closing blue purple over the road in front of me. "My head is killing me, and I need to pay attention to what I'm doing here."

"Drive safely," Archie said.

"Always." I clicked the "End" button, laying heavier on the gas.

I had a solid trail on Zayne. Maybe Nicky Richardson could help me shore it up, provided he felt like talking.

41

I flashed my ID at the nurse working the ER desk and smiled when she held up one finger, tucked an escaped lock of brown hair behind her ear, and yelled for someone to please clean room four.

"What can I do for you, Officer?" she asked, turning back with raised brows and an *I have sixty-four things waiting for my attention, so be quick* stare.

"I'm looking for—" I didn't get the name out before a nasally bellowed "Get the fuck out of my way. That little faggot broke my goddamned nose!" rattled the glass in the doors and sent the nurse sprinting down a hallway to the left.

Four steps behind her, I broke into a run when Darren Richardson raised his fist to punch the orderly blocking the doorway.

"Mr. Richardson, I'd stop right there if I were you." I didn't have to shout. My head was thankful.

Richardson spun to face me.

And began to laugh.

"If it isn't Ranger Barbie." He sounded like an old radio recording of Howard Cosell, the deep-black bruises under both his eyes disappearing under a plaster-and-gauze cast encasing his nose. "What're you going to do, sweetheart? Give me a makeover? If you'll excuse me, I have an important lesson on respect to teach my idiot son."

The orderly, stocky and young but two heads shorter than Richardson, bent his knees and planted his hands on the doorframe.

"Sir, I'm going to have to ask you again to watch your mouth. And return to your bed." Good for him. His voice was shaky, but only a little.

"And I'm going to have to tell you again to go fuck yourself, shorty. Move out of that door before I move you."

I kind of wished he'd try.

"Please, please give me just one reason to put cuffs on you," I said, moving to Richardson's side and widening my feet into a punching stance.

"I got a better idea. Let me take care of this and I'll put them on you." Richardson leaned sideways with a leer and stumbled, crashing into the wall.

Gross. Not even if he wasn't ten years too old and three sheets too drunk.

"Mr. Richardson, please." The nurse put a hand on his arm to help steady him, and Richardson roared and flung her to the floor.

That was all I needed. I whipped my cuffs free as Richardson pushed off the wall, blowing his breath out in a huff. I got a whiff of bourbon strong enough to make my eyes water. Jesus. It's a wonder he was upright.

The nurse scooted backward across the tile, her ankle already twice its normal size and tears dripping down her face. When she reached the wall, she braced her back against it and used her good leg to push herself to standing.

"Please return to your own bed," the orderly said through clenched teeth.

Richardson drew his fist back again, and I stuck one boot out in front of his knee as he spun to throw the punch, sending him skidding across the tile on his face.

"You little bitch!" he howled when he managed a sitting position.

Blood streamed anew from his nose, soaking through the gauze packing and running down his face to rain red spatters on the white tile.

"I warned you," I said, glancing at the orderly and the nurse in turn. "Y'all okay?"

"I've had better days," she said, whimpering when she tried to put weight on her foot. "But I'll live."

The orderly just nodded, not budging from the door. Behind him, I could see Nicky rolled up in a ball on the narrow ER bed, his face varying shades of black and purple and still slightly bloody besides. I turned a *Try me* glare on his narcissistic douche of a father before I opened the cuffs and stepped toward him.

"I'm afraid you're taking a detour through county tonight, Coach," I said. "Good luck getting your pain meds there."

"You can't arrest me!"

"Oh, but I can. One count of assault"—I pointed to the nurse—"and one count of attempted assault." I jerked my head to the orderly. "You folks want to press charges?"

"Please," the nurse said.

"Yes, ma'am," the orderly said.

I smiled, laying an obvious hand on my gun. "So, are you going to give me your wrists, or are we doing this the hard way?"

Richardson glowered. Opened his mouth. Snapped it shut. Folded his wrists one over the other behind his back and turned so I could reach them.

I knelt and closed the cuffs a little tight before I hauled him up by the collar as hospital security and two male nurses rounded the corner at a dead run.

"Gentlemen," I said, pushing Richardson toward them. "Assault and attempted assault."

The largest cop grabbed Richardson's arm when he stumbled. "Rough night, Coach?"

Richardson nodded. "My nose."

"We'll have someone look at that," the cop said, waving for one of the nurses to make that happen. Rolling his eyes, the blond one gestured to an empty room.

I turned back to Nicky's door, mostly so I wouldn't clock the sympathetic cop. He was just starstruck, and he hadn't heard the hateful bullshit Richardson spouted at Nicky. Or that's what I'd tell myself so I could focus on Nicky, anyway.

"May I?" I nodded to the orderly.

He kept his eyes on Richardson's retreating back, moving just enough to the side to let me squeeze through. "My brother is gay. And, kid, your dad is a dick. Nice job on the nose."

Nicky raised his forehead from his knees, his long, muscular arms still wrapped tight around his shins. "I've never been good enough, you know? Not before I knew I was gay, not for one single day since."

I wanted to tell him how wrong he was, but the hard truth was, it wouldn't matter what I said. I wasn't his father.

"What happened?" I stepped to the side of the bed and winced when he turned to me. Up close, the bruises on his face were deep and blood speckled and downright frightening.

Tears trickled across the black-purple-red palette, pelting the green-and-navy hospital gown tented over Nicky's knees. "I tried so hard. But it was always his work. Always his players. Hours in the gym and I just couldn't play. I didn't fit." He sniffled, scrubbing at his nose with one fist. "From as far back as I can remember, I was the queer man out. I think he knew it, too. Maybe before I did. The only time he looked at me or spoke to me, he was always trying to toughen me up. Make me stronger. More like him. You know he gave me a subscription to an online porn service for my twelfth birthday? Said I might as well learn how to give girls what they wanted if I was going to be a man." Nicky's eyes were fixed on a poster about hand washing over the sink, his voice flat, disconnected.

I watched his hands, tightening on the skin of his forearms as he talked.

"I was the coolest kid in the seventh grade because of who he was, and then everyone wanted to hang out at my house and watch those videos. Problem was, I didn't get it up looking at big tits or watching girls give blowjobs. But then I found a male/male section and . . . I knew."

"And there's nothing wrong with that." I couldn't help myself, stepping closer to the bed. "Your dad is wrong. Pretty often, by my guess. But I meant today. I need to know what happened tonight."

Nicky shook his head, pulling in a hitching breath. "He was drinking. Started at like, three. I heard him calling me when I came in from school. I should know better, you know? My brain really is broken. I keep going back, looking for approval. Affection. Something besides contempt. I stuck my head in to ask if he was okay."

The tears fell so fast they drowned his next words. He flicked them away, mopping his face with the collar of the gown, and took a deep breath. "He asked me what I'd miss about Tenley. I told him her laugh." Nick let go of his knees and plucked at a thread on the blanket next to him. "He said she was probably better off. That a hot girl who was a lousy piece of ass wouldn't find a husband before she got too old and fat. I was so mad. So mad I actually couldn't see. I thought that was just a saying, you know?"

42

"So you hit him?" I forced the words past a heavy lump of disgust.

Piece of ass?

I'd convinced myself on the speed-racer drive back that Richardson was full of horse shit, talking a big game to his dealer about screwing a teenage girl. Tenley Andre was smart. Accomplished. Admired.

Surely . . . *surely* she wasn't sleeping with her best friend's abusive father, for Chrissake.

Nicky shrugged. "I guess. I don't remember anything until after we got here. But he says I did." He held up his left hand. "My knuckles say I did."

I bit down on a *Good for you, kid.* Encouraging him to go around punching people wasn't exactly my job. Objectively, there were extenuating circumstances surrounding this particular violent outburst.

The orderly applauded from the doorway, and I smiled at him. "I don't suppose you could ask someone to send his doctor in?"

He nodded. "Sure thing." Disappeared.

I turned back to Nicky. "Where's your mom?"

He glanced at the clock over the door. "Probably passed out on the family room sofa."

Oh. I started pacing. "Does she drink, too?"

Nicky shook his head. "Pills. When my dad goes off the deep end, she takes pills until she goes to sleep."

Which meant she stayed asleep.

"Nicky." I stopped. Flexed my fingers in and out of a fist. The question was shitty all the way around, but I had to ask it anyway. "Was Tenley having an affair with your dad?"

Nick sniffled. Dropped his head back against the pillows. "So, she finally told me last summer that she'd lost her virginity. Said it was an accident, she didn't really mean to, but the whole thing was over before she had time to say no. The guy was too old for her and I'd be pissed at her, but she had to talk through it with someone."

I nodded. "You were her best friend."

"I thought I was, yeah." He shook his head. "She didn't tell me it was him. But I didn't ask, either. Maybe part of me didn't want to know. She even said it was in the locker room before the last meet of the season."

"Was your father there that day?"

Nicky nodded. "There was a guy from California there to watch T run. Old friend of the coach. He went to the locker room to give her a 'pep talk.'"

That was the fifth time the kid had referred to his dad as "the coach." I found it funny because my teenage self called Chuck McClellan "the governor," too, and people always said I was "so respectful."

I wanted to hug this boy. It was like I'd found a kindred spirit.

Focus. "Nicky." I paused until he looked at me. "Honest truth. Do you think your dad could've hurt Tenley?" I held my breath. Jessa was a student at the university. A student Tenley and Nicky both knew. What if she found out about this? Tenley was seventeen. Darren Richardson would do just about anything to protect his reputation, and a statutory rape charge would ding it something fierce.

Shit. I believed that Lenny didn't have anything to do with anything, because twelve seconds into eavesdropping on his conversation with Erica, I knew he wasn't smart enough to pull off this sort of cover-up. But what if Zayne Davenport was just a regular-variety entitled teenage asshat instead of the murdering kind?

What if these cases could stop flipping every time I thought we had a good lead?

Nicky's wide eyes filled with fresh tears. "God, what if he did? What if I could've stopped it if I'd just gotten her to talk to me?"

I grabbed his hand, careful not to squeeze the knuckles. "This is not your fault. You hear me?"

He shook his head. "I loved her. I wish I was normal. That I could've loved her the way she needed me to, you know? I tried . . . everything."

"She knows you loved her, Nicky. You did the best you could. It's all any of us can ever do, isn't it?"

He sniffled again. "I should've done more." He shook my hand off, slammed his swollen knuckles into the bed rail and pulled in a deep breath. "It wasn't enough."

I stepped backward. Searched for words that would stop him from hurting himself.

A rap on the door saved us both.

"Hey there, Nick." A young man in scrubs stepped in, smiling as he held the door for a woman in sky-high heels, a pencil skirt, a silk blouse, and a lab coat. "This is Dr. Lindgren. She's got a few questions for you and then we're going to get you a room, okay?"

Nick didn't bother to nod. Scrubs guy smiled at me and jerked his head in the direction of the door. I followed him out.

"You're admitting him?" Thank God. I wouldn't have to worry about him trying to get home only to find an empty house and sedated mother.

"We'll keep him for twenty-four to forty-eight hours. Just make sure everything's okay."

I nodded. "Thank you. I may have more questions for him later."

"Of course. Such a sad situation. I hear I missed the big commotion with Coach Richardson when I took my break."

"He put on quite a show." I gestured to the floor. The red drops from Richardson's nose gleamed undisturbed under the fluorescent lights, but I couldn't hear him shouting anymore. "Hopefully a little time alone will calm him down."

"I saw him getting in a police car on my way in." An alarm sounded in a nearby room and the doctor turned. "That's my cue."

"Thanks for your time." I eyeballed the orderly's cart.

Q-tip. Baggie.

I knelt and brushed the cotton swab over the top of the largest blood droplet, then sealed it in the bag and tucked it in my pocket before I turned to wave goodbye to Nick.

"Nicholas, how many—" Dr. Lindgren began, pushing the door to his room shut.

My phone buzzed a text.

Archie: *I got a traffic camera that puts Quentin Davenport's car a block from the bar Jessa went into that night.*

I stared at the phone. Touched the baggie in my pocket. For the love of God. Could we chase one goose at a time, please?

Excellent. But hold up. I have a story for you, I typed.

I clicked another screen and texted Graham: *I don't suppose you ever heard from your scientist friend?*

Dot bubble. Buzz. *Yeah, actually. She got back in town this afternoon. Waiting for samples. I texted Jim, he didn't answer.*

I'll find him. Send.

I dialed Jim's cell on my way to the truck, smiling when he picked up as I climbed in.

"You're working late," he said by way of hello.

"How much do you love me?" I asked.

"Enough to put my beer down to take this call. Beyond that, it's dicey. What do you want?"

"I need a favor. A superspeed DNA run."

"I don't do DNA."

"Graham has a lab tech on standby."

"What do you think you've got?" Curiosity laced the words.

"I need what you took from Tenley's nails and genitals run against a blood sample I just snagged and a couple of DIS files we can send you. And I need them all checked against swabs from Jessa DuGray, too."

Jim whistled. "No shit? Boy, that'll be a big collar."

"You have no idea. Can you help?"

"Why not? Graham's friend at Travis County, or do I have to pack up samples and take them somewhere?"

"I'll find out. Be there in ten minutes with the counter-check."

"I'm waiting."

I hung up and opened my texts. Graham. *Jim is on board. Is your friend at Travis?*

Buzz. *Yep. She can be there in twenty.*

I pecked at the screen with one thumb as I started the truck. *They ought to be booking Darren Richardson into county on assault right about now. VERY IMPORTANT that he not bond out until tomorrow.*

I backed out of the space. The phone buzzed in the cup holder. Graham: *On it.*

I pulled in a deep breath. My gut said we had our solution, one way or another. Archie was on the Davenport kid, Richardson was locked up.

Nobody was in immediate danger. Now I just needed to make sure it stayed that way.

43

I screeched to a stop in Jim's driveway just after nine, grabbed the baggie, and ran to the door whispering a prayer with every step.

Please don't let him get out.

Richardson might be hard-pressed to hide in Austin, where more than half the city drove past a thirty-foot rendering of his face on the way to work every day—but with a head start, he had the money to avoid law enforcement for longer than I wanted to think about.

Jim met me at the door of the Craftsman postwar bungalow he and his wife had raised four boys in, stepping onto the porch and putting a finger to his lips. "If you wake the dogs, they'll wake Sheila, and she's not feeling so hot these days."

I tipped my head to one side, holding the bag out. "What's wrong?"

"Cancer." He spit the word at his slippers.

"Oh, Jim." My hand flew to my mouth. "What kind?"

"Carcinoma of indeterminate origin." He shook his head. "Fancy way of saying they can't find where the hell it came from, only where it's spreading to. She's taking some sort of superchemo twice a week. She's been so sick. And this all started because she thought she had a kidney stone and went to the ER."

I put a hand on his arm, guilt bubbling in my chest for getting so out of touch with my old friends. I swallowed it. Wishing the past was different does nothing but wreck the present and steal the future. Right then, I was standing there. So right then was what mattered. I squeezed his arm.

"I'll keep y'all in my prayers, but please let me know if I can do anything."

He looked up. "There's a drug trial at Anderson her doctors are trying to get her into. They say it's her best shot, but there's a lot of red tape and they're having trouble. I've called everyone I've ever so much as shaken hands with, begging, but people keep telling me they don't have enough pull to help . . ." He let the sentence trail, his eyes filling with tears.

People. People who weren't my father. Chuck McClellan had enough pull to move mountains, but Jim still didn't want to ask. I didn't wait for him to, nodding. "I'll talk to him."

The tears spilled over, Jim grabbing my hand and pumping like oil was bound to gush forth. "Thank you. I can't tell you how much I—"

I cut him off by pulling him into a hug. "That's what friends are for. Why didn't you ask me before now? I've seen you twice this week, and it's not like you don't have my number."

"I always got the feeling you wanted to keep your distance from your family. I don't know the whole story about what happened to your sister, but I heard whispers. I thought it was too big a favor."

Jesus. I waved a hand. "What the hell do my daddy issues matter next to your Sheila's life? I'm happy I can help. Or at least try to."

He hugged me again before he took the baggie. "One Q-tip? You're not serious."

"I got lucky to manage that."

"Are we going to find a match in LDIS?"

"I doubt it. But check it against our victims. And I'll send you the link for the other profiles."

"I'll let you know as soon as we have something."

I nodded, squeezing his hand. "Thanks, Jim."

"Anything you need, kid. For the rest of my days."

"She'll be okay. She's too tough to lose this fight."

"That's what I tell myself. Some days it works better than others." His eyes filled again and he swiped at them. "Sorry."

"For being human? I'd be offended if you weren't crying. You two are like a fairytale forever with a Texas twang."

"Hoping for the happily ever after."

"I'll do everything I can to help you find it." I jogged back down the steps, hoping like hell I could make good on the promise to help. My mother was right about one thing: the governor had a stubborn streak ten miles wide, and he could be a vindictive son of a bitch. I wouldn't put it past him to refuse to make a three-minute phone call as punishment for what he deemed my poor life choices.

My own stubborn streak had work to do. There weren't many things anybody loved more than the governor loved his power, but my love for my friends could give him a run for his money.

My phone buzzed. Archie: *Call me when you get this.*

I started the truck and touched the phone icon next to his name.

"They got a computer match on the audio in the DuGray assault video," Archie said when he picked up.

The low, even tone meant he was trying to hold himself together. I stopped breathing. "Who?" I managed.

"Bobby Wayne Otis."

"What?" It burst out so loud I made my own headache worse. "The guy who just confessed to killing the porn dude? That Bobby Wayne Otis?"

"So says the software. I'm on my way to county to have a chat with him."

"I'll meet you there," I said. "They have a new overnight guest I wouldn't mind chatting with myself. Darren Richardson seems to be the mystery man Tenley was hiding."

"You're not . . ." Archie paused. "You know what? Of course you are. I can't even pretend to be surprised by that tonight. On our way."

I dropped the phone back into the cup holder, turning away from headquarters and toward the county lockup. Maybe Archie and I could get some answers the old-fashioned way while Graham's friend worked whatever DNA magic she could.

If I'd been a gambler, I'd have bet the house Darren Richardson wouldn't love being questioned by Ranger Barbie.

So I'd go do just that.

* * *

Walking through the back door at the jail, I handed my ID to the officer on duty and laid my keys and my gunbelt in a tray before I passed through the metal detectors.

"Evening, ma'am." The fresh-faced second-shift desk officer smiled. "What can we do for you?"

"I'd like to have Darren Richardson brought to an interrogation room, please."

"Coach Darren Richardson?" His rust-colored eyebrows disappeared into his hairline.

I nodded, then tipped my head toward the computer in front of him. "I imagine he's been here about an hour now."

"Okay, then." He started punching keys. Twisted his thin lips to one side.

"What?" My stomach twisted with the kid's lips.

"I can't see the whole status because somebody locked it, but I think the coach bonded out about twenty minutes after he got here."

I shut my eyes. "Locked it?"

"Yes, ma'am. Only command staff can do that."

"They let him go and locked the computer access." My voice was flat. "To keep the arrest quiet."

Too bad they'd probably sentenced his son to the death penalty in the process.

The kid shrugged. "I'm sorry?" He said the words to my retreating back as I spun on my heel, out the door in four long strides.

In the parking lot, I pulled out my phone and clicked up a contact I'd never once had cause to use. Desperate times and all that. Knowing who got Richardson out of jail might give me a road to who was trying to cover up Tenley's murder.

Three rings. Come on.

"Yes?"

"It's Faith McClellan. Darren Richardson was booked into county about an hour ago for assaulting an ER nurse at UMC and beating his teenage son. He's already out, and the computer files are restricted from access even by deputies."

"Someone high up had to have done that." Pause. "Why are you calling me?"

"Because the last thing he wants is to be all over the TV for this, and you're the most annoying TV reporter in town. I'm only asking one thing in return. If you find anything, text me at this number."

"Why should I help you?" Skye's voice could've frozen the third ring of hell.

"Because you want the story worse than you want to be a pain in my ass. And because your ratings stunt with hunting down the porn guy the other night actually got him killed, and me a thousand hours of nightmares. You need to balance your karma."

She paused. Sighed. "I'd say thank you, but somehow I think this will work to your advantage as much as mine."

"If I'm right, he'll be back in jail in a few hours and you'll have the scoop of the year. Get your story, Skye. Just make sure you don't get in my way." I hung up and squashed an urge to wipe the phone with Clorox before I put it in my pocket, moving back toward the truck just as Graham and Archie turned into the lot.

"What gives?" Archie asked, putting the passenger window down as his Crown Vic rolled to a stop.

"He's gone." I shook my head.

"Who? Richardson?"

"Yep. And the deputy can't even see how or who was responsible."

Graham slammed a hand down on the steering wheel. "I called three different guys who swore on their mothers they'd make sure he spent the night."

"Money and power play a whole lot bigger game in this city than we like to think," Archie said. "I'd wager your friends are no match for the coach's."

"That's okay. I just sicced Skye Morrow on the whole lot of them," I said, patting myself on the back when Archie turned with a slack jaw.

"Way to play hardball, kiddo," he said. "And I know how hard it was for you to make that call."

"Some things are more important than personal feelings," I said, watching Archie kick the door open. "You really think Otis is going to talk?"

"According to the APD, he already has. Telling everyone who will listen to him what a good deed he's done for the city, the state, and the entire internet."

I put one hand on the top of the door and paused as Archie moved to the jail entrance. "Arch."

"Yeah?" He turned.

"Something isn't right here. Keep your guard up with this guy."

"Whysat?"

"I know politicians. He's talking about this hand to keep people from looking at what he's doing with the other one. Or hiding with the other one."

"Have you read this guy's bio? He's not sane enough to be that clever."

"If that's him on the video, he killed Ray to keep anyone from finding that out, and he wanted his secret kept bad enough to assault a police officer carrying the McClellan name." I touched my stitches. "The governor cares way more about an attack on his family than he does about me, and this guy is a politician. He had to know the risk when he hit me. Chuck McClellan's wrath is way scarier than a rape charge, even one this horrifying, and this guy already confessed to one murder. Just give me a few minutes and let me see if I can figure what the smoke and mirrors are about. I'll text you what I come up with."

"Politics isn't the same nowadays as it was when your dad was in the mansion, kid. Plain old crazy gets elected to more seats every year." Archie stepped toward the door.

I shook my head. "Nah. It's just that greed gets better at talking a good game and people get more divided and gullible. My gut says Darren Richardson is in this up to his fake-baked hairline, Arch. What if the gifts Tenley bought weren't about goodbyes, but because she was running away? From him, maybe? People around her said she seemed happy lately, for the most part. A hundred grand would've taken her about anywhere she wanted to go."

"Why was she at the dam, then?"

"Thinking. Getting her courage up. Her folks said it was a special place for her." Graham's voice came from inside the car.

"Exactly," I said. "And if she was having some sort of bizarre affair with Richardson, he knew that, too."

My fingers tightened on the door, the variable my brain had been teasing since I left the trailer park popping neatly into stark relief. "And Richardson knew Ray Wooley."

That made Archie let go of the door. "He what?"

"The dealer Erica Andre went after today said it—actually he said it twice, and I caught it but it got lost in the rest of the case," I said. "His buddy Ray went for the big time in Austin and got himself in with the basketball coach, that's what he said. And then he said Richardson was bragging about sleeping with Tenley. And there are a hundred reasons why the two of them might've wanted Tenley dead, depending on how many of their secrets she knew."

Archie nodded. "Makes as much sense as anything else around this. Find the coach. And holler if you do happen to find anything on Otis."

I slid into the passenger seat, turning to Graham. "This feels right."

"The whole damned thing is crazy. And you were the only one who saw it."

"Thanks for believing me." I opened the browser on my phone, and a text alert flashed at the top of the screen.

Skye: *Sen. Bobby Wayne Otis's assistant signed the coach out six minutes after he cleared processing.*

I stared at the letters. A headline. Different words in a bigger font from fifty-six hours that seemed like three lifetimes ago.

Shit.

Buzz. *My guy says Otis is sitting in a cell. Mix-up?*

"No." I shook my head. Tapped *I don't think so.* Send.

I touched the search bar. Tried to stop my hands from shaking as I typed Otis's name. Please, let my stupid photographic memory be wrong this time.

Graham hung a right out of the parking lot. "Where to?"

Search results. News. Top hit: *Mom says pastor's miracle camp "cured" lesbian daughter of demons.*

Shit, shit, shit.

"The hospital. They're after Nicky." My voice sounded hollow and far away, my brain racing faster than my heart as the magic rock finally came up off the answer: Nicky Richardson was the secret at the center of this case —both girls, his dad, Otis . . . every trail led back to Nicky.

"Faith?" Graham stopped at a light. "What's wrong?"

I didn't answer, clicking back to my messages. *Skye, there's a bigger story here than you can imagine. Go to Richardson's home and make sure he's not there.* If he was, if I was wrong about them wanting to hurt Nicky, so be it. But I knew in my bones I wasn't.

New text to Archie: *Otis runs a religious podcast and a conversion camp for gay teenagers by day. Jessa DuGray was a teaching tool, Arch. His office got Richardson out. Please be careful asking about that video—it's the thing he's trying to hide because it'll kill his cash cow.*

"Graham, they were trying to convert Nick to heterosexuality." The words sounded hollow as I clicked back to the article and scrolled. "Prayer. Lectures. 'Innovative proven therapy.'"

"That's code for electric-shock treatments," Graham said. "And we hear whispers of stuff that's a whole lot darker."

Jessa.

Dear God.

"Nicky's hair used to be shorter." I flicked on the lights and siren. "Darren Richardson is absolutely the sort of man who'd slip into a hospital and smother his sedated kid to cover his own ass. Go."

44

The angel smiled.

It had to be a sign, the way she looked at him. The way her lips curved up, beckoning him closer. The way she practically begged him for it. No more wondering. No more waiting. The monster was fully awake and off its chain.

Showtime.

And then the angel started to talk.

"You know those days your whole life turns on? Today is one of them for me. I'm quitting track." She raised one perfect honey-tanned hand without looking up, words tripping out of her mouth so fast he had trouble keeping them in order. "The truth is, I can't be a champion forever. Maybe I can't be one at all. Missing the Olympics last year nearly killed me. I appreciate every sacrifice people I love have made to see me run. I even got gifts." She pointed to the bag, pausing for breath.

He stared, face blank, eyes hard. Why was she telling him this?

The monster didn't care. His feet moved closer, blocking her exit path.

The angel didn't back away. Didn't recoil. She actually reached for his hand.

"I did a stupid, stupid thing. With your dad. And I'm so sorry, but I'm not sorry because he shot off his big mouth and . . . Nicky, I know. Shock therapy? Are they kidding? You knock that shit off. I mean it. You are amazing and I love you exactly the way you are. I'm buying off that asshole the coach hired to do this to you, I'm getting everyone I love out from under all these lies, and you and me are

getting the hell away from here. I can still go to Stanford on academics, and you can wrestle! I'll be your biggest fan. God, I'm so—"

He tipped his head to one side, a smile spreading across his face. Wicked. Wolfish. Chilling. The monster's smile.

She stopped talking.

"Nicky?" She drew the word out, unsure, a tiny wrinkle fracturing her perfect forehead when her brows drew together. "Are you okay?"

He would be. In just moments, he'd be better than okay.

They had promised.

He raised his left hand and drew his index and middle fingers across her right cheek. "You will quiet the monster. And when he's done with you, I will set you free. My angel. So perfect." The low, gravelly whisper was laced with danger.

She froze. Twisted. Pushed off with her back leg.

Ran.

She was fast.

But not fast enough.

His hand shot out, closing around her arm in a wrestling move that gave her no choice but to move back to him—her wrist would snap otherwise.

Almost like she knew that, she yelped and returned to him. Her eyes searched his face, terror making a bright-white ring all around the light latte amber.

"I thought you loved me," she whispered.

His breath slowed for five beats as he fell into those eyes. He would love her. He would worship her. Never forget her. She would set him free. She would make him normal.

The monsters swore she would.

His grip tightened, his foot shooting out and taking them both to the ground.

Every bit of air forced from her chest by the fall, the angel struggled to pull in more.

She twisted and wriggled, working her arm free as she pulled in enough air to scream.

"Go ahead," the monster crooned, warm, sticky breath spilling over the angel's face. "Let me hear you."

Nothing came out of her open mouth before he covered it with his.

He let go of her arm to work at his jeans, the monster's voice as hard, as painful, as the erection he needed to free. "Come on, sweet angel, scream for me. Scream as loud as you want. Nobody's here to hear you but us."

The angel's eyes went wide, her breath shallow and fast.

"Please, Nicky, no."

He slid his zipper down and tears leaked from the corners of her eyes.

"You can't do this. You can't be this. You're not like your father." Her half-whispery pleas fell unnoticed. She pushed at the solid wall of his chest, and he could feel her muscles coil and fight. She was strong. But no match for the state wrestling champion.

The monster forced a hand under her skirt, groping for her panties. Shoving them aside.

Thick, rough fingers shoved inside her, tearing and burning.

"There. That's what I need. Open your legs like a good little whore."

Her palm flew into the side of his face, stinging, her nails raking fire across his arm when he grunted and corralled both of her wrists in one hand, pinning them over her head.

"Don't you ever call me that again," she sobbed. "Nicky, please. What is the matter with you?"

Her voice was raw. Terrified. Nicky stirred. And the monster faltered.

Just for a moment. But it was long enough.

He had strong hands.

His angel had strong legs. He'd watched her for hours. He should've been ready.

But he wasn't.

Her right knee rocketed up, her thigh slamming into his balls and sending pain to the ends of his hair, his guts coiling under a breaking wave of nausea. A sharp breath snuck in through his teeth, his grip loosening for the split second the angel needed.

She pulled the knee down. Shot it up again, this time jerking both hands straight down in the same instant, shoving with everything she had until he landed on his side in the dirt.

One hand cupped his crotch, the other reached for her as she scrambled across the gravel.

"You know you're not supposed to drink with your meds." The words came out between ragged breaths as she stood, her hand closing around a gold locket nestled

in the hollow of her throat like it could keep her safe. "What the ever-loving hell has gotten into you?"

Twin beams pierced the darkness, lighting her perfect face with an otherworldly glow.

Tenley.

His Tenley. His angel. His deliverance.

Nicky blinked. Buried one hand in his curls and reached for her with the other.

God what had the monster done here? Why was she looking at him that way? He pushed off the ground, stretching toward her, fumbling with the front of his jeans when he felt them slipping. His fingers brushed her ankle and she jumped backward, her heel catching on a half-buried rock near the edge of the dam.

She stumbled.

The whole world rocked and wavered, rushing past them too fast to shift fate.

Her arms spun behind her, finding no purchase but the dewy predawn air.

So fast.

So quiet.

She was there.

She was gone.

There wasn't even time for her to scream.

45

We left the car in the fire lane outside the ER. I sprinted through the doors, my lips moving in a repeated prayer for Nicky's safety.

Graham caught up as I reached the desk. "Breathe. He's in a safe place."

"Your lips to God's ear." But the same unease I'd had in Ray's apartment settled around my shoulders like a granite-lined cloak, and I couldn't shake it.

"I need someone to check on a patient," I said, flashing my ID. "I'm afraid he may be in danger. Nicholas Richardson. He was admitted through the ER about an hour and a half ago."

"Are you family?" The young man behind the counter smirked. "Because I can't confirm anyone is here unless you're on a list the patient gives us."

"His family is what you need to be worried about," I half shouted.

Graham put a hand on my elbow. "I'm Travis County SO, she's Texas Rangers. This young man is in your care and could be in danger. If you're not comfortable sharing information about him, perhaps you could find me his physician?"

The guy shrugged. "I'm not saying he's here."

"I know he's here, I saw him here not two hours ago," I said, every ounce of control I could muster barely keeping me on my side of the desk.

"Kid. If you don't want to go to jail, go find me a doctor." Graham's tone was pleasant, but firm. "Any doctor will do."

The kid rolled his eyes. "Just keep your gun in its place there, Officer." A snide twist hit the last word. "Excuse me."

He sauntered away and I turned, folding my arms across my chest and scanning the room. "Why is everything so hard today?"

I spotted the friendly orderly from earlier at the far end of the hallway to the right, wishing to hell I'd asked his name and patting Graham's hand. "Be right back," I whispered, starting that way.

"Where are you going? Faith." Graham's voice was low, but I waved a *Be quiet* at him over my shoulder, holding up one finger and working to keep my legs from racing down the hall and calling attention to myself.

"Hi there," I said, stopping behind the young man as he emptied a wastebasket into his cart.

"Hey, Officer," he said. "What're you doing back here?"

I looked around and lowered my voice. "I need to find Nicky Richardson," I said. "His father bonded out half an hour ago, and judging from what I saw earlier, I'm afraid for the kid's safety. Dr. Lindgren was admitting him. Any idea where they took him?" I stuck out a hand. "I'm Faith, by the way."

He removed his latex glove and tossed it into the trash before he shook my hand. "Earl. Did you say Dr. Lindgren?"

I nodded. "She came in right before I left."

He furrowed his brow. "Well then, he's up on seven, though I'm not sure why. Seemed like a fine dude."

I tipped my head to one side. "Isn't seven the . . ."

"Locked psych ward?" Earl nodded. "Yep."

No.

I turned back for the doors just as my phone went nuts.

Call from Jim. Text from Skye. I clicked the call first.

"Did you find a match?" I hurried my steps as the smirky desk guardian and a man in a lab coat approached Graham.

"Yes and no. Yes, the tissue under Tenley's nails matches one of the profiles in the vaginal swab from Jessa DuGray that Waco tested last week."

My eyes fell shut.

God, please no.

"Then it gets weird," Jim continued. "We triple-checked the accuracy, but it's the damndest thing. Match on five loci, one exact allele on each. Like . . ." Jim paused. Or the phone cut out. I pulled it away to check bars, my heart free-falling to my knees.

"Jim?"

"Can you hear me now?" he asked.

"Like the blood I brought you was from a relative of the perp." I didn't bother with the question mark, grabbing Graham's hand and hauling him toward the door.

"That's what we got, yeah. You okay?"

"Nope. But that doesn't mean I don't have a job to do." I thanked him and touched the "End" button, then opened my texts.

Skye: *Richardson just left in a little Mercedes convertible. And there's a Jaguar SUV pulling into the driveway.*

Can you follow him? I tapped back.

He's gone.

Shit. I didn't break stride. *The Jag white?*

Buzz. *Yep.*

Keep an eye on that and let me know if it gets interesting.

I stashed the phone and quickened my pace. Why the hell was Erica at the Richardson house? Hadn't she caused enough trouble for one day?

No time to wonder right now.

"Can you take a breath and fill me in?" Graham asked, breaking into a jog to keep up. "They said the Richardson kid is gone."

Of course he was.

"It's him. Jim said the DNA under Tenley's nails came from someone related to Darren Richardson, not from the coach himself. And it turns out that doctor I talked to earlier was a shrink. Nicky was admitted to the psych ward." I walked faster, the words punching hard. This was so fucking unfair.

"Electric-shock therapy. Pills. Twice, he looked dead at me and told me he wanted to be in love with Tenley. I saw a fucking picture of the two of them on top of the dam, for Chrissake. How could I miss this?" I didn't need Graham to answer.

I'd seen what I wanted to see. And I did not want to see Nicky Richardson as a murderer. But there'd be time for overanalyzing and beating myself up later.

"What?" Graham broke into a jog to keep up. "It was the kid? The one who was her friend?"

I nodded. *Think. Where would he go?*

I paused with my hand on the car door handle. "Do we still have Tenley's phone?"

"It's in my bag."

I dived into the car, sucking in a deep breath after I closed the door.

Tenley. Jessa.

Nicky.

I was right about the main variables, but I'd put that last one in the wrong place. My brain was stuck, not wanting to process the new information. I liked Nicky. Nicky couldn't be a rapist. Or a murderer. He loved Tenley and she loved him.

The whole universe had flipped clean upside down.

I snapped gloves from the first aid kit onto my hands and groped through Graham's bag until I came up with the phone. Pressing down on the tape over the home button, I whispered, "Please."

The screen came to life. I raked my thumb left to right and typed *Find My Friends* in the search bar. Opened the app. Nicky was the only name on the list. I touched the screen. Watched the wheel roll.

"He's almost to the dam," I said. "Dammit, Graham, he's going to jump."

Siren wailing and lights flashing, Graham peeled out southwest.

I stared at the still-green dot on Tenley's screen, praying harder than I'd prayed since Charity died that we'd get there before the worst could happen again.

46

A nurse shut off the lights as the doctor droned about being responsible with his meds, avoiding alcohol, and keeping up with therapy.

"Why haven't you been seeing your doctor regularly?" She did pretty well masking the admonishment in her tone, but Nicky could hear it anyway.

Because Pastor wasn't *a doctor and the fucking electroconvulsive therapy was causing massive headaches. That they hadn't warned him about. The memory lapses, they did. He was fucking tired of those, too. And the lying bastard said six weeks. Six weeks had come and gone since his last treatment and he still couldn't remember chunks of where he'd been, what he'd done. Like Monday night. He dropped T off. He was amped up and pissed at himself that after eight months of this conversion therapy bullshit he'd let his dad talk him into, he still couldn't get it up for the hottest, smartest, sweetest girl in Texas.*

He remembered pulling out of her driveway.

And then nothing until another headache woke him up on Tuesday afternoon. It had been almost eight weeks. Why hadn't they stopped?

Nick shrugged at Dr. Lindgren. She seemed nice enough. But she couldn't help. Nobody could.

This was just him. His fate. Nothing could stop it: not prayer, not bleeding himself every time he thought about another guy. He'd literally tried everything up to and including apparently breaking his fucking brain.

Therapy his hairy white ass.

Therapy was supposed to help you. Not make you sick.

The coach had lost his shit, storming about, screaming that nobody warned him the treatment could induce bipolar disorder in teenage boys. Or maybe just surface what was treading under. Either way, Nicky was caught in full-on rapid-cycling mania, the actual doctor said.

His mother cried and took more pills as she begged Nicky to take the ones they gave him.

He tried.

They made him feel like he was watching his own life. A bystander. Not in the story, but reading it.

He hated them. Was almost relieved when his dad had a fit about the pharmacy bill in November and stopped buying them.

He blinked. This new doctor, Dr. Lindgren, was holding a syringe. "Just something to help you sleep. We'll work on getting your meds straight in the morning."

Nick leaned his head back and closed his eyes.

A bolt of pain ripped through his head, laying a memory he'd lost bare in its wake.

A recent memory.

My God, he'd been there.

He could see his Tenley, his princess, his favorite person in the world, lying broken on the packed sand.

He shook his head, tears falling as Dr. Lindgren finished pushing the syringe into the IV. "You need to sleep, Nicholas. I'll be back in the morning to check on you."

He couldn't sleep. That was the problem. His brain raced around the clock, sleep an elusive enigma that might visit for a few hours around dawn, and then only if he was lucky.

He tried wearing himself out. Pushed hard at the gym.

Took those damned pills his dad started bringing home around Christmas. "Same stuff, half the price. If Mexico can get it right, why the hell can't we?" he boomed as he shoved the bag at Nicky.

They didn't fix him. He lost more time. Got more angry. Felt more helpless.

He tried swiping some of the coach's bourbon. Seemed to work for the old man, right?

Just left him off-balance and pissed off at the world.

The internet wasn't much help, either. Bipolar mania is supposed to be a euphoric state, the articles said. Except when it's not. A very small percentage of people get black-hole-caliber depressed. Become a danger to themselves.

But nothing and no one had warned him he might be a danger to others.

He squeezed his eyes shut, jaw locking against the pain, and pushed through the noise, reaching for the memory.

He'd been a danger to Tenley.

He couldn't manage how she ended up on the sand, but he could see her. Could smell what was left of the water as he sped down to the shore with the windows down, feel the dew on his skin as he sprinted to where she lay.

Her eyes stared at nothing, her face at peace.

The barest ring of blood showed just around the crown of her head, the sand soaking up the rest.

Her arms were sprawled at unnatural angles, her legs twisted half around from her torso like a broken mannequin.

She stared up at him.

The monster leapt. Howled.

"No." It slid through Nick's teeth, low and loud at the same time.

The monster couldn't have his Tenley. Couldn't touch her. This part of his life was off-limits to the seething anger that hated nothing more than it hated Nicky.

She deserved the very best the universe had to give. She deserved to be free.

He hit his knees next to her. Pulled his knife from his pocket even as he wondered how it got there in the first place. Moved her thin silk skirt up over her hip. Drew the blade up sharply over her flesh.

But the blood didn't come.

Of course not, stupid. Her heart wasn't beating. He couldn't help. Couldn't save her. Couldn't set her free.

He sobbed until he ran out of tears, orange light peeking over the water as he scrubbed at his face and reached for her, arranging her carefully in her favorite sleeping position: flat on her back with her arms crossed over her chest.

"I always, always loved you best." He kissed her forehead, already cold against his lips. "I wish I could've made things different for us. Given you your happily ever after. Be free, princess."

He stood and turned back to the car, and the memory fragmented, Pastor Otis standing near the trunk, a fat yellow envelope clutched in both hands. His red, squishy face flickered like a broken TV set, darkness rushing in from all sides.

In the hospital bed, Nicky fought, ripping the tape off the IV needle and pulling it free, watching blood trickle over the back of his hand.

Cleansing.

Freedom.

He struggled to sit, pushing himself from the mattress and unplugging the beeping IV pump.

Clothes. Shoes.

He splashed water on his face and strode from the room, down the hall, out the doors behind a nurse on her way home, and into the stairwell before anyone had time to notice him.

Everything had been fine until the coach brought up that damned camp. Not fine enough for the coach, but fine enough for Nicky. He let himself be talked into it, though, the possibility of a normal life, of Tenley and babies and a white picket fence and all the things he'd been taught to want since before he could talk just too damned perfect to walk away from.

"Perfectly safe," they said the first time they strapped him to the table and put the headband on. "It'll just straighten the neural pathways, so to speak."

"Perfectly safe," Pastor Otis told the coach the first time he took a scalpel to Nicky's thigh to bleed the devil out of him. "Surgical grade and sterilized, you have my word."

He walked into the cool night, glad he'd driven himself there, swearing he could smell rain in the air. Tenley loved the rain.

But Tenley wasn't perfectly safe. Wasn't here to smell the storm. Because of him.

Because of them.

He owed the coach a long chat. And a little drive.

47

Tenley's parents were looking for Darren Richardson, too.

I shook my head at the text from Skye informing me of that. "The coach should've stayed in jail. He'd be safer there."

"What now?" Graham asked.

I held up one finger, staring at the gray dot bubble in the corner of my screen. *His wife is swearing he's not here. The dead girl's father looks like he wants to kill someone.*

I wasn't about to tell Skye Morrow why Brent Andre was pissed. *If you see the coach, let me know, please,* I tapped back.

I turned to Graham. "The Andres are over at the Richardson house. Looking for the coach."

"Oh shit. Should we send a patrol car by there?"

"As long as the coach isn't there, there's no need. And his wife says he's not."

"Probably halfway to Mexico by now." Graham shook his head. "There's something inherently unfair about a jackass like that guy fucking up so many lives and literally walking away from the consequences."

I tapped one finger on the side of my phone case, staring at the still-green dot on my screen. "We'll find him. But we have more pressing matters to handle right this minute." I meant it. I would make it my personal mission to bring Richardson up on whatever charges we could make stick. Very publicly. But it could wait until his kid was safe.

I looked out the window, silent neighborhoods blurring by as Graham took the dark, twisty road as fast as he dared.

Another buzz. *Did Tenley Andre get into a car crash going to pick her drunk mother up from a party?*

I stared at the letters. "Somewhere she didn't know how to get to in the middle of a school night," I muttered. "Damn."

I didn't answer Skye that time, letting my head fall back against the seat. "Tenley's folks paid Stella Connolly off because Erica was drunk and Tenley was going to pick her up. Alone. In the middle of the night. With just a permit."

"So maybe Tenley flipped that around on her folks because she felt like the mom owed her?" Graham asked. "Damn. No wonder the kid was blitzed when she died. Keeping all these people's secrets straight could make a nun start slamming shots."

"Right?" I rubbed my temple. "Like my head didn't hurt bad enough already."

My phone buzzed again. Skye: *Coach's wife says her son has been depressed. Cutting himself. Not sleeping, going up to the dam at night. He was close with the Andre girl, but . . .*

Damn. I rubbed my head harder. "Nicky's mother says he's been going up to the dam at night. Can't sleep. Cutting himself." I was talking half to Graham and half to myself, typing a reply at the same time.

On my way to him now. Send.

"That would've been good to know a couple of days ago." I glanced at Graham.

"So did he just see her up there and happen to attack her?" he asked. "I'm still trying to work this out."

"Me too." I sighed, dropping my phone into the cup holder. "He loved her. No way he was lying about that. How could he do such god-awful things to her?"

I stared at Tenley's phone screen. The dot was still there. Nicky should still be alive. I wondered if even he'd be able to explain his friend's death.

Because Nicky did love Tenley.

That woman in Houston probably loved her babies, too, but she still drowned them in her tub. I'd seen a handful of similar cases in my years in homicide. Severe mental breaks can make people wholly not themselves. And the green dot still couldn't tell me if we'd make it up there in time.

"Three minutes," Graham said. He'd always had a weird way of knowing what I was thinking before I said it.

"Park at the bottom of the hill," I said. "The last thing we want to do is startle him."

I folded my hands together so tightly they were both cold from lack of blood by the time he cut the engine. We climbed out and started up the shoulder in silence, gravel crunching under boots and short breaths the only noise save for the katydids. Blooming honeysuckle drifted to my nose on the stiff breeze.

I needed the excuse for quiet. My head was warring with my heart for what could cause me the most pain right that minute. Nobody would ever say it, but some cop I was. I didn't simply miss this. I flat-ass refused to look for it. Every last road and rock led to Nicky. But he reminded me of myself after my sister died: same lost look, same unimaginable bastard of a father.

The dark, naked truth was that I hadn't wanted him to be guilty. Hadn't dug far enough to see that he was sick.

And now he might end up dead because I fucked up.

Pretty shitty consequences to live with for one lousy mistake on the job.

"Stop it," Graham murmured in my ear. "This was not your fault. Nobody else got it either."

"You didn't talk to him."

"Did the kid seem like a killer to you either time?"

"I didn't want him to be."

"If we're playing true confession, I wanted it to be the little snot quarterback. I'd still like another crack at that one." Graham huffed. "We're sure it's not him?"

"DNA is sure." I didn't break stride, my words clipped. Wanting it to be anyone was the biggest misstep we'd taken here. There's a reason circumstantial evidence doesn't carry much weight—any cop worth their shield can stack up indicators against a suspect they can't stand. Seeing the guilt I didn't want to see was so much harder. "Zayne sure made for an easy train to jump on, though, didn't he? And Darren Richardson was just as good a villain. What the fuck kind of parent sends their kid to get electric-shock therapy because he's gay?"

"The kind who pats himself on the back for not kicking the kid out in the street," Graham said. "I see it every day, working major crimes. Kids who trusted their parents, or maybe were outed by a bully or a teacher—and the parents just show them the door. Cut them off like they never existed. They end up on the streets, stealing, or begging, or worse."

We both nodded, falling back into silence.

"Thanks," I whispered ten steps later.

Graham bumped my shoulder. "What friends are for."

The top of the hill in sight, I stopped, catching him by the arm when I heard voices. At least two. Both male.

What the hell else was I wrong about?

We crept closer.

"You promised it would make me normal!" Nicky screamed. "Do you have any idea what I've done? You made me a monster!"

I swallowed hard, my insides going cold in the warm night air.

Jesus, no.

"You were trying to fuck a woman at least, were you not?" That was Richardson, I thought, but the words sounded slurred. Like he'd hit the bottle again after he got out of jail. To my right, Graham froze.

I took two more steps, just trying to get above the sight line.

Nicky paced, probably five feet from the edge of the dam. The light from the almost-full moon glittered off the blade in his left hand, dark liquid dripping from the tip.

His father stood a half step from death, blood running from a gash on his cheek, wide eyes following Nicky's every breath. Richardson's arms and hands trembled violently enough for me to notice from fifty yards out.

The fingers on Nicky's free hand disappeared into his curls, twisting around them as he shook his head. "My God, there's really no hope for you, is there?" He stopped, squaring up to his father. They were roughly the same size, I noticed for the first time—the elder Richardson just seemed larger because of his overinflated ego. I'd noticed that about many a politician, growing up. A good scandal to take them down a few pegs and they never looked quite so big again.

"Right there." Nicky kicked the dirt. His father flinched. "She was right there when she fell. Begging me, the person she trusted most, not to hurt her. Because of you. Jump, you heartless prick. Now!" Nick swung the knife.

Richardson scurried two steps to his right, rocks scattering over the edge into the void behind him. "I only wanted what would be best for you," he said.

"Bullshit," Nick shouted into the gusting wind, stepping toward his father. "You don't even know how to want what's best for anybody but yourself! Not me, not your team. Feeding those guys pills until they leave broken addicts who end up on the streets. And you don't care. Not about anyone. Not Mom. Not Tenley. You know, she told me what happened. She just didn't tell me it was you. You raped my best friend on the field house floor when she was a virgin and then called her a lousy piece of ass. You miserable bastard!" He screamed the last words from a raw throat and swung the blade again. "Don't make me push you, Coach."

Lightning brought the night sky to blue-purple life overhead, a whopper of a Texas storm brewing over the thirsty lake.

"Nicholas, stop." Richardson's voice jumped three octaves. "I don't want to die. And you don't want to kill me. I know you."

"You haven't ever known me. Not even a little." Nick swung again, lunging. "I'll see you in hell."

Richardson scuttled sideways again.

Shit. My legs pumped, lungs burning and head throbbing as I sprinted for them.

I opened my mouth to scream for Nicky to freeze.

Before the words hit the air, he hit his knees, the knife falling to the dirt, his chin dropping to his chest.

I slowed, my breath coming easier. He couldn't do it. As vile and possibly deserving as his father may be, Nicky—this Nicky—wasn't a murderer.

I pulled my cuffs from my belt. "Darren Richardson, you are under—" Crashing thunder swallowed the words. I cleared my throat to try again.

And the night erupted.

Bright blue white lit everything in sharp contrast, the honeysuckle perfume swallowed by the sting of fried ozone.

An engine roared. Gravel and feet flew, yet the world slowed, not a blink or breath unnoticed.

I spun to find headlights dead-leveled at Graham.

His name ripping from my throat, I charged. Leapt. My shoulder exploded when it hit his chest, all my wind rushing out in a *whoosh* as I rolled, rolled, rolled us both, opening my eyes to a tire speeding past our noses. Tears leaked from my eyes as the stitches in my head ripped, blood running over my ear and down my neck.

More footfalls. A higher voice.

"Look out!" Skye? Who was she talking to?

I pushed off Graham's chest, raising my head as brake lights washed everything in blood.

Erica Andre's white Jag skidded to a stop a foot from the edge of the dam.

"Dad!" Nicky bolted upright, his hand shooting out.

The sky opened up.

Darren Richardson pitched backward.

He fell so fast the rain couldn't even catch him.

48

A pair of butterflies, one orange and one yellow, played tag over the hyacinths at the gates of Texas State Cemetery Saturday morning.

Storms gone, the sun bathed Tenley's memorial service in warmth, purple flowers popping against the flat steel of the casket, the end-to-end blanket of petals enough to make the whole city smell like spring.

Graham stood beside me, his hand finding mine during the opening prayer. I laced my fingers through his and smiled at the sparks racing up my arm. Maybe now we'd have time to figure out what that electricity might mean.

The Marshall High choir sang "Amazing Grace" and "Jesus Loves Me," and then broke into Katy Perry's "Roar." I glanced around, people filling the graveyard as far as I could see, news vans lining the road for day two of the scandal of the century.

Skye broke the story Friday morning on two hours' sleep, and the web just kept spreading, ensnaring another Austin power player every hour, it seemed. New this morning: the university president was paying for the illegal prescription opiates four of the five starters on the basketball team and more than half of the football players were abusing. Archie's cyber team found a nice trail of bank transactions and recorded conversations in Darren Richardson's laptop. A narcissist always covers his own ass first.

And I still knew my politicians: Bobby Wayne Otis sold Ray Wooley the video of Jessa DuGray's assault for twenty-five hundred dollars. Since there were no faces visible on camera, Bobby Wayne thought if he killed Ray and swiped his laptop, he could stop himself from being thrown under the bus in a plea bargain if Ray went to trial. He found the laptop, but not the memory stick he'd given Ray with the original video, which he took from my pocket after he coldcocked me in Ray's apartment Wednesday night. He said he confessed to the murder because the scene was gruesome enough to pull the news cycle off of Ray's website, and he "liked his chances of drawing a hung jury on account of Ray being such a disgusting human being."

"Takes one to know one" was never so true: in the enhanced original video of Jessa's final hours, the cattle prod Otis had hit Nicky and the other boys with as he screamed at them to "take her" was visible, and his voice was a dead identical match. By dawn Thursday, he'd admitted that she'd stopped breathing at some point, though he couldn't be sure when, and he'd burned her body to hide evidence and buried it on his back forty.

I would enjoy watching that man go to prison for a long, long time.

Nicky, his memory vomiting horror in fits and starts, told a story about sneaking out to Otis's place and moving Jessa's remains on a bitter winter night after he saw her parents pleading for answers on the news.

Even Skye Morrow did a good thing every now and again.

The choir fell silent, Jake Simpson taking the podium.

"Tenley Andre was a superstar. Many admired her light, but few got close enough to see past it to the wonderful soul within."

Wow. Deep, and lovely for someone who came across as so self-involved. Simpson went on about Tenley's accomplishments, his eyes never leaving a tall, lanky boy in the back row of folding chairs.

I scanned the crowd: blotchy-faced, sobbing teenagers packed tight among the trees. The entire Marshall High student body was at the cemetery. With one painful exception.

Erica Andre called Friday and invited me and Graham over to ask if an exception could be made for Nicky to attend Tenley's service. "You might think I've lost my mind, but I know how much that boy loved my daughter. Nicky wouldn't have hurt Tenley. Or anyone else." She did an admirable job of talking around her tears, a shaky breath bringing her husband's hand to her shoulder. "Not before they went messing around in his brain. I hate with everything in me that we all have to live with this, but it's cruel to make him miss her funeral. He should be there. She would want him there."

I called everyone I could think of up to and including my parents. Erica asked Governor Holdswaithe's wife, but nobody had enough pull to drag that mountain: Nicky was in a court-ordered locked psych program. Hopefully good doctors and good therapy could repair the damage Otis had done. But they couldn't make him forget, and I feared the memories, once he had them all, would end him.

Erica and Brent sat next to each other in the front row, heads bowed and hands folded in their laps, as person after person stood to talk about their daughter and what they remembered best about her, what they'd miss the most. It was hard for me to listen to without tearing up, and I'd never spoken to Tenley, though I felt like I knew her all the same.

People sometimes told me I was brave, chasing murderers, jumping in front of bullets. Maybe. But these people, sitting in this massive crowd missing and remembering their daughter—they were braver.

Nicky, looking up at me Thursday night, tears streaming, wrists crossed in front of him, confessing patchy recollections of doing horrible things to Jessa and Tenley before he asked me to put him somewhere he couldn't hurt anyone else—that was valor.

Police work can force a person to see the world around them as black and white.

Every once in a while, a case comes along that brings out all the gray in the middle.

I started Tuesday with a promise to help Tenley's family find peace. I'd raced through the week determined to avenge two bright young women who had life stolen from them far too soon. Like Charity. Except I could do for Jessa and Tenley what nobody had done for my sister: I could deliver justice for them. Could leave their killer to rot in a cell forever.

But it wasn't that simple this time. My heart ached for what the victims lost, but it hurt just as gravely for Nicky—for what people he trusted had done to him in the name of "normal." The presumption that such a thing exists is the biggest lie people tell themselves every day.

"The hard ones stay with you, kid," Archie had told me over margaritas at the Work Horse Friday evening. "It's the ones where the bad guy is a human, not a demon, that haunt you when you do this job long enough."

Right again.

Sitting with Nicky in the emergency room, I'd patted his back as he sobbed. "Aren't you supposed to take me to jail?" he asked. "I did god-awful things. Things I didn't even know I was doing. How can your own mind just betray you that way?"

I couldn't answer, unsure what to make of that myself, even with my psych degree. So many years in police work will make a person think they've seen everything, but talking to the doctors about Nicky was a crash course in what not to do with mental illness. Electroconvulsive therapy had come a long way since the early days of practically lobotomizing people via current, they said, and had shown to be effective in treating serious depression.

But administered by an unqualified person to a bipolar teenager in the early days of his first manic phase, it had created the perfect storm in Nicky's head, sending his brain into a rapid-cycling form of depressive mania that had him cutting himself, blacking out, and struggling to survive a life he'd been pretty happy with just a year ago, by all accounts.

Brent stood and made his way to the podium. I smiled when Graham squeezed my hand. Forensics deemed the front bumper of the Jag unblemished, and Brent swore he wasn't aiming for Richardson, but trying to stop Nicky from doing something else he'd regret. Truth? Maybe. Maybe not.

Given the press around the case, Captain Jameson let it go.

Brent gripped the sides of the podium, his chest puffing out with a deep breath. "Erica and I would like to thank you all for coming here today to honor our beautiful Tenley. She was brilliant, she was special, and she was loved just as fiercely as she loved in return. We may not have been given as many days with her as we would've liked, but we will cherish every memory that much more for knowing how fleeting they were.

"We will miss her every day, but we will move forward, we will love bravely, and we will find our smiles again. Tenley had such a beautiful smile, and she'd have been the first to tell anyone here that yours is just as radiant, just as valuable, and just as necessary. If I could ask y'all a favor: do one thing every day that makes you genuinely smile. That is the best way I can think of to remember my little girl."

He made it to the last word before he choked up, nodding as the minister patted his shoulder and asked everyone to stand for the closing prayer.

The Andres shook a thousand or more hands as people filed past the casket. Erica stopped the line to pull me into a hug.

"Thank you for believing us," she whispered. I squeezed her shoulders tight. If there were words to answer that with, I couldn't put them together.

I followed Graham back to his cruiser, where I leaned against the side and watched as the crowd dissipated. Erica stayed until they lowered the casket, but turned away when time came for the shoveling to start.

She and Brent walked to the waiting limo in lockstep, his arm draped around her, her head tipping to rest on his shoulder. I smiled, the ease between them not what I expected after the dynamite at Lola Savannah just two days ago. Good for them. Finding love in tragedy is a much tougher dig than finding blame.

Turning to open the car door, I spotted my mother fifteen or so yards away, pulling open the back door of a town car. Catching her eye, I nodded.

Ruth McClellan tilted her head forward and disappeared.

Jim's wife was in Houston getting prepped to join the drug trial. I had a mandatory lunch date with my father in an hour. Small price to pay, looking around.

As Graham drove out of the cemetery, my phone buzzed. Boone: *Nice work, McClellan. I have something that might interest you waiting on your desk when your "vacation" is over.*

Graham laid an easy hand on my knee. "Everything okay?"

Tenley's family had an answer. I had Graham back in my life, even if I wasn't sure exactly how yet. And Boone had used my actual name in that text. All things considered, it seemed I'd done some good and had the karma to show for it: "New Girl" had officially moved up in the world.

A rippling sea of bluebonnets blurred past the window as I put my hand over Graham's.

"Today, everything is way better than okay," I said. "And tomorrow will take care of itself."

Leave No Stone: Faith McClellan #2

A missing woman.
A sadistic serial killer.
And a Texas Ranger running out of time.

Shortly after a young mother mysteriously disappears, a serial killer begins leaving corpses and clues across the Texas Hill Country. Texas Ranger Faith McClellan and her mentor, veteran Ranger Archie Baxter, are assigned to the case.

But this killer is more clever—and sadistic—than any they've ever encountered, and the list of seemingly unrelated female victims is growing by the day—an attorney, a pastor, a stay-at-home mom. Each murder features a missing ring finger, severe head trauma, and a cryptic message carved into the corpse. But these gruesome calling cards provide more questions than answers, and with the best coroner in the state unable to identify the murder weapon, Faith and Archie are flying blind.

With the young mother still missing and a mounting body count, it's up to Faith and Archie to solve the mystery. Before the killer strikes again...

ACKNOWLEDGMENTS

"Write the book that scares you." Every author has heard those words, but I never really knew what they meant until I started this novel. I stay involved in my littles' lives, and I like to think I have the kind of bonds with them that mean I really know how they are, what they're thinking, and if anything is bothering them. But what about the twist of fate you don't see coming? That's the fear that keeps me awake some nights, and it was the question that grew into this novel, which has been through too many evolutions for me to remember over the past two years. This book challenged me, surprised me, pushed me to venture inside some of the darkest capabilities of humanity, and stretched my ability as a writer.

I owe thanks to several folks for their help getting it into your hands: my agent, John Talbot, who saw something in Faith McClellan I missed, and never gave up on this project; my friend Rick Campbell, who has played the role of publishing guardian angel for me for the past couple of years; Andrew Watts, Mo Metlen, Keris Sirek, and the rest of the team at Severn River Publishing, who work incredibly hard to help my books reach readers, and make being part of this team such fun; Julie Hallberg, Donna Andrews, and Tara Laskowski, who read drafts for me, said nice things, and offered insightful comments that made this a better book; Art Taylor, who gives the very best writer pep talks in the world and also listens better than most anyone I know; Hank Phillipi Ryan, who continues to set high bars both professionally and personally, a gifted author who is also one of the best people I've ever met; Jessica Gardner, who has the sharpest eye of any editor I've ever worked with; the men and women of the various Texas law enforcement agencies I covered during my journalism career, who taught me firsthand about police procedures and what motivates good cops to go to work every day; Jody Klann, who is ever-patient with my lab and forensic questions; and Justin and my littles, who never complain about having pizza again or laundry that still hasn't been folded—I love y'all with the fire of ten thousand suns.

And you, wonderful readers: thank you for reading, reviewing, telling your friends, and sending lovely notes that mean more to me than you could possibly know. I hope y'all love Faith as much as I do. As always, any mistakes are mine alone.

ABOUT THE AUTHOR

LynDee Walker is the national bestselling author of two crime fiction series featuring strong heroines and "twisty, absorbing" mysteries. Her first Nichelle Clarke crime thriller, FRONT PAGE FATALITY, was nominated for the Agatha Award for best first novel and is an Amazon Charts Bestseller. In 2018, she introduced readers to Texas Ranger Faith McClellan in FEAR NO TRUTH. Reviews have praised her work as "well-crafted, compelling, and fast-paced," and "an edge-of-your-seat ride" with "a spider web of twists and turns that will keep you reading until the end."

Before she started writing fiction, LynDee was an award-winning journalist who covered everything from ribbon cuttings to high level police corruption, and worked closely with the various law enforcement agencies that she reported on. Her work has appeared in newspapers and magazines across the U.S.

Aside from books, LynDee loves her family, her readers, travel, and coffee. She lives in Richmond, Virginia, where she is working on her next novel when she's not juggling laundry and children's sports schedules.

Sign up for LynDee Walker's reader list at
severnriverbooks.com/authors/lyndee-walker
lyndee@severnriverbooks.com

Printed in the United States
by Baker & Taylor Publisher Services